A Killing
Frost

Also by Sylvia Wilkinson

Moss on the North Side

A Killing Frost

A NOVEL BY

SYLVIA WILKINSON

HOUGHTON MIFFLIN COMPANY

BOSTON

1967

in memory of Mama and Papa George

Contents

Dummy . . .

Miss Liz, my grandmother, is sitting in the pew beside me. Tonight she is wearing her red dress made of bumpy nylon that makes a noise like a tiny saw when she pulls it from under her legs. Because she has her flannel nightshirt on under the dress, she still smells of hot biscuits and bacon grease from breakfast. Before we left for church tonight, I watched her take off her bib-apron, turn it around because she couldn't remember if it still had a clean side, and hang it on the refrigerator handle. Then she pulled on the red dress and sat at her dresser, beating her chest with a big white powder puff and coughing in the dust. I went over to her, rubbing the white dust into her skin and said,

"Mama, your undershirt is showing at the neck."

She looked at me a moment, her eyes glazed and yellow, before she began to shake her head and mumble, pinching together the top of the red dress and fastening it with a rhinestone pin.

"There, there now. That better, Ramie? That better?" She held back her head, looking in the mirror.

I see the tanned V at her neck showing now, some of the white powder still on top of her skin.

I am Ramona Hopkins and just turned thirteen, but the girls at school say I don't look thirteen. Miss Liz pats me on the knee now, just like I am a little girl, and I take the hymnal from her and find the number of the song. When she first stands beside me, Miss Liz always bumps against my arm, wobbling a little while she fluffs out her dress in back. As I look at her big square head, I think of a picture of her on a square sheet of paper. She is square, her shoulders, her head, even her feet seem to have corners on them. I like to paint pictures of her. I think the next picture will be in that red dress, with the flowers on the nightshirt showing through, with her hymnbook in her hands and her mouth pinched shut, not singing. She never sings. I could make the picture show that she never sings. Sometimes she doesn't even stand up, just sits there with the book in her lap and follows the words with her finger. I used to paint before I was sent off to St. Anne's where I go to school now, but I never painted people. Then when I got there, I decided to try to paint Miss Liz. I painted her seven times and every time my teacher liked the painting, but never knew they were all the same person. I think I never painted people much because I couldn't make their eyes match, but Miss Liz's eyes don't match anyway. I carved her in wood once with a cornstalk blowing around her. Her body was heavy and her feet that in real life look like wood *were* wood and the corn leaves were wrapping around her shoulders and legs, bending around the corners of her body. She looked like the wood I made her from, especially after it dried out, but the cornstalk kept breaking; the leaves wanted to curve away from the wood grain and would keep snapping off under my knife until the stalk only had two leaves. But Miss Liz stood there made of wood like she was saying to me,

"I am wood. I like to be made of wood but it is no longer wood; I have made it me."

When I looked at the statue, it was a little living Miss Liz that would talk to me, but the cornstalk broke and broke again, like it was death not to be green and soft. So I carved it away from her, though it made me sad to give it up, and the chips of it looked like dead things, like leaves that had fallen, and I threw them out. Sometimes it makes me sad to paint her because the picture comes alive and is talking to me long before the paint is thick and nice as I want it. Often I'm scared and afraid to touch it then and Miss Liz is saying to me from her picture that she dares me to touch her again and I have to leave the paint thin with the paper showing through.

The people in the church are singing now and Miss Liz and I are just holding the book between us. I don't usually want to sing in this church either. To try to hear your own voice or to try to sing with them; I don't know, it all sort of gets lost. And the sound that they make is one big voice, only it's rusty and tight like an old machine:

> You got to walk that lonesome valley,
> You got to walk it by yourself,
> Ain't no no no bod body else . . .

They can't get that line out right. It's the third time they've tried the chorus and never got it out right; this time they all even stopped before the "nobody," that is all but one of them. I grow irritated at the sound of the singing and wish it was over; sometimes it is one sound and gives me a dizziness, but now when they stumble on the words, it is like the swarm of greenflies in the swamp forest that go up and down and around you when you disturb the wet ground.

There is somebody in here that's singing too loud and messing up the "nobody" every time. There it goes again, and now I know who it is. It's that old woman on the end in the choir; I know her face and her round mouth and her hateful voice. I know she will try and try until the organ plays it her way and the people give up and sing with her, letting her get her way or else. She's got her wish now. They have all given up to her and when the organ paused and gave up to her, I felt Miss Liz's hands tighten and pull on the songbook.

> Some folks say he was a Christian,
> But he was a Baptist too.
> . . . .
> You got to walk it by yourself . . .

And she held the "self" too long, which would make me ashamed. She is not ashamed of that. You can tell she wants everyone to hear her hold the note longer than anyone else. The choir is singing an "amen" and the people are mumbling it as we drop into our seats and close our books. I look at the old woman in the choir one last time and she sits in her white robe with her arms folding her songbook against her chest.

It is silent now and the preacher is walking in front of the altar. On my arm I see one of the greenflies from the swamp. He has been around me all night, going up and down and bouncing on the people and disappearing when the singing starts. But I hear him buzzing now; I hear nothing but his buzz, and he buzzes and stops and does it again close to me and tickles the hairs on my arms. When I brushed him, I hit him. I think he is very slow and tired because November is too late and too cool for flies. I see him walking under the pew in front of me, dragging one wing, but I can't reach him with my foot.

It's time for the saving now. The people never pay much attention to it here. They are all ashamed to go up except for some of the girls my age who stand up there and blush or look all white and washed out. They have pimples on their faces with no powder over them and dull hair and their clothes have no color. Every night some of them have been up there, always in pairs like they planned it ahead of time to go with their friends. I bet they would be ashamed and afraid if they stood up there alone.

But I know one person who'll be up there tonight and every

night for that matter—Dummy will. I have seen him all my life when I come to the farm visiting but if Miss Liz is around, she always pulls me away when he comes up. When I looked over my shoulder, I saw him back there, leaning against the back door like he did last night and the night before, waiting for the second calling. You can tell that he tried to shave for tonight because there are clean patches on his face and spots of dark blood in his gray whiskers but he still has a face full of whiskers, not all gray really—some reddish and straw-colored like his hair. I think he is very old but it is hard to say; his hands and cheeks are like an old man's, covered with brown-and-white spots and creases. When he pinches his nose and scratches it, you can see his fingernails, bright yellow like kernels of dry corn.

Dummy has started up the aisle, twisting his head back and forth at the people on both sides and frowning at them. And when he swings his arms back and forth as he walks, you can see the great dark circles of sweat under them. Dummy makes squeaky sounds when he walks, his arms swinging, the belt that dangles down from the buckle on his pants, and the folds of his trousers where they have been doubled over around his waist, all squeaking when he moves. Everything about him looks dirty, but he squeaks like your hair when the soap is washed out and it is clean.

The preacher just stepped back for him to go by and I hear Dummy's shoes sucking in and out on his feet. Dummy just turned sharply in front of the preacher and is standing with his chin up and his eyes looking at the rafters. He heard some of the boys snickering at him and his eyes rolled down at them and squinted, then looked back up at the rafters. I just caught myself looking up there too but back down again as Dummy knocked his heels together with a loud thump. Just as the preacher calls for the people to come congratulate the souls who have gone to Jesus' flock, I hear the back doors go open and the people start out.

The people in front of me stand up to go out and I am looking through them, trying to spot Dummy. There he is, shaking hands and grunting at people.

"Mama, look quick," I say. "Look at old Dummy up there again."

Miss Liz pinches her clouded eyes together a minute, looking at Dummy, then jerks her face around to me, saying, "He ain't got no business up there. No business a t'all. He's just found out that's a way to get your hand shook."

She starts walking down the row to the aisle, and I follow her until we are out in the cool night air. I can see the local boys all looking at me now, but they don't really know I can see them. They always drop out of the light from the door and talk and smoke after the service and I always see them look at me. I can hear Dummy's grunts from inside the church and see him now at the door with the preacher pressed against the wall behind him. Dummy is still shaking hands but almost all the people have turned away from him. He just saw me looking at him, so I turned back to Miss Liz and the woman she is talking to, but I can feel Dummy walking toward us.

He taps my arm and when I look up at him, he begins to smile and tap the top of his head. The woman talking to Miss Liz just excused herself and Dummy is pointing at Mama and back at me.

"No, Miss Liz is not my mother," I say, trying to talk to Dummy. "I call her Mama, but she is my grandmother." Then I repeat "grandmother" and he begins to nod his head. His hands are excited and moving in a sign language that he doesn't know how to do. While I watch him, he rolls his eyes back and stands on his tiptoes and bounces up and down like a little puppet. Then he puts his fingers under his nose and begins to curl the ends of his moustache. I started backward as his body bent forward almost as if he were falling, but he is only shutting his eyes and resting the side of his face on his folded hands.

"Mama, what's he saying?" I ask.

"If I've seen him do that once, I've seen it a thousand times. Pshaw, couldn't grow a moustache like Papa's on that sorry scraggly face if he tried. He thinks he really knows something because he remembers Papa and that he died."

I saw Dummy's eyes flick back open like little blue flowers in his speckled face when Miss Liz said the word, "died."

"Oh," I say, "that was a moustache like Papa's. Then he was making like he was dead."

I feel Dummy's hand close on my arm; he has never touched me before really; he has only tapped me, and even now his hand is like a twig that can't really close and hold anything. Miss Liz startles me as she grabs his wrist and says, "Go on. Get on, you! You know more than you play like." Dummy smiles at me and turns quickly, stumbling away toward another group of people.

"He's nothing but a nuisance," Miss Liz continues. "Don't you pay no attention to him, you hear, or he'll pester you to death. Whew! And don't he stink something terrible. All this outdoors air and he still stinks to high heaven."

I can't see Dummy now but I can hear his grunts above the other people as we start to walk home.

"Can he hear really good, Mama? He always acts like he hears good and knows words and all."

Miss Liz is silent a moment, which is her way when you ask a question, then she says, "Who, Dummy? As good as anybody."

"Then I don't see why he can't talk. He can make a noise," I say.

"He hasn't got any sense, that's why," Miss Liz says sharply. "He hasn't got biddy brains in that ugly head. Not for one minute would I put up with that good-for-nothing sleeping on my place. Not for one minute. I seen your Grandpapa let one hobo burn down our barn sleeping in there and rolling up our tobacco and smoking it. And Dummy's good for no better than that.

Help those that helps themselves," she says, then adds with a dry laugh, "he helps himself all right."

"He lives at Vernon's, doesn't he? I saw him over there this summer playing with the children. But I didn't think he used to live there."

"He's lived in everybody's hair but mine, I'm proud to say. And Vernon Stiles's the longest yet and they feed him to boot. Never does a lick of work and they feed him to boot. I'd put a stop to that and send him out away from here."

"Did you ever know of his family? Papa used to tell me he didn't belong to anybody. He was just there one day and never gone again."

Miss Liz answers, "He was here long before Papa came here; long before Papa came. Dummy was a young man here when I was a girl. He was somebody's bastard and they saw he didn't have good sense and got shed of him. If he was kin of mine, I wouldn't make no claim to it. Best that he die and they put him in a hole somewhere."

Miss Liz stops talking a minute and her face softens a little when she says, "You might not take to this, Ramie; you might think I'm just telling a tale but he led folks to believe he could talk. He walked in the store one day a stranger and stuck his nose in the air and he was dressed to kill then, letting on like he was too good to talk to us. Had on a suit coat in the summertime and shoes and colored socks. He came in the first day anybody saw him, dressed up and slicked down and stuck his nose in the air and people ran around and looked at him and they got him up a bunch of stuff from the store, bread and sugar and such. I was there, reason I'm telling this, the first time we caught sight of him. I was in the store jarring up honey when he walked in and he pranced around a-pointing at this and that and we bundled it all up. And Tessie Allbright turned to me and said, 'Well, this one's a fine one. So fine he won't talk to such as us,' and Tessie and me looked at him taking the sodie crackers out of the barrel and eating them with his nose in the air. And we all just watched him prance around and I said to Tessie, 'There's a fine-looking man if ever I saw one.' I said that was a fine-looking man. And he kept that up, just buying and buying stuff and eating them sodie crackers with no notion of paying for them like they was being served to him on a platter. Had a wad of money in a leather folder and rented a room at Tessie's mother's; just walked in Tessie's house that first day and stood there till her mother took it he was looking for a room and she showed him one and he pointed to a fine one across the hall and settled there. It was a fine room he had then."

Miss Liz stops to laugh a moment and I wait for her to go on.

"Well now, I'm getting right jealous of Tessie at this time, this 'fine-looking man' staying at her house. And I want to tell you what was the end of it all. He came in the store one day and I was feeling right proud he had taken notice of me and looked at me working there, nodding his head and sucking whole sodie crackers in his mouth with one bite. And that day I was so proud, Tessie's Papa said, 'That'll be five, twenty-seven,' and the man pulled out a five-dollar bill and I seen in the folder there wasn't any more there. His nose started pinching up and he started hitting his pockets, puffing and blowing out cracker crumbs down his front, but there won't no jingle in his pockets and it was an awful thing to see. His hands going up and down like they was going to shake off and waving this way and that, and he started into that grunting, puffing out them crumbs all over himself and in Mr. Allbright's face and we all just set there with our mouths open. It occurred to us that in a whole week, he hadn't spoke nary a word to any of us and here he was grunting and shaking and didn't have no more money. Why we just set there watching him carry on awful, and he cried and grunted and

Tessie said to me, 'I declare the man's crazy as a tick!' She just kept saying it over and over and there he was, couldn't talk a word. Couldn't talk a word for the love of him."

Miss Liz is laughing and can't talk anymore. She is about to choke up from laughing but I can't feel a laugh.

"I never seen him anything but happy," I say to her.

"Oh, he's a happy one now, he is," she says, almost choking on her words. "But that won't a happy man then. It was a long time till that man was happy after that. They told about him a thousand times, I bet, down at the store. And my little brother, I remember well him saying it. He said, 'I seen him at the fair. I seen him on this man's knee. I seen him with a wooden head and jaws working and a little suit on like a person.' My little brother said that and carried on about it. 'That's where I seen him,' he kept hollering. 'I seen him at the fair and he set on this man's knee talking up a storm and I seen the man put him down and he couldn't say a word. I seen him balled up on the floor and he had a hole in his back and workings inside and couldn't say a word.' And my little brother would say to Dummy 'fore he had a name, 'The man put the dummy down and he don't say a word.' And we used to get tickled and call him the dummy. And Tessie's mother had got shed of him quicklike and he was sleeping around the barns and the dummy got dirtier and dirtier; he had one suit of clothes to his name and one day when he had got filthy and stinking my little brother was saying, 'The man put down the dummy,' 'cause he knew he could make us all laugh when he said that, and Dummy started laughing and jumping around to beat the band. It was a sight to see and it had us so tickled we couldn't stand it, and my little brother just popped up in front of him and said, 'Dummy, dummy, dummy'; and Dummy just laughed and nodded his head and my little brother said, 'Lizzie, look Lizzie, look! The man done picked him up again. He done picked him up and's making him work.' And I'll say the man done picked that Dummy up for good because for weeks we'd yell out, 'Dummy, dummy, dummy,' and he would jump and carry on for us till we all got wore out from it and it won't funny no more. And he was Dummy since then. Only he won't funny no more. He won't nary bit funny."

Miss Liz's face tightens again as she says, "Not nary bit funny. Pest! Never done a lick of work and getting a roof over his head. I wouldn't have it, not for a minute."

She turns to me and says before we go in the house, "Don't you go feeling sorry for him. He gets the best of everybody that does. I've seen him work people many a time looking like a beat dog. You stay away from him, you hear?" I am glad she has stopped talking and we are in the quiet house.

I go to my bedroom but turn around and see she is at the door. I undo my dress and get ready for bed but she stands there for a long time looking like my wood carving of her. Finally she moves and goes to pull the red nylon off her nightshirt and gets it caught on the pin that held the neck up to keep the nightshirt from showing at church. I can't see her head as she fights under the red dress, searching for the pin; and she makes red shadows on the door frame as the light comes through the dress like a flame. Now she wads the dress up in her fist and the flame on the door disappears, but I feel I have to stand on the cold floor by the bed until she says what she has to say.

Miss Liz speaks now, "You mind what I say. Don't you get around him." She is still standing there a moment, dark in the white nightshirt, then she is gone to her bed.

I am in my bed and my feet are tucked up against me and beginning to get warm. I am almost asleep and I try to think of Dummy but I see a painting of him with two heads, a sad, clean head and a dirty head that laughs, and both heads go away and there is left a little black face and body dancing in front of me. When I see the little black dancing boy, I remember for a moment when I am almost asleep and can't keep my mind straight, I remember a time when I was outside a colored church. I remember that I was there once with some people from school and listening to the singing inside and I'm there again, but I am by myself. The colored people inside the church are singing "Lonesome Valley," but the song is not like tonight. I hear it like I heard it then with tambourines jingling and thumping and hands clapping, and I am almost asleep but there is a trumpet that keeps me awake, and I hear in my mind after each verse the trumpet I heard that night when I was in the car listening to the singing and watching the people bounce up and down through the open door and the little black boy is dancing in front of me. I am almost asleep now and I remember the face of the little black boy, popping in the window of the car. His eyes are laughing and he says, "How many sodie crackers in this box . . . how many . . . how many sodie crackers in this box?" and he dances away and I am almost asleep. I am in the box and the box is the church but not the colored church, the church tonight, and the people are more sodie crackers than I can count for the little boy, but he is gone now anyway. I see the old woman in the choir and we are standing to sing but there is no sound; the old woman is singing "no . . . no . . . no . . . nobody," but she makes no sound and I see that she is a sodie cracker. I am afraid and I turn to Miss Liz, but she is a sodie cracker too and in the pews the people are all sodie crackers, but I can't look at me to see if I'm a sodie cracker, but I have no legs and no arms and I am asleep, and I'm a little square and I open my mouth, but I have no hands to hold the songbook and I cannot sing and all is silent.

Little Bird . . .

As soon as the first light appears in the window in the morning, shining pale green through the trees, the chimney swifts wake up outside, singing like they're in the quiet time before a storm, their sounds going up and down as they chase the flying bugs across the fields. Long before the wild things woke up, a rooster crowed somewhere in the distance, probably at the headlights on the highway. The single cry of the rooster, awk-ak-awk-k-k-k, lingered in the fields; the noise seeming to puzzle at itself a moment, wondering why the sun had disappeared so quickly. Then he was fooled again, awk-awk-k-k-k-k-k, until finally the orange circle of the sun swelled from the earth and everything woke up around him, drowning out his voice with its noises. The great orange circle pushes up slowly under the air of frost and melts the frozen earth, the plants in the fields giving up their silver covers, and shining green and gold and wet while the orange circle fades yellow-white like the ground.

But deep in the woods, the swamp forest is still dark as night. I know it has no frost and it has no sunlight; only under the wet leaves it has a buzzing sound as the greenflies burrow into the earth to get away from the cold. No one sees the swamp forest anymore and no one walks on the wet ground that bubbles with a spring if you press the ground with your foot. Down there the air smells thick and heavy, like things are rotting, but when things are decaying with clear spring water, rot is not a bad smell. And soon when winter comes, the running cedar will make green lace across the earth and change the rot smell to cedar spice. The ground in the swamp forest is green and black and very dark but for the little lights that pop up under the leaves and shove the leaves away. The little lights are the mushrooms, orange and white and red in all sizes and shapes, circling through the shadows making a fairy ring.

The swifts go up over the swamp forest and wait for the buzzing greenflies to fly up from their wet leaves on the ground. The birds snatch the flies that rise over the treetops and pinch them until they are silent on the way across the open fields to the house. The swifts drop to the edge of the chimney, but trembling now as the smoke and heat come up to them, smoke that wasn't there when they built their nest. The birds will let the bugs drop from their beaks into the dark chimney and fly away, leaving the screaming late family that hangs suspended and crying in the smoke.

* * *

"Hush up! Oh, for goodness' sake, hush up!"

I get out of bed and dress and walk to the front room where the squeal of the birds is loud and steady. Miss Liz is fanning the smoke back up the chimney with her skirt tail and when the birds finally get quiet, she sighs aloud and shakes her head at me.

"Another family," she says. "It won't enough they had to fall down and yell their heads off in the summertime. Now they won't let me build a fire in my own fireplace."

A shower of dirt and sticks hisses in the fire and Miss Liz says, "Oh, my goodness. What am I going to do with them if they start falling? I just can't put off the fire no longer. The dampness will muster up everything in the house. Oh, my goodness," she says again.

More dirt is falling and the screaming of the birds is loud again as Miss Liz begins to mumble and fan the smoke back at the fireplace. Then she jumps away from the fire and snaps her skirt down.

"Oh, my gracious! There's one of them already."

In the dry darkness in the back of the fireplace, I hear the screaming again without the hollow sound of the chimney. Miss Liz squats on the hearth and reaches into the dark corner, coming out with a little squealing bird cupped in her hands. It looks like it is made of twigs and mud, but in the center of the round, rough ball is a head with no neck and two dull, dusty eyes beside a bright yellow beak.

"Just look at that ugly thing with his mouth wide open and yelling. Just look at him!" Miss Liz says and cups her hand over the little bird's back until he gets warm and shuts his eyes and mouth. "Well, I'm not going to stand here holding you the rest of my life just to shut you up," she says to the little bird, peeking at him through the crack in her hands.

"What can we do with him?" I ask. "He's not able to fly back up there."

"Not a thing to do with him. Not a thing. He just has to die, I fear."

I feel my heart hurt inside my chest as I watch him back deeper inside Miss Liz's hand on little legless feet. Miss Liz says quietly to the little bird, "Now what in the world am I going to do with you?"

"Can we set him out in the yard?" I ask. "Maybe his mama will hear him and come get him or feed him or something."

"The cat'll get him in a minute. Besides his mama won't have a thing to do with him once he's been touched by people. She'll act like he ain't none of hern. Now don't fret, there's a million more," and she sets him back down in front of the fireplace. The logs smoke and glow red behind him. He blinks his eyes open and opens his mouth and starts squealing again. I look at Miss Liz as she wipes her hand on her apron and says, "Dirty as he can be. Messed in my hand," and she spits in her hand and wipes it on her apron again.

"I can get you a speck of raw meat to poke in him, if you're a mind to keep him," she says as she walks into the kitchen.

I watch the little bird whose round body comes apart, flapping up a cloud of dust in the ashes, his wings spread out like a dead leaf. He doesn't look up at the flames beside him and seems to watch my feet from behind his dusty eyes. He is quiet a moment until he hears his brothers and sisters start hollering again inside the chimney, then he starts screaming with them but never looks up.

"Here, pinch some of this off and run it down that big mouth with some water," Miss Liz says from behind me and hands me a piece of red chicken liver.

I go into the kitchen and take the bird with me, setting him on the edge of the sink. He looks funny and black on the white sink, but he lifts up on his claws and holds on so he won't slide off. When I pinch off the chicken liver, it sticks between my fingers like glue. Inside the little bird's mouth I can see the piece of liver when I drop it, beating up and down with his breathing like a little red heart in his throat. When I drop water on it, it goes down and leaves pink bubbles that rise and pop in the dark hole.

"Looks like a wad of dust," Miss Liz says. "Be far better if I could scoot him out the door with the broom. That infernal squealing, fine mother he has letting him plop out like that, leaving him on us."

The little bird closes his eyes and his head sinks down when he closes his dead-leaf wings around his body again. Then he shakes his head, slinging red drops of water on my hand.

"Mama, he's not choked on it, is he?" I ask.

"No, no, he's all right. Just telling you he's had his fill. He'll be yelling again soon enough. Ain't that something, just like a little baby." I look at Miss Liz and her eyes are light-brown and bright in the morning light and she is smiling at the little bird though her eyes drop down in the corners like someone frowning. She reaches over and scratches the side of the little bird's head until he pulls it down and his round body sinks and he tucks his feet underneath it.

It seems sometimes that Miss Liz can just touch things and make them well; she can make anything grow that's sickly. I guess that's why I love her, though she does say things that make me sad at times. I can remember her sleeping with the weak biddies under the covers with her at night. I used to ask her how she kept from mashing them and she would say, "If they can get out of their fat mama's way, they can get out of mine." Miss Liz and I would go to the incubator and see how many little sickly ones there were and take them out and in the house. And if there was a speck of blood on one, we would take him out quick or they'd peck him to death. Miss Liz said they didn't mean any harm by it but if they saw a dark speck, they'd all just naturally start pecking at it, trying to be the one to get it for himself. Then once she caught up a corn bug and put him in with them to show me what she meant, and the biddies ran and fell and pushed over each other, darting in and out, pecking up and dropping that bug until one of them swallowed it down. After that they got quiet again and it looked strange to see them all quiet and huddling around the light bulb. That's what she meant about the blood; they'd all run in and peck and instead of going away like the bug, the blood spot would get bigger and bigger until they pecked him to death. Miss Liz would bring in the chick with the blood spot and lick the end of her finger to wash it off and then put a drop of soot and spit on it and put the biddie under the covers of her bed.

I put my little bird down in a box of rags and tuck them around him and set him on the hearth. His brothers and sisters are still screaming but he is quiet now with his eyes closed tight. I move the box out a little so the sparks won't pop in it and so he can stay warm. He doesn't make a peeping noise when he is warm, like the little biddies used to when I went in Miss Liz's room to listen if she had any under her covers.

I go to wash my hands and Miss Liz is setting my breakfast on the table. When I finish eating I reach under the cover plate over the bread platter and get a piece of last night's cornbread.

"Ain't you going to put a thing on it?" Miss Liz says as I start to eat the cornbread. "There's butter and jam a plenty and a piece of cold meat."

She always says that when I eat plain bread. "Like it plain," I say, and finish the bread and hold my mouth under the spigot to wash the lump in my throat down with water.

"Can I get you to save me some steps this morning?" she asks, and I nod yes. "You run Vernon's butter over for me, please. It'll just take me a minute to sack it up."

Miss Liz reaches in the refrigerator and takes out two of the bright yellow cakes from the shelf. When she wraps them in wax paper, I see the milk bubbles on the surface of the cakes spread out under the paper. In the top of each one is an acorn print from her butter mold. She whipped me good one time when I was little for making mud pies with her mold, but the acorn was much prettier in the mud when it dried than it is in the butter. I made five of them and kept them for a long time under the house until the chickens busted them up.

She puts the butter in a sack and I go out the back with it. There is a string of red peppers on the porch that looks like a necklace of long red teeth. As I go across the yard all the things around me are Miss Liz. Her pile of kindling that my uncle who makes furniture gave her is wrapped in an old quilt under the smokehouse shed. I want to go through the stack and take out the walnut and mahogany to carry back to school to carve with, but I'd have to hide it from Miss Liz so I guess I'll do without. I can't stand to see her burn the pieces of walnut and cherry like they are nothing but kindling, but I guess it's all the same to her, just scraps and not good for anything. The reason I'd have to hide it from her is she talks and worries all the time about running out of kindling in the winter and she always gets more wood than she needs, and I've seen it just lying there and rotting in the springtime. It's no time to ask her to let me take any of it now since it's already getting cold. She's like that about the water and everything, won't let me flush the commode but once a day for fear it's running the well dry, and then if I forget and flush it, she comes running in there and watches the water whirl down like she's about to grab it and stop it. They already told her the well had enough to last the rest of her life but she said, "How you know so much how long the rest of my life is going to be?" Her other well did go dry though, and Papa and me used to have to go to the spring in the swamp forest and tote up the water. We'd dump it in her black pot over there and she would build a fire under it on Saturday morning and stir the dirty clothes in it with a stick. She's got a sink now but she says she doesn't use it and I can see burnt wood under her pot and where soapsuds have dried on the grass.

I'm in the trees now where it doesn't look like Miss Liz, and when the wind goes through overhead, the seeds and leaves shower down on my head. The persimmon tree that was ugly in the summertime with tent caterpillars in it now looks like it's holding to their webs to keep the bony branches together. We burned holes in the webs with a kerosene wad on the end of a bamboo to let the wasps and birds in to get the worms but the caterpillars just closed up the holes and spread on around the rest of the leaves. The ground is still spotted with the black droppings of the worms, like no one has walked through the trees since summer. When I walk through the tall grass in the fields, my shoes fill up with little seeds and the grass seems to fling grasshoppers through the air at me, and they'll stick to my legs if I don't reach down and knock them off. Here and there are tiny, bright-green tobacco leaves budding from the dead stalks like they are trying to grow again before frost. The light frost has already burned away in the sun and is not strong enough yet to kill. The pumpkin vines still have a tinge of green, but the pumpkins don't seem to be growing from their own vines, but look like they're growing from the morning glories that bloom all around me, bright as the colors in a paint tube and sticking up like little trumpets. It is strange to see them still wide open like this, with dark veins running down into the mouth of each flower, because I am not usually out early enough to see them before they twist and wind up in the sun.

There is one light fence post in the pasture, cedar with its bark peeling off like old skin. Papa put that post in over five years ago; the year he died he put it in. A day never went by that Mama didn't mention that post, how it was rotten and going to fall and let the cows loose. And Papa always said, "I'll get on it one of these days, Lizzie," like he did about most of the things she nagged him about. Then Christmas morning when we were all there, Papa came in and threw a log on the fire and said, "Recognize it, Lizzie?"

He took her to the window and showed her where he'd put in the new post and I looked out and saw a red ribbon tied around it. Papa said, "Merry Christmas," to her and we all laughed when she chased him across the room and swatted him on the rear with a present box.

I see the side of Vernon's barn, and when I walk around the dark side of it out of the sun, I see some of the morning glories have gone up the wall and died. I love to take off the seed bun-

dles on the dead vines to see if I can get them off without breaking their covers. I pick a whole bunch of them and put them in
my hand and pinch the little covers so I can feel them crunch. I
blow away the husks that fly off like paper and look at the black
seeds. They have cut sides, like you could stack them all together
if you knew how and make a circle with them like one of those
Chinese wood balls that I got apart and couldn't get back together. I throw them against the barn and listen to them tinkle
and fall in the grass.

Then I hear a sound that is not the seeds; it goes ak-ak-ak-ak-ak
and I jump and look behind me and there is Dummy. He is
pointing at me with his finger like he's making a gun and going
ak-ak-ak at me.

"Hey, Dummy. What you doing?" I ask.

He pulls at my arm and starts to point under the trees where
I see a bunch of little kids playing. I guess they're playing soldiers
and that's what he means.

"No, Dummy. I can't go play. I've got to take Mrs. Stiles her
butter for Mama."

He reaches toward me and I duck my head, but he has already
snatched a tree seed out of my hair that I must have got walking
over here. Then he holds it under my nose and shakes it at me.
When he gets close like that, his breath smells bad because he
breathes hard and all over you, just coming up with more and
more breath and grunts and never getting anything out but noise.
His teeth are all brown and yellow, the ones he's got, and they
lean and slant about like a bunch of tombstones. He's still shaking that seed. Then he squashes it in a ball and thumps it at my
face. I start to walk away from him, but I hear him coming behind me again. He taps me on the arm and when I look at him
this time, he starts brushing the straw off his pants, taking a big
piece of the straw in his fingers and sticking it under his nose on
top of his own moustache, and starts screwing up his mouth try-

ing to hold it there. His eyes roll around, trying to look at the straw under his nose. Then it falls off and when he bends over to pick it up, I see straw all woven in his hair. I start walking again and Dummy still comes behind me. Finally he runs out in front of me and starts waving his hands for me to stop.

When I stop, he starts making his moustache turn up like he did last night and closes his eyes and plays dead again. I am getting tired of messing with him.

"Yes, that's right. Papa died," I say.

He points at me and starts pouting his mouth and whimpering, making lines down his cheeks with his fingers like they were tears.

"Are you saying I cried when he died?" I ask.

He doesn't nod his head but keeps making tears and pouting and starts jumping around.

"I was crying when he died. We were good friends," I say. "Good friends." He won't stop doing it, and now he's making a crying sound and laughing at the same time and he's making my eyes start to burn. I don't remember him there at Papa's funeral. He must have been there, but I just remember Miss Liz and how when she started crying, I did too. I couldn't stay with her with her crying and went back of the people and cried where nobody would bother me. I don't like it when people try to make you stop crying because it makes it worse, and I don't like Dummy doing that either and he won't stop. I don't like to think about Papa being dead; in fact I don't think it would really seem like he was dead if Miss Liz hadn't made me look at him with that satin and just half of him showing like that, like he was chopped in two or stuck down in a hole. I was real little and kept thinking he might sit up and not really be dead. But when I told Miss Liz I was thinking he might sit up and talk to me and everything would be all right, she said they took people's blood and insides out before they put them in a casket. I didn't know they did that before and she said they cut out the back of their clothes and all and there was nothing much left but what was showing on top. When I was sitting around in the room with the people that night, I was thinking of going to see if I could lift Papa and see what they had done to him. Then when they put me to bed I was still thinking I was going to, and was trying not to go to sleep so I could when they all left, but I started getting sick with all those flowers smelling up the house and those white ones that Papa had his feet under. And getting sick because they cut up Papa and stuck their hands in a hole in his back, and I was trying to remember how he talked and what he used to say to me and couldn't before I went to sleep.

I don't know why Dummy just keeps doing that but I'm about to get mad at him. He keeps jumping around and grunting and crying until I want to hit him in the head and make him stop. Dummy grabs my arm only it's not like last night when I could hardly feel it. It's tight and I'm scared and pull away and run to the steps of the house and start knocking on the screen.

I watch Dummy coming toward me and my heart is beating fast. I pull on the screen, but it's hooked on the inside. But Dummy's not looking at me now. He's started looking at a plate full of biscuits and eggs that I stepped over on the steps.

"Your food's outside, Dummy. I ain't got time to bother with you today."

I jump at the loud voice from inside the house. Now Dummy takes the plate and sits down and starts picking the eggs up with biscuits and stuffing them in his mouth.

"It's me, Mrs. Stiles. Ramie," I call.

I hear her walking toward the door and the pots on the shelf by the screen start shaking a little when she comes across the porch.

Then I see her through the screen. She says, "I declare, I thought it was Dummy banging on the door." Then she unhooks and opens the screen and says to me, "Come on in, honey."

"I just brought your butter from Mama," I say. "I better not come in. Mama expects me right back."

"I declare, you didn't have to walk it all the way over here. I could have sent one of the kids after it." Then she stops and says, "I'm real glad to see you again. Been since early summer, ain't it?"

"Yes, Ma'am," I say. "I'm just out six days for Thanksgiving and wanted to see Mama again before Christmas."

"And Miss Liz? We haven't had a talk in an age."

"She's doing fine as ever."

Dummy bangs his plate on the steps and I turn around and see him stick out his tongue at me before he starts shuffling back across the yard. I pick the plate up and hand it up to Mrs. Stiles and almost laugh, especially since he made that face at me like a little kid, because I was scared of him a while ago.

Mrs. Stiles wrinkles up her nose when she takes the plate. "Look at that ugly thing, poking out his tongue," she says. "I'd smack a youngun in the face for that."

"I think he's mad at me because I wouldn't pay any attention to him," I say.

"Well, you sure did right by that." She frowns at the plate and sticks it on the shelf inside the porch. "Humph, he sure licked it out today. Feel like I have to scald everything he touches. Wish he was like a cat and would just take up and leave when you're sick of him." Then Mrs. Stiles looks sad and says, "Miss Liz don't think much of me for not throwing him off the place. She don't ever come over and sit anymore." I don't say anything and Mrs. Stiles shakes her head. "I get embarrassed to death every time somebody new comes by, and feel like I have to tell them he ain't no kin. Honestly if I had somewhere to send him, I'd send him tomorrow and not think twice about it."

"He enjoys playing with Lyndie and the other kids, doesn't he?" I ask.

"I reckon that's the only reason I let him stay," she says and lets out a deep wheeze. "Every time I make mention to Vernon I'm going to run him off, the kids start cutting a fit and making me feel bad about it. I ain't got time to amuse them so I guess it don't hurt them to put up with his foolishness."

I can't see the tree where the kids are playing now, but I hear them laughing and squealing and think of last night when Miss Liz told me about her little brother calling him Dummy and making him dance. And it really seems funny when I think that little brother is a grown man now and is my Uncle Buck who makes furniture and brings her the wood for kindling.

"I'll be going, Mrs. Stiles. Miss Liz is expecting me back," I say.

"All right, honey. Now you be seeing us again before you go back?"

"Yes, Ma'am. Goodbye," I say, and start walking across the yard and hear the screen thump on her rear end then shut easy. I go back to the side of the barn and see the little children again. They've got a hopscotch course drawn in the dirt and I see Dummy in the middle of it, trying to hop through holding his foot up in front of him. He's wobbling sideways in his old spread-out shoe and waving his arms in the air. I hear a tinkle of laughs and hear Lyndie Stiles say, "No, silly, put your foot in back of you like this."

She shoves Dummy's knees and he wobbles a minute and plops backward in the dirt. Lyndie throws a rock in one of the squares and starts hopping all around Dummy. She doesn't look at him as she hops, and her hair bobs up in the air when she lands straddle-legged in two squares. She reaches in her pocket and gets another rock and throws it in a square, then bites her bottom lip and jumps over two squares. Dummy slaps his hands on his knees and waves his arms in the air, squeaking inside his dirty shirt-sleeve, until Lyndie hops around him again.

I walk over close, but none of them can see me for the tree. Dummy's face looks all dry, but his eyes are real wet and his wrinkles seem like they're going to squeeze his eyes shut. When I look at him, the ground starts looking all hazy and too bright, like the heat is coming up from it in little waves, but Dummy just sits there all wadded up in a little ball and has quit making grunting sounds. He still looks all dirty, his hair full of straw, but his eyes look real clean and blue and I watch him let them shut slow under his white lashes, then pop back open before I turn and start walking back.

The sun is real bright now and getting warmer, and all the morning glories have closed up since I came through before. If you try to pull them open they'll just twist back up. Now the field looks green and brown with no colors. Even the pumpkins look faded out in the sun, but real pumpkins never are orange like they are in pictures. When I squint my eyes shut in the sun, I see black balls that the sun makes, like when you look at a light bulb, and the birds flying around make little specks in my eyes like they are just moths.

I remember my little bird in the house and wonder if he is hungry again. When I get to the shade spot where the trees with the black spots under them are, I stop and think a minute that Dummy looked sort of like my little bird sitting there all balled up like that, but I guess my little bird doesn't pay any attention to people like Dummy does.

Persimmons . . .

Miss Liz is cooking lunch now, filling the kitchen with strong smells, more than I can stand to breathe for long. I am on the porch, but the cooking smells even come out here. It would be OK if I was hungry, but she always starts her meals so soon I'm not over the last one yet and it's hard to get used to a hot meal at noon. As I walk down the steps, I see the skeletons of Miss Liz's hydrangeas all around the bottom of the house; all dead and almost transparent like they are ghost plants. The huge dry flowers that shatter if you touch them were bright blue in the summer. Yet when I took one to town with me and rooted it at Aunt Cecie's house in our yard, it grew with pink flowers instead of blue.

I hear the children laughing down in the sage field below the tobacco barns. All morning their sounds have gotten louder and closer to Miss Liz's house and now, as I walk across the yard, I can see the colors of their clothes when they dart through the yellow sage. In a square of golden light through the dark tobacco shed, I can recognize Lyndie Stiles rolling in the sage.

The yellow grass and the sun make me squint to keep from sneezing. I walk under the shed where it is dark and damp, almost cold, and sneeze anyway. The walls are dotted with dirt dauber nests, but nothing buzzes around them now; nothing's left but the quiet fingers of dirt they stuck on the wood. Miss Liz and I busted one of them open once and found fourteen spiders that the mother dauber had left with her egg, all limp and drugged so they would be fresh when the egg hatched. There was a tiny black widow mixed in with the ground spiders.

Against the wall of the shed are two rotten bales of hay and I almost sit down on them when I get that feeling I sometimes get — I have done this same thing before . . . and that I shouldn't do it now. Maybe it's because I just thought of the black widow in the dauber nest. I look at the bales, their yellow string brown and rotten now, and holes and burrows in the hay where the mice and birds have gone in after the seed. I touch one of the strings and it breaks, sending the hay down on my feet in a square chunk. As I jump back, the hay in my shoes and sticking to my socks like beggar lice, I remember what it was about the hay. It was the copperhead. I turned up the hay and thought it was a little ground snake, but it was a copperhead that hadn't grown all its colors yet, and Papa stomped it to death with his bare feet. I remember his feet with the white calluses and the dirt under his ankle bones that Miss Liz called "rust"; and I remember I was more scared for Papa's feet than I was for me. I saw Papa pop the head off a chicken snake many times, pick up its tail and pop it like a whip, sending its head rolling off, but chicken snakes can't hurt you.

"Hey, Miss Ramie!"

I jump and look behind me and there is little Lyndie Stiles. I think Lyndie is the kind of little girl that is prettier when she is all dirty with grass in her hair than she is dressed up; dressed up, she looks like her clothes are too tight and she can't move, but now she looks pretty, like a little animal sort of.

"Well hey, Lyndie. You sneaked up on me."

She giggles and looks proud of herself. "Whatcha doing? I

heard you sneezing." She walks over to the hay and picks up the square I broke off, shaking it over her head until it shatters across her hair and shoulders.

"Lyndie, don't do that. You're going to itch to death until you get a bath."

She bends over and beats her hair, "No, I ain't either. It don't bother me none 'cept when I get chiggers."

"You better not mess around rotten hay anyway. My Grandpa killed a copperhead under a bale I turned up once. It had been setting like that one has, in the shade."

"A copperhead!" Her eyes pop open wide.

"Yeah, it was just a little one but they're just as bad."

"One of the niggers got bit last summer."

"One out here?" I ask.

"One of ours, John Junior's little sister." Then Lyndie giggles. "Though it hadn't ought to been funny, it was. It bit her on the butt while she was setting under a tree."

I can't help but laugh at Lyndie and then we both laugh to-gether. "She got well, didn't she?" I ask, feeling a little ashamed for laughing.

"Oh yeah. She couldn't set down for a long time though. Pa said that would kill a nigger faster than anything, not being able to set down under a tree." Then Lyndie turns and points out into the sage. "She's out yonder now. You can't tell it none now but her butt was twice as big last summer."

I see the little colored girl with her knotted pigtail head and in a blue dress, dark around the waist where the sash is torn off. She squeals loudly, then she ducks and holds the top of her head as a shower of dirt breaks behind her, scattering against her legs and her skinny little rear end.

"Mattie Ruth, is that John Junior and them busting them clods?" Lyndie calls.

The little colored girl runs over to the edge of the shed where we are. She doesn't know me and looked at the ground when I said hey to her. Now she looks at Lyndie and the white spreads through her eyes.

"It your brother and mine and that Dummy, that what it be."

I hear a yell from the other side of the shed and the little girl jumps inside, snatching my arm when another clod of dirt breaks at her feet. Then a walnut bounces across the tin roof and Mattie Ruth starts to tremble and clutch my arm tighter, like it doesn't matter whether she knows me or not anymore; I'm just bigger than she is.

Lyndie puts her hands on her hips and tightens up her nose. She walks to the edge of the shed.

"They think they're something 'cause they got all the ammunition down there."

"They're down behind the dike, aren't they?" I ask.

"Yeah, that's the fort and them ain't their walnuts. Me and Mattie Ruth picked up more than they did, and it was rules not to throw at each other."

I see Dummy for the first time. He jumps to the top of the trench with his arm swinging from behind. He swings all the way around to throw but forgets to let go of the walnut until his arm goes behind him and he throws the nut backward across the field. Lyndie starts to laugh as Dummy loses his balance and falls back down behind the dike.

"Dummy, Dummy, Dummy! Can't hit the broad side of a barn!" she screams. "Clumsy Dumsy!"

Dummy pops back up again. This time his body seems to stiffen inside his baggy clothes like a puppet with strings on his arms and legs but not on his clothes. He slams three nuts on the ground in front of him, making them skid along until they come crashing through the shed. One hits Mattie Ruth in the side of the leg. She yells and then starts whimpering, almost tearing my sleeve holding on to me.

"Hey, that busted a whelk on Mattie Ruth's leg. You better watch that. And you made her cry besides!" Lyndie yells.

She wasn't really crying before but she is now.

"Sissies! Why don't you fight back, sissy girls!" one of the boys calls from the ditch.

"That was Little Brother, thinks he's so smart. If he was down there by himself, I could make him run like blazes." Lyndie looks up at me. "Now you watch what happens." Lyndie calls out again, "Mattie Ruth is hurt bad. She's already red and swollen."

John Junior's black face comes over the edge of the dike and screams, "Niggers don't turn red!" I see the flash of his white teeth and hear him start laughing as he drops back behind the dike.

"They bleed red!" Lyndie hollers.

Mattie Ruth is crying louder now and has let go of my arm, dropping to the ground beside my feet. I look back toward the dike and see Dummy coming slowly over the top, his hands in the air over his head. His yellow-white hair and skin is almost the color of the broom straw, only the broom straw is shiny in the sun and Dummy is dull and dirty looking.

"See, yonder's Dummy like I figured. You can make him feel bad easy. I knowed that would make him feel bad, what I hollered about Mattie Ruth being hurt and crying."

Dummy is stumbling through the field, his shoulders hunched forward now, his hands brought down and dangling at his sides. He is as baggy looking as his clothes, walking like he's going to fall any minute.

"You can get Dummy to change sides in a fight easy as anything. He most always wants to be on me and Mattie Ruth's side anyway, don't he, Mattie Ruth?"

The little colored girl looks up from the ground and starts sniffing, her eyes like water with the sun shining on them.

"I reckon," she says softly, and whimpers again.

"You reckon? You knows."

Lyndie looks at me and laughs. Dummy stands by the edge of the barn now, hiding half his face like a kid that's been bad. He looks at me so I guess he thinks I'm going to fuss at him.

"Give it to him, Miss Ramie," Lyndie whispers to me. "He is figuring you're the grown-up here and is waiting for you to cuss him out. He'll stand there until you do."

"Why should I cuss him out?"

"Because he busted Mattie Ruth in the leg," she says in surprise. "But let me do it anyway. "I'll show you, I can do it better than most grown-ups."

Lyndie walks to the outside of the shed and Dummy leans back against the wall, his eyes frightened as he watches the little girl at his feet.

"Dummy! You know what you done, you Dummy? You busted Mattie Ruth in the leg and hurt her bad, you know that? And you are hateful and mean and at least three times bigger than she is and she is setting there just bawling her eyes out . . ."

Lyndie turns to Mattie Ruth and frowns because Mattie Ruth is not crying at all now, just staring up wide-eyed at Lyndie. But Dummy doesn't even notice she's not still crying, he's looking at Lyndie, scareder than ever.

"Now, are you sorry you done what you done? Are you good and sorry you hurt Mattie Ruth?"

Dummy nods his head and his eyes open wider. Lyndie turns and smiles at me before snapping her face back toward Dummy who starts nodding again.

"Dummy!" Dummy jumps back against the wall of the shed. "Dummy, you get down on your knees in front of Mattie Ruth. Right there in front of her," — she points — "and hold your head down."

Dummy makes a thump like a sack of feed falling as he drops down in front of Mattie Ruth. Lyndie says, "OK, Mattie Ruth, bust him a good one in the head."

Mattie Ruth bites her bottom lip and hits him with a little black fist that just bounces off the mat of yellow-white hair on his head. Dummy doesn't move or look up.

"OK, you're friends again and you can be on our side now, Dummy." Dummy looks up and smiles at Lyndie and starts to slap his hands on his knees like he did this morning when they were playing hopscotch. That's the first time I've seen him happy since then.

He starts to point at me and jumps up and down in front of Lyndie, waving his thumb in her face.

Lyndie starts to giggle, and says, "He wants me to tell you about his thumb, Miss Ramie. You know what that Dummy done last Sunday at church?"

She laughs again and Dummy jumps around in circles and gets so dizzy he has to rest his hand on the wall.

"That Dummy got his thumb stuck in the candle-holder on the back of the pew. He did, and everybody got up to leave and went out the other end of the row and me and Little Brother was planning on tripping him up from behind the door . . . only he didn't never come out and when we looked in and we seen Dummy all bent over, we thought he must have been praying for something, but he was trying to hide that he caught his finger and it was all puffed and swollen so bad from his pulling on it, it won't never likely to come loose."

I look at Dummy and he has his hands over his face and is peeking between his fingers at me. "My daddy had to go to the truck and get a screwdriver and take the candle-holder clean off the pew so Dummy could leave and they could be locking up the church, and me and Little Brother told him we was going to have to saw his finger off, and made Dummy cry."

Dummy traces a tear down his cheek and pouts, just like he did this morning when he was mimicking me at Papa's funeral.

"Anyway Papa got out his saw," Lyndie says, "and you ain't never seen Dummy run so fast, run off and left his shoes, and we didn't even see him till he turned up at revival last night and didn't have no candle-holder on his thumb."

Suddenly a shower of walnuts hits the tin roof, sounding like someone has dumped hailstones on us.

Lyndie steps up near the wall of the shed and whispers, "Dummy, you go up under the persimmon tree and get some hard ones and some squishy ones." Another walnut comes rolling under the shed and one rings across the roof and off the other side. "And Mattie Ruth, you collect up all the walnuts they throw up here. But don't you try to throw none of them, you hear? You give them to me or Miss Ramie because you can't hit nothing." Mattie Ruth picks up the walnut that hit her in the leg and gives it to me before she runs off in the grass to hunt for the other walnuts. Lyndie hands me two clods and says, "Bust one on top of the dike, Miss Ramie. That'll make John Junior mad and he'll throw every which a way."

I toss the clods, and as the second one breaks on the top of the dike, I hear John Junior start cussing. About ten walnuts roll through the shed where Lyndie and I lean against the wall. I see Mattie Ruth come around the corner and start to fill her cupped skirt with the walnuts. Over the sound of the walnuts ringing on the roof, I can hear Miss Liz beating on the tub on the back porch.

"Miss Liz is calling me to lunch, Lyndie. I'm sorry I can't play but I'll try to see you again before I go, OK?"

"OK. Bye. Wish you could stay and fight though."

I meet Dummy coming around the edge of the shed as I leave, his shirt cupped up in front of him, like Mattie Ruth has her dress. I see the orange juice of the persimmons seeping through his shirt and dripping off on his white stomach. As I start up the path I hear Lyndie call out, "Oh Dummy, you gooed them all up before you got here."

When I get to the top of the hill, I hear all the children start to laugh and shout. The boys have run over the top of the dike. Lyndie and Mattie Ruth have come from the shed and are standing in the edge of the field. Dummy is dancing in circles through the sage, clutching at his red-stained shirt with both hands. When he falls in the straw with a thud, a loud squeal goes up from the girls and I turn my back on their laughter, catching in my eye before I turn, the red-spotted Dummy in the pale yellow sage.

Writing Spider . . .

Miss Liz and I are down by the pond and it's afternoon now. The water has a green skim of pollen on it and as the ducks swim toward the bank, the green stuff swirls and trails along behind them, breaking in spots so you can see the water which looks cold and gray like metal. I run down to the edge and the frogs stretch out in the air and land in the water. Then the little holes they made in the pollen close over and I wait for the frogs to come back up. I see them now, their eyes peeking out of the water, watching me with light green pollen on top of their heads.

"Baarrup!" I yell and they pop back under again.

I start laughing and when I see them all come back to the surface, I turn to call to Miss Liz. But I stop and don't say anything when I see her. She's not looking at me, just staring down at the rushes and the water willows. The redwing blackbirds fly up from the cattails and I can see their old nests hanging in the plants like brown sacks. The birds make a cawing sound when they fly that's like a crow, only softer, and sounds a long way off. When I look back at Miss Liz, I see that her eyes are watching the birds go over our heads, their black bodies opening and diving after the bugs and a red spot glowing in the black each time they flap their wings. Miss Liz has her apron held up and full of biscuits for the ducks and she's crumbling them up with her hand but not looking at what she's doing. I start to walk back up the hill to her but when I look down, I see little red frogs hopping all around my feet.

"Gee, Miss Liz. Look at all the little frogs."

She turns her head slowly to face me and stares at me like she's trying to remember who I am. I feel funny for a minute; I'm afraid to move because I'll step on the little frogs, and I feel I ought to move and say something to Miss Liz. Then she starts to blink her eyes and walk slowly toward me. As soon as she gets close to me, I scoop up one of the little frogs and hold it up to her; it's the color of red clay and sits in the middle of my hand.

"Piss frog. Put it down!" she snaps.

I look back at the little frog but it's already gone, though I didn't even feel it leave.

"Piss frog?" I say.

"Go wash out your hand. You'll get warts sure as you're standing there."

I walk down and stoop where the water juts in around the cattails. When I stick my hands in the cold water, the pollen feels gritty. The pollen gets slimy as I rub my hands together, trying to dry them and warm them back up. I jump up as a shower of biscuits hits the water beside me, the ducks squawking and diving toward them.

"Where's the other one, Miss Liz? I don't see but five."

"Fox got him. Found his feathers and all, over there where they roost in the willows."

"Oh, he got him while he was asleep. I've never seen them come out of the water since I set them out."

"They'll learn to sleep in the water or there won't be a one of them left. Only I don't feel no envy for them having to sleep with their bottoms in that cold water."

The ducks were my Easter present from Miss Liz. I had to

leave them here when I went back to town and I can't really feel they're the same ducks, because when I left them they were still yellow and fuzzy, and when I came back they were white and almost as big as they are now. They were real cute when they were little; I let them take turns swimming in the commode, but they'd get scared sometimes if I put them down in there. I always thought, wouldn't it be awful if somebody slipped and flushed one of them, but I had to let them swim and Miss Liz wouldn't let me run a sink full of water.

The ducks are smacking at the water and tearing up the pollen skim. Most of the bread is broken apart and sinking now.

"Don't you think we ought to try to feed them on the bank so so much of the bread won't sink?" I ask.

"No, they'll be needing the water to swallow. Don't want them so fat they get slow and lazy anyway. They'll get caught for sure."

We leave the ducks to start up the path to the house. I run right into the back of Miss Liz as she stops. She takes me by the arm and leads me around a writing spider web that is woven over the path. The spider is yellow-stripped and its legs bend like long fingers as it works.

"Boy, it's mean looking. I didn't even see it when we came down," I say.

"He won't there," she says and I feel chill bumps go up my arm.

Miss Liz is looking at the web. "They make a fine web," she says. "Don't no spider I know of make a prettier one."

"I don't like spiders even if the web is pretty. I can't even look at them without getting chills all over. That one's almost as big as my hand."

"He's a pretty thing with all that yellow on him. Looks like he's made out of gold. They used to tell me if he wrote your name, he was carving your tombstone for you and I used to see him write out 'E.M., E.M., Elizabeth Marshall,' over and over, and think he was carving my name."

Miss Liz points to the center of the web. "See it?" The spider sees her finger and runs up a strand to the top, trailing a silk string behind it. I get chills again and see his zigzags in the center that could be made out to be an E.M. if you were looking for it.

"I hope it can't make R's and H's," I say. "That makes me feel creepy."

"No, he can't make them. Only letters that zigzag," she says.

The spider drops back down the silk and starts to work in the center again.

"See, he's busy carving a tombstone for me and won't have me disturbing his work."

"Mama! Quit saying things like that. Let's go back. I can't stand to watch him."

"He ain't got no poison. Not more than enough to kill a bug," she says, and I watch her big body start back up the path.

"If I saw him on me, I think I would just die from the look of him," I say. "A black widow has enough poison. I read it had enough to kill a cow, and a black widow isn't half as big as that." I don't know why I started talking about spiders again. I sure didn't want to.

Miss Liz stops at the top of the path on the edge of the woods. "They have enough, they do," and her eyes look watery in the sun as she stands there. "You don't remember Gregory, your little brother?"

"No, not really. I just remember he was a little baby when he died, and he used to play out in the yard. I remember Aunt Cecie told me he died."

"I reckon you wouldn't remember it, how it happened that he was to die. I blame myself to this day, to this day for that." Then she starts walking and I catch up with her. "He was always prone to pick up specks. Had little eyes sharper than a tack and would crawl around on the floor picking up dead flies and bits of paper and such. He'd spot a speck of something all the way across the room and would just scoot over and get it and hold it under his nose in his little fingers. And I'd try to keep an eye on him to keep him from handling them dirty flies."

A shudder goes through her big shoulders before she starts talking again. "I hate myself to this day. It was an awful thing. You was just a little bit of something yourself, three if I remember correctly, and your mama was just dead and left you both on my hands. Little Gregory was still in diapers so I was to keep you both, it was decided, until we got things straightened out — after that was when Cecie took it on herself to take you with her. Just me and Gregory was at the house and he was just too much little man for me to keep check on so I let him amuse himself. Papa was out of hearing down at the barns and Gregory was setting out back playing by the woodpile, wasn't bigger than a minute and could amuse himself stacking them blocks. Then I heard him start into yelling and thought he had got himself into a nest of hornets and went running out back and there was his little hand already swelled up big as his head. It was unnatural big and I was still thinking a hornet had him when I seen that hating spider, pinched up in his little fingers. He still had him pinched up in his little fingers and had picked him up like he was always prone to pick up specks and there was that hating spider."

My hands are shaking and Miss Liz just talks faster and walks faster like she doesn't even hear me. I have to almost run to keep up until I just want to stop and ball up on the ground.

"Well, he'd turned him up one of them boards and seen a speck and picked it up, that's what he had done. And it was that hating spider. I slapped it out of his hand and just stomped it to a pulp, but I could see that red spot on it when it curled up. And I toted him in and put on soot and butter and everything I could think of and wrapped him up with him hollering his head off and started out to find Papa to see if we could get him in to a doctor, and that little feller just swelled and swelled like he was going to bust in my arms. Then he got quiet and whimpered a little and died right there with me toting him. Just died right there in that blanket from that little bitty spider, and he was as healthy a little man as ever anyone had. Just as strong a baby as anybody could have wanted to have. Would have grown to a fine man, you could feel it in his hands when he was a mind to pull on you, strong as a little mule and he died right there with me toting him."

Mama keeps saying the same things over and over. We sit down in the porch chairs with her still talking but I don't listen to her anymore. I am looking out under the shade trees and watching a Dominique hen scratch in the leaves, humming to herself as she picks up the leaves with her feet and pecks in the dirt.

"Mama!" I yell, and she looks up quickly at me and gasps. I caught her right in the middle of a sentence. She looks mad at me and I'm trying to think of something to ask her quick to get her to talk about something else.

"Mama, I saw Dummy playing with the little kids today and it's really funny to see an old man like that, out there trying to play hopscotch. And playing war down at the dikes just like a little kid." I hear my own words and they sound frightened. Miss Liz is glaring at me, not saying anything and looking like her eyes are going to burn out. She grips her mouth shut, still staring at me.

"Didn't I tell you to stay away from him?" she says sharply.

"I did stay away. I was just watching him and the little kids, and Mrs. Stiles was saying that's why she didn't run him off, because they liked him."

She still stares at me, making my heart beat fast. I can hear it beating and it hurts my chest. Miss Liz has never talked sharp to me like that before.

"I'm a mind to tell you about him. I'm a mind to," she says.

"I'm a mind to tell you something you ain't even got no business thinking about," she adds angrily.

"Mama, I didn't see him on purpose. You sent me with the butter and I couldn't help but see him over there. And he was playing with them just below your barns, I couldn't help seeing him . . ."

"You oughta know. You're big enough that you oughta know."

"Know what, Mama? Honestly, I just saw him playing with the little kids, and he acted just like one of them only he was old and couldn't do anything right."

She didn't listen to me and my eyes start to burn. Now she stares out across the yard and when I look out there, I see the Dominique hen come from behind the tree.

"I ain't set foot on Virginia Stiles's place since. I seen it last summer and it was her kids with him, I seen that," she says. Then Miss Liz's chair starts to rock and her voice sounds like she's walking as it jars up and down and her feet slide back and forth across the grit on the floor.

"I was a mind to walk down to my pond one day after you had gone back to town, and throw some biscuits to the ducks," she goes on, "when I heared all this screaming and fussing and splashing and knowed the little Stiles kids done took to go swimming in my pond again. Well, they hadn't seen fit to ask me, and since I feared that one of them might drown down there and figured they didn't have no one watching over them, I started rushing off down the path. Now I want you to know I won't going to be hard on them for swimming. The sun was hot enough to suck the juice out of a mushmelon and the cows had taken to standing down in the slop holes to cool off. So I set on off down there with it in my mind to tell them I wasn't against their swimming but I thought their Mama ought to watch over them. Well, I'm walking along and get about to the dam where that minnow seine is rigged up and where them water willows grow so thick, when I see a sight I never want to see again. I just let my apron go and let those biscuits go rolling. I seen little bits and snatches of clothes piled all around the edge, and they was all in there swimming and splashing just as naked as jay birds, which I ain't got no objection to them being little younguns, but in their cutting up and splashing with them was that sorry sight. That sorry sight Dummy was jumping up and down in there with them without a stitch on and there was that filthy thing, a grown man, right in front of those little children with his business showing bright as day. And there was two little girls, that little Lyndie Stiles and one of their little nigger tenant girls, jumping around in the water without a stitch on and that dirty thing in there with them. It just made me sick to my stomach. I don't even like to speak of it now; it was just a filthy sight, him showing himself in front of those little girls like that. And ain't no telling at all what he's been up to when there won't no one around to see him. I was a great-minded to go tell Virginia Stiles what she was letting happen right under her nose, but I just kept my mouth shut, I was so sick to my stomach. If she ain't got no better sense than that, being a mother to that little girl, well, I say she can just suffer for it. It just made me sick to look and I went back to the house and was thinking things so terrible I hate to make mention of them. Them little girls not knowing no better and that dirty thing with them all the time, why I'm telling you, he's just apt . . . Oh, my gracious alive! I won't think about it anymore, I just won't. It's just too terrible a thing to put your thoughts to."

I am hearing every word Miss Liz is saying now. My hands feel all cold when I touch them together, worse than they did when I washed them in the pond. And I see my hands pick off a dirt dauber nest from the porch post and sling it in the yard, busting it beside that old hen who goes running off and squawking. She stops running and walks in circles, stretching her neck

up and making that humming sound again. I'm wishing I had
that old hen on the chop block and had an ax in my hand and
was cutting that neck in two and she would stop making that
noise.

"And you being a big girl and starting to develop, why there
ain't no telling what that sorry thing has on his mind," Miss Liz is
saying. My feet and legs are feeling cold and I'm hating the feeling when they touch together. I'm not able to put anything
straight in my mind. I'm seeing Dummy's clothes stacked up by
the pond where I was today, all dirty and smelly and looking too
filthy to touch, and him out there in the water hopping around
naked, and Lyndie and Mattie Ruth shoving his naked body
down and him sitting there in the water with his skin all showing
and looking up at the little girls.

But his eyes, his eyes are like they were today, they are, Miss
Liz. They're like today and they are clear and blue, and he's got
his clothes back on and he's watching the little girls play hopscotch and he is wishing he wasn't old, so he could play hopscotch like that. And he loves the little girls, Miss Liz, he loves
them because they can jump all around and are young and can
jump through the squares like it wasn't anything, and it makes
him all tired and breathless because he is so old. And I feel tears
coming in my eyes and burning, but I feel like crying because
Dummy is so old, Miss Liz, and can't hop through the squares
like the little girls can, and he's watching them and loving them
because they're so pretty and little and can hop all around him
under the tree. He will jump around the same as when your
little brother called him Dummy, and he will play dead for them
in the sage with persimmon stains on his shirt; he will do it to
make the children laugh.

The Web . . .

Miss Liz just walked over and put her supper plate in the sink. She stands in front of the stove, pouring her third cup of coffee. As the coffee goes into the cup, she frowns at the clumps of grounds that splash from the spout. When she sits back down across from me, she tips the coffee over the edge of the cup into the saucer. I watch a circle of brown spread around the bottom of the cup that she has set on the tablecloth. She lifts the saucer and sucks the coffee into her mouth.

The clock in the living room is striking. I count six strikes and know that it is over fifteen minutes slow. "Mama, are we going to start getting ready for church soon? It's getting late."

"I've decided against our going," she says with the saucer of coffee still at her mouth.

"Oh, I didn't know."

Miss Liz sets her empty saucer on the table, sighing and looking up at me. "I'm great-minded to tell Ione myself. Somebody ought to, and though I ain't certain it's my calling, I'm still great-minded to tell her," she says.

"Ma'am? I don't understand."

"About her singing. That hateful voice," Miss Liz says sharply. "She'll get peeved at me, I'm certain of that. But an old woman showing herself that way and messing up the singing.

Why, it ain't even a pleasure to listen at the singing with all that squawking going on. I'd as soon listen at a nest of jay birds in the yard. Just ruins the songs. Standing up there with her mouth puckered up like she sounds so fine.

"Well, I guess she ought to know what she sounds like since she has to hear it too. She probably thinks she sounds good. I guess somebody could tell her she didn't sound good and she probably wouldn't believe them. Anyway, somebody let her in the choir." Then I laugh and say, "She'd sound just as bad out front though."

Miss Liz splashes her coffee over the top of the cup again before dropping her chin down and blowing the coffee into little waves. I don't think she has even been listening to me. She wrinkles her nose, shaking the brown drops from her chin whiskers, and says, "An old woman showing herself like that. It don't get to be no laughing matter having to listen to such as that every week. I just might take a notion not to go anymore."

"You mean not to go to church at all? Just because of the singing?" I ask.

"That ain't all of it. That ain't all of the reason. It ain't the first time I've put my mind to it. Having to see them younguns every week, going up there so they can flooze up for each other, with no notion in their heads what they're supposed to be there for. And their folks going, cause if they don't, they'll have to take into explaining why they won't there. That preacher goes out and spends his week prancing up in this and that yard saying, 'You feeling poorly, Mrs. so-and-so? I seed you won't gathered in with us on Sunday last.' I've seen ten or more preachers come and go at that very church and that's the worse one yet. Come here thinking he was so fine and had to put on like a nigger when he was talking to us. 'You feeling poorly, you laid up in the back, reason you won't gathered in with us,' " Miss Liz mimics. "Thinking he's so fine he's got to talk down to us to get understood. Up there talking about saving and telling us we got to go up and play the fool in front of everybody to keep from going to hell. I just bet that keeps that sorry Dummy out of hell. It'd take a sight more than preaching and saving to keep that sorry filth from burning."

Miss Liz stops talking and I don't say anything while she reaches for the coffee cup. Her fingers stop moving and she stares at her hand that rests on the table. "And when Papa passed," she goes on slowly. "You should have seen that preacher's airs when Papa passed. Well, I guess you remember his carrying on so at the funeral like he was Papa's best friend. After the burying he got those women up there to cook up stuff and he come bringing me a basket of fruit and such, like I was an invalid. I just flat told him I'd raise my own fruit, thank you, and he went pit-patting off across that yard like I was going to hit him with the broom."

"I think that's what they always do at churches, Mama," I interrupt. "I don't think he meant any harm really."

Miss Liz looks up at me and then grabs the coffee cup, her hand shaking and splashing the coffee into the saucer. "You don't think so. You don't think so, do you? Well you got a lot more living to do. You'll see what people got on the back of their minds soon enough. Papa won't in the ground a week before they was all showing up here trying to buy me out. Won't offering me a sight better than half what the place is worth and stood around carrying on how I wouldn't want the place to run down and what a shame it would be to let such a fine farm go to ruin. Won't a week after Papa was dead and they was already buzzing around like hornets, so I just put them straight quicklike. I told them they had another think a-coming if they thought they could talk me down like they did Papa, and they could just pack themselves right off my place, that I was the one who managed when Papa was living and him being dead won't going to change none of that. Not in my way of thinking."

"Aunt Cecie told me what a fine job of managing you did," I

say quickly. "She told me all the time about how they never had to go hungry even if the crop went bad."

Miss Liz is silent a moment. She starts smiling at me. "Cecie said that, did she? I would never have thought Cecie ever took notice of nothing since she thinks she's so fine now."

"Oh yes she did, Mama. She always talks highly of you to Uncle June."

"And then she prisses around here saying how dirty this and that is. Running those prissy fingers through the dust on the furniture, like I ain't got nothing better to do than swish around with a dust rag."

"But she is always talking about how hard it was to live through a winter on what the crop brought, how sometimes even in a good year the tobacco didn't bring anything at market, and how you always made sure they had enough to eat and all."

"So Cecie said that. Well I declare, I never would have thought it."

Miss Liz stands up, knocking her body against the table, jarring the dishes. She picks up my plate and puts it in the sink. She is smiling now and I am glad I said what I did.

"I'll have time to wash everything up tomorrow so Cecie won't have anything to find fault with on Sunday. Reckon the stove could stand a scrubbing. Let's just leave everything be tonight and go set in the front room."

"OK, and I better feed my bird again."

"You run on in and stir up the fire and I'll fetch him some meat and water."

I go into the living room and take my bird's box from the hearth. He's still quiet and has snuggled underneath the rags except for the top of his head. When I shove the logs in the fireplace with the poker, they begin to crackle and flare up. Miss Liz walks up behind me and takes the poker from my hands, handing me the meat for the bird and a cup of water. The flames on the logs have died back down again.

"Now, that ain't no way to get a fire going." As I drop the food in my bird's mouth, Miss Liz starts ripping the pages out of a magazine and wads the paper in her hands, stuffing it under the logs. Then she crams kindling over the paper and soon the fire is so hot my face burns. When the flames begin to pop, my little bird starts trying to hop around on the rags. He flaps his wings a little but falls on his side until I set him back up.

I pick my bird up and hold him in my hand, his wings opening across my palm. "He already feels heavier. Look at him close his mouth, Miss Liz. He's gotten stubborn since this morning."

"They'll turn against the hand that feeds them, they will. It's hard to raise a wild thing. Give him a little pinch in his jaws. He'll open up." She stoops beside me and presses her fingers against the sides of his beak and his mouth comes open. "Now not too much more. Don't want to bloat him up. His craw is about stuffed. See, feel him here." She washes a piece of the meat down his throat while I feel the little bird's neck. As the liver in his mouth disappears, I can feel a tight throbbing puff of feathers under his beak. Miss Liz takes the rest of the meat and tosses it on the fire where, for a moment, it smells like it is cooking then it disappears. When she stands to pour the rest of the water in the flower pot on the mantel she says, "Set him on the floor a minute. Let's see him hop about."

When I put him on the floor, he flaps his wings a moment until he has his balance. Then he scoots across the rug and under the sofa.

"Woo, look at him run," Miss Liz laughs.

"Gee, I didn't know he could get around like that already."

"It don't take an animal long to be up and around. It's just human babies that are a nuisance."

I reach under the sofa for him and when my hand closes around his warm body, he tries to squirm away.

"Just look at that ugly thing now," Miss Liz says. "I'm glad fancy Miss Cecie ain't here to see that, I am. Now don't you let him run under things and collect a wad of dust like that for her to harp on this Sunday."

The little bird is covered with gray dust, and draped across the top of his head is a dry spider web.

"You told on me, didn't you, you little rascal," Miss Liz says as she takes the bird from my hands. Then she wraps his body back up in the rags and picks the web off the top of his head. His little eyes shine black now like they have grown with his body since morning and the fire makes a jumping red spot in them.

"Wonder what happened to the others in the chimney, Mama?"

Miss Liz looks toward the fireplace, silent for a moment. "I reckon they're all dead by now. I hadn't thought to notice that they won't making any more fuss. Their mama just run off and left them, I'm suspecting. Don't know as she could do much else though. I seen a cat tote her little ones around by the neck many a time if they didn't choose to be born in a fitting place but I don't know as how a bird can do anything."

"I wonder if Aunt Cecie is going to let me take my bird back with me. Oh, and I almost forgot, Mama. I want to go out before dark and fill me up a jar full of tadpoles to take back with me."

"Ain't a thing down there now but bullfrogs. What you want those big, ugly things for? Come spring you could get some little ones but I wouldn't have one of those big ones."

"Well, I promised my teacher I'd get some tadpoles for biology class when I came home, and she said get bullfrogs so they would be big enough for us to watch their legs come and all. She said they'd be the only kind we could get to study in the winter since it takes them longer to develop."

Then Miss Liz laughs and says, "It's a good thing you ain't got to take the bus back toting all those varmints. They'd put you off 'fore you know it. Woo, I remember the tale your Uncle Buck used to carry on about of when he was taking the bus back to the army and this fat old woman let a whole box of biddies get loose on the bus. He said they was running around under everybody's feet and she was bending over in the aisle to catch them and just breaking wind out loud every time she bent over. Woo, it was the funniest story when he used to tell it . . ."

Miss Liz laughs a minute, then she puts her finger on top of my head and says, "You're going to get yourself caught with a room full of bullfrogs. Then what you going to do, when they start croaking and hopping out all over the place? I declare I can remember as good as yesterday when you were a little bit of something, you had this house so full of critters I couldn't walk for fear of stepping on one or stepping in what one of them left behind him. You remember that old terrapin, the one you wrote your name on? That was some sight seeing that ugly thing with 'Ramona' on his back."

"I remember. And he wouldn't come out of his shell and we'd set him in front of the fire until he'd get hot and scoot across the floor. But my teachers says land turtles are turtles, that terrapins are something else."

Miss Liz starts walking toward the kitchen and says, "I'll poke some holes in a jar for you. I declare it ought to please me to find a youngun who'd be satisfied to get a doodlebug for Christmas."

I hear Miss Liz getting a jar from the cabinet and I go to the door and watch her put the ice pick against the lid and bang it with her fist until it makes a hole in the top. Then she says, "I reckon it ain't going to be easy finding any since the ducks are down there gulping up everything they see. You won't find too many up shallow where you can reach them so I'd advise sneaking up behind the dam, so they won't be likely to see your shadow."

"You know what my teacher calls them, Miss Liz? Pollywogs. And she calls a crawfish a crayfish, and a lightning bug a firefly, and calls a fishing worm an earthworm. She just keeps on going until I have to look at a picture to find out what she's talking about. Sometimes I feel ashamed to ask a question for fear she'll laugh at me for the wrong word. But one day I did tell her after class that you called a towhee a swamp robin. Miss Robinson just thought that was wonderful and said a poet told her one time that a towhee was a perfect robin."

Miss Liz is laughing now. She hands me the jar and says, "You remember when you first started at that school, the day you come running up to me with a handful of flowers and said, 'Look, Miss Liz, forget-me-nots,' and what was that other name you had learned, I forget . . ."

"Bluets?" I say.

"That's the one, and then you asked me if what you had in your hand was a bluet or a quaker-lady or a forget-me-not. And I told you it was a piss flower." Miss Liz starts laughing again and says, "Piss flower, that's what it was — piss ants, piss flower, piss frogs, piss pots, and you like to had a fit, you did. You screwed up your face at me and said, 'Miss Liz, that's a dirty word.' But I declare to this day they're piss flowers to me. I ain't never heard them called nothing different."

"I didn't mind telling my teacher what you called a towhee, but I sure didn't tell her what you called a forget-me-not. And it's not a piss ant, it's a termite."

"And what was it you called that pretty little gray bird with the peak on his head — a tuff-tied titmouse. Woo, a titmouse. I declare that's the funniest word I ever heard."

"It's a tufted titmouse," I say. "My teacher wants to come home with me sometime and see if you'll let her catch some stuff for class. She said she could pick up water moccasins with her hands and just let them bite her . . ."

"Let them bite her!" Miss Liz shrieks.

"That's what she said, and that it didn't even hurt because she was immune."

"Snakes! You mean she handles snakes? I won't have any such woman on my place. She picks up them hating things?"

"She's not even scared of them. She has a whole shelf full of snakes and spiders in jars. They're all dead and pickled but they sure look real as everything."

Miss Liz is mumbling as I go out the door, "Snakes and spiders, Woo." When I hear the screen slam behind me, the squeals of the night bugs start at my feet. Overhead the sky is pink-orange and full of flying things. My eyes get blurred at this time of day and I can't see clearly; it's hard to tell if the birds are barn swallows or blackbirds or bats, except the bats dart around faster. I look up toward the chimney of the house until my eyes get used to the light. I can see which ones are bats now, because they don't have tails and the swallows have long forked tails and look like something graceful that loves to fly, while the bats look nervous and scared. High up overhead are little dots in great clusters of the birds migrating and you can hear their whistling sound, sort of sad and way up. The swifts that are still here don't land on the chimney anymore and fly away up above the smoke that is coming out. I go to the pond the back way behind the dam, and when I climb up the back side, I hear my ducks splash into the water. I can still smell the fireplace smoke and see it in a cloud out over the water. The red-wing blackbirds are down here catching bugs in the smoke.

I can see tadpoles huddled in the edge of the water, but my ducks are swimming toward me and will frighten them away. I throw a clod in front of them and the ducks squawk and slide behind the cattails. When I scoop my jar down for the tadpoles, they roll over in the water, showing their white stomachs. I get five in two tries, which should be enough, but the water is so dirty I can hardly count them.

As I go back I decide to take the path that comes out in the field. The woods are dark since the light of the sunset can't come through the trees. The trees seem to close you up in a little dark box, almost as dark now as the swamp forest. I feel chills come on my arms and something is bothering my mind, but I don't know what. Then across my face I feel something like silk threads. I hear my voice shriek through the air and my jar drops when I fall to my knees.

He's in my hair. He's in it. I yank the rubber band out of my hair and hit at it. I know he's in there. The tears are hot on my face and I feel him crawling on my neck down my shirt.

"Miss Liz! Miss Liz! Come quick!"

It is dark and I can't see if I've knocked him out on the ground anywhere. I feel him all over me and feel the cold water gurgling out of my jar and running under my knees.

"Miss Liz, please come. Please hurry!"

I hear her come down the path, but I can't move when I feel her arms lift me up and start to lead me up the path. We are in the thin light at the edge of the field and Miss Liz is shaking me back and forth but when I try to look at her, her face is blurred.

"What is it? What is it?" she says. "What happened, Ramie? Tell me quick."

"The spider . . . in my hair."

I drop to the ground at her feet and feel her rough fingers lift my hair and rake across the skin on my neck, pulling my collar back. Then she takes my hair in her hands and shakes it and I scream again, because it feels like he ran down in my face.

"He ain't on you, honey. He ain't on you nowhere. Believe me, he ain't. Now don't you cry no more. He ain't on you. Come on, get yourself up now."

I feel her lift me to my feet again and my skin is crawling all over. I put my hands against my face to keep my hair from touching it. I feel her hand on my arm, rough and hard like scales, and the silky feeling of the web starts to go away as we go up the steps into the house.

The Closet . . .

I HAVE MY FACE in Miss Liz's lap and she is brushing my hair out across her knees. All the tangles are out now and I feel my body relax and sink as the brush glides through my hair.

I hear her talking and saying over and over, "You see, he ain't in there. That old spider is down there in the woods trying to patch up that hole you made in his web. He ain't in your hair, honey. He is more scared than you were. He looks like the biggest spider in the world to you, but he ain't a bit big when you consider how a person must look to him."

Her voice is slow now and I feel small like a child. The fire is warm and there is no sound but the flames popping and the logs falling every now and then. The sound of the night bugs is shut outside the doors. I hear a gurgling sound like water in the spring coming from Miss Liz's stomach. Her heartbeat is very slow and steady, and as I shut my eyes and press my face deeper, I remember once when I felt a heartbeat against my ear. It was a little hammer beating at me. I couldn't see anything; it was very dark and I was very small, so small that all of me was in my mother's lap and we were inside the dark closet under the steps. Miss Liz had always used the closet to throw things in when company came, but once my mother and I were in there. It was too low to stand up in, and my mother's head hit the ceiling and dirt showered down on my face if I looked up.

I can hear Miss Liz's voice like I did then, outside the closet and muffled sounding. Only then she was saying, "What you want coming around here? You ain't welcome, you hear. She ain't here and you ain't going to see her."

Then I heard a man say over and over, "I come to get her and I'm going to find her. I'm going to take her off with me."

"You ain't touching her or the youngun, you hear? You'll get off this place or I'll get the law to you. I will, don't you think I won't," Miss Liz said.

And my mother squeezed me tighter, and though my eyes were wide open, I couldn't see anything but a line of light under the door. The man's voice grew loud and frightening until the front door crashed shut. When I heard him walk across the porch, the floor shook in the closet and dirt sifted down in my hair.

I stop thinking and sit up quickly. Miss Liz starts backward and her face is blurred until my eyes get used to the light.

"Well, I declare," she says. "You ought to give a body warning when you decide to come to life. Scared the stuffings out of me."

"I'm sorry," I say, and push my hair back from my eyes. "I'm all right now. I just got awful scared."

"Well, you sure scared the life out of me, hollering down in the woods like something had holt of you."

"I'm sorry, Miss Liz. I didn't mean to."

"Oh, now don't you go feeling bad. I know you didn't." She smiles at me and taps the brush on my knee. "I can see he gave you an awful scare."

"Mama," I say. "I'm trying hard to remember something that I never thought about until today when you mentioned my mother."

Miss Liz turns her face from me and folds her hands in her lap, staring across the room. She doesn't speak.

"You know that closet over there? Were my mother and I ever in that closet? It seems that I remember being there with her and that's the only time I even remember her at all. I couldn't see her because it was dark and I don't even recall what she looked like."

"She was the spitting image of you except a mite skinnier. In looks she was, but that was all. That was all; that girl didn't have a smart bone in her body. She never said one word that made good sense." Miss Liz pauses and asks, "You say you recollect being in that closet?"

"Yes, I think I do."

Miss Liz turns and stares across the room again.

"Miss Liz, won't you tell me about it? Don't you want to?"

"Some things it's best you don't hear tell of."

"But I want to know. It'll be bothering me until I know. I remember a man that was at the door and you were talking to him and he wanted to take us away."

"He wanted to, but not on my life would I let him," she says sharply. I don't say anything and Miss Liz begins to tap the brush in her lap.

Then she starts to talk slowly. "That man you heard was your father. And he was headed off to the army and thought he was going to come and take you with him. You and your mama both. I knowed him. I knowed what he would do. He would take you and Maylean, that was your mamma's name; he would take you and Maylean and get her pregnant again, then run off messing around and leave her without a cent. I knowed him. That was all he was good for. He done it once and he'd do it again. But he got to her. To this day I don't know how, because I thought I had her under my coattail until he was gone again. After he had left for the war, Maylean was moping around here big as a barrel in four months' time. I ain't never been so mad. I wanted to knock her in the head and she just walked around stupidlike and would watch me look after you, just stare at me and never lift her hand to help me. Well, she had that baby, that was Gregory, God rest his little soul. She had that baby, and if she ever had a lick of sense before, she didn't have none then. She took to hollering and yelling at me and trying to pull that baby out of my hands with me trying to wash it and would just get soap all in his eyes and had me so scared she was going to drown him in the washtub that I . . . I hauled off and hit her in the side of the head. I never felt tempted in my life to hit a youngun in the head, but she was so trying and aggravating, I couldn't keep my wits no longer. I could hear her teeth rattle I hit her so hard. Then she just stared at me like she didn't feel it. She never got in my way no more. Cecie could tell you about Maylean, you just ask Cecie."

"Mama, Aunt Cecie won't tell me anything. She just says that my mother died and that was that."

"Well, you ask Cecie sometime if Maylean won't off in the head. It was like she won't no child of mine, she was always off in the head, couldn't do nothing in school and Cecie would try to help her until she'd just have to give up. Then Maylean got messed up with that man, took advantage of her, knowing she didn't have good sense."

Miss Liz stops talking and is banging the brush up and down in her lap.

"Why did she die, Mama?" I ask.

"Lord, I don't know why she did. Why she done it. Papa walked in . . . Papa walked in one day and he had Maylean in his arms and he just stood at the door not making a sound with Maylean soaking wet and dripping off a puddle on the floor. We had got word her man was dead, and I hadn't seen fit to even tell her, but Papa had told her. I reckon that's the only explaining it there is. And when Papa stood there holding her, that was the only time in all of Papa's days I ever seen him cry. But he had found her down there drownded and had carried her up to the house and Maylean just hung there from his arms like a little wet baby."

Miss Liz turns to me and says quickly, "Now don't you go getting upset again. I declare I didn't want to bring you out here to stay with me and make you all upset over something that is dead and gone."

"I'm not upset, Miss Liz. I don't remember her. I just wanted to know, and Aunt Cecie wouldn't tell me."

"She was right by that. I ought to be beat for opening my mouth. I should never have told you such a terrible thing."

"No, I wanted to know, Miss Liz. I want to know about my father. He was killed in the war, I know that. But I want to know everything you know about him."

"There ain't no more to know. He left and didn't come back and they sent his body, but I didn't go to the burying and I didn't put no stone there. I won't spending a cent for no stone for him and if I'd had any say, he wouldn't be down there by my folks. He won't none of us."

"That's all you know about him?"

"That's all," Miss Liz says and pinches her mouth together.

"I think I'll go to bed now, Mama. I feel awful tired."

"Oh, now I went and made you go fretting. I should have known to leave well enough alone."

"I'm just sleepy, Mama. I won't fret. I wanted to know."

"But don't you even think about it."

"Aunt Cecie bought me a wreath to put on my mother's grave. She got a plastic one so it would last."

"We'll walk down tomorrow and set it out. Now don't you think about it or you won't sleep good. They won't your folks. Don't you think they was. Well, Maylean was but he won't, and don't you even think Maylean was. You just go to sleep and know that Cecie is your folks and loves you, and I love you better than any of the others. To this day I don't know how Maylean ever had such a bright little whip as you."

"Night, Mama," I call from the door.

I undress and get in my bed and can hear Miss Liz in the living room saying "Oh, Oh, Oh," over and over. Her chair thumps the floor as she moans. Aunt Cecie wouldn't tell me, Miss Liz. Don't be sorry you did. I asked and asked, and all Aunt Cecie would say was they died. Over and over that they died. Miss Liz knows everything. But even Miss Liz won't tell me about my daddy. I want to know what he looked like, I want to paint his picture. Mother looked like me, so I have nothing of him in me, nothing but that he made me. And I am a bastard. And Gregory was a bastard, only he is dead and will never know it. Everybody is dead, everybody but Miss Liz, and even Miss Liz is old and will die before I will. Aunt Cecie acts like she's my mother, she's not. Her with all her prim and proper and making me put everything away and not letting me have any animals and making me stand up straight. I hate her. She wouldn't tell me, she won't tell me anything. She asked me why I never painted her picture; she has no face, I will never paint her. Her face is like the paper before I put a picture there.

Please, Miss Liz, don't be sorry you told me, please stop moaning, please. I wanted to know, I want to know about my daddy, what is a man like. Uncle June is not like a man, he is weak and red-faced and tells stories that are too long and always has something wrong with him. What is a man like who says, I have come to get her and I am going to take her off. I am sleepy and I can't think but I hate, I do, I hate Aunt Cecie. Please stop moaning, Miss Liz. The heavy quilts press me down, and on my arm that is out of the covers, I feel the satin and wool and corduroy of the quilt, and the satin is my dance costume, the scraps that were left, Aunt Cecie takes me to dancing, and the quilts are heavy, and my eyes drop shut.

Rainbow . . .

FROST IS ON THE WINDOW, and when I sit up and look outside, the fields are silver, almost like they are covered with snow. The air is so cold on my back, I crawl back under the quilts to get warm again. It is quiet outside this morning. I only hear sounds inside the house; the fire is popping in the living room and the bed creaks under me when I move. I don't hear Miss Liz in the kitchen, but the air smells of bacon. I reach on the floor for my clothes, grabbing them quickly and putting them under the covers with me. Their cloth is cold. I tuck them under me until they are warm before I stick my head under the covers and get dressed. When I get out of bed and stick my feet in my shoes, the leather feels wet and clammy. From my suitcase I get my black tights and go in front of the fire to put them on. My legs look skinny and crooked with them on. I laugh out loud in the quiet house when I remember once my roommate and I were walking down the sidewalk in our black tights, and we heard some boys yelling and whistling at us from a car. When the car got in front of us, we saw they were Negroes and they saw we were white. They jerked their faces back inside and rolled up the windows.

I reach in my bird's box and feel his sides, bristly and warm and going in and out. I'm always so afraid that he'll be dead when I touch him, that it makes me feel good to touch his warm body. The only wild thing that I have ever had live from a baby, was a rabbit and he grew up and turned on me, scratching and clawing at my hands until I had to set him free. I never knew which one of the young rabbits running on the farm he was.

I go into the kitchen and see a rainbow of colors flickering across the table. On the window sill over the sink, the sun is shining through a jar. It's the jar I carried to the pond last night, and now it's full of tadpoles. I count nine in there; the water is clear except for a net of green algae. Tangled in the algae on the bottom is an almost transparent little crawfish who tucks his feelers down each time the tadpoles swim over him. I look back at the table and put my hand in the rainbow; the colors dance across my skin and the blue is very beautiful.

Through the window in the back door, I see Miss Liz. I had forgotten that it was Saturday, wash day, and she is standing over her black pot with her back to me, stirring the clothes with a stick, the fire burning at her feet. The elbows are worn out of her sweater and her legs are muddy looking because of her cotton stockings. Everything in the yard is covered with frost except the path where Miss Liz walked to the black pot, and a circle in the grass around the pot that has been melted away by the fire. I watch her stand there stirring the clothes, only her shoulders and arms moving as she works. The veins swell in her legs under the tight stockings when she lifts the clothes out on the end of the stick, wrings them out, and starts clipping them to the line. Soon I can see her only from the waist down as she moves behind the line full of clothes. The soap and water just hit the fire when she tipped the pot up on its side, and a sizzle goes up that I can hear through the door. Miss Liz walks out of the cloud of steam and starts toward the steps carrying a big piece of soap in her hands.

Since my breath has spread on the window, she doesn't see me until she is at the top of the back steps. She jumps back and her mouth drops open, then she smiles at me. I step back as she opens the door and say, "Morning, Mama."

The cold air comes in the door that she shuts quickly behind her. She sets the soap on the table and begins rubbing her hands together.

"Woo-ee, it really took a drop last night. Winter's on us now, I fear."

"That's a killing frost, isn't it?" I ask.

"That it is." Her eyes are cloudy as she looks up at me. "I set your breakfast in the stove to keep it warm for you. You didn't get it?"

"Not yet. I just got up. I almost slept all day."

She opens the oven door and sets my breakfast on the table. When I sit down to eat, I see her pat the side of the coffee pot and pour herself a cup of coffee.

"My hands ain't got an ounce of life in them," she says, and sits down across from me, folding her hands around the steaming cup.

"You went down and got me some tadpoles this morning, didn't you?" I say.

"And that hating crawfish got in with them. He pinched me good when I tried to fish him out."

"Oh, I like him. I'm glad you got him. We had to cut up those big pickled ones at school, but I'd like to have a little one for a pet."

"Pshaw, some pet he'll make. You won't be able to change the water until he decides to die."

I laugh and say, "I appreciate your getting them for me. I sure made a mess of getting them last night."

Miss Liz begins to run the back of her hands around the hot cup while I eat my breakfast. She is silent for a moment then she says, "I seen that that spider is still down there. Had him a greenfly in the web this morning. And his web was all frosted up like it was made of glass. You could see it a mile away today and no one would never know you even broke it. He won't be finding pickings so easy now it's frosted, but I suspect he's got a bunch of bugs balled up somewhere for winter."

I carry my plate to the sink and see that all of the dishes have been washed. "It looks like you've lived half a day since I've been asleep," I say.

Miss Liz glances up at me and squints before looking back down at her coffee. She didn't understand me. She says, "I used to tell Papa we ought to up and move down where there won't no winter to speak of. Folks that has been down in Florida tell me they don't have no winter a'tall, that the fields is green year round."

"That's where all the vegetables in the grocery store come from in the winter."

"Pshaw, they ain't fitting to eat. They been picked green, you can tell it by the taste of them. I wouldn't have them and I ain't giving no man a quarter for a mater what ain't got no more sweetness about it than a persimmon."

"You'd probably get tired of hot weather all the time, Miss Liz. I thought about it last year at school when I was looking out of my window when spring came. They have all these rows of pink cherry trees down the middle of the campus with little fences around each tree, and the trees look just like weeping willows only they have flowers. And you should see how we all acted when we saw our first robin at school. I do love snow now and then too, Miss Liz, and the girls who came up from Florida never even saw snow before. We would snitch trays from the dining hall and go out sliding on the golf course. And there was this one girl from India, you should see her. She wears long dresses made of silk and has a red dot drawn between her eyes. I saw her go out in the snow and pick it up in her hands and just look at it until it got too cold to hold. I would see her out there in the snow in those silk dresses that had the middle out and I would wonder what kept her stomach from freezing."

"She wore her stomach out of her dresses?"

"That's the way they dress over there."

"Well, that sure must be a sight."

"Oh, she's very pretty except she has dark hair under her nose that almost looks like a moustache."

Miss Liz laughs and picks at the fuzz on her chin. "You ought to have heard how Cecie used to carry on about my chin. I don't know why it come frizzling out like that, it won't always there. Cecie used to tell me I had more hair on my face than Papa which won't so, not a word of it. Papa'd shave his chin off right but he'd go around looking like he had a wad of corn silks stuck under his nose. And I'd just have to sit him down and snip them off or he'd go walking out with half his breakfast dangling in them."

"You know something, Mama? I try all the time to remember Papa when he was alive, because I really want to. When I'm thinking really good and all, I can remember his overalls and his brown brogans and his yellow hair but I can hardly ever remember how he talked."

Miss Liz smiles and says, "Well, he won't prone to talk much. Guess he was figuring I'd talk enough for both of us. You were such a little bit of something, I'd be surprised if you ever saw above his knees. And him towering up like he did, skinny as a rail. It won't a few times I seen him bang his head on the top of that door. If he was here today, I reckon he would tell you he remembers the top of your head the way you ran around under his feet all the time. You most certainly didn't suffer no lack of attention where Papa was concerned. It won't an uncommon sight to see him make an awful fuss over you."

"He used to lead me around on old John mule, didn't he?" I ask.

"And I seen the stupid thing lead you right in the barn on him one day and just dump you off on the ground. He didn't do it but once and he learned, but you just plopped off on the ground without letting out a peep and I feared he had busted you wide open. But I declare you didn't cry a lick. You just set there and I watched him dust you off and then you jumped up and started laughing at him. Papa paid you more mind than he did his own younguns, he did. I recollect clearly the day he took you out to show you his sign he won when he become a member of the Hundred Bushels of Corn Club. He was the only man around here that had got a hundred bushels off a acre, he got a hundred and five in fact, and he took you out there to show it to you, just showing off and you jumped around and clapped your hands and didn't have no notion in this world what it meant. Papa was just as pleased as punch 'cause it tickled you, and I would catch him looking at that sign every chance he got. It's still stuck up out there on the crib in fact. I reckon it'll be there until the crib falls down behind it."

I think of the tin sign that is tacked on the crib. I can see it in my mind with five ears of corn painted on it, spread out like a fan; but I don't remember when I first noticed it. The rainbow of colors is flickering over the back of Miss Liz's head, catching in the top of her gray hair. She looks up at me and blinks her eyes.

"Scoot your head over a little." I move my face and she says, "No, the other way, that's it. You got a rainbow on your face. What's a making it?"

She leans back and turns around before I can answer and says, "Oh, it's them tadpoles wiggling around. Just look at that sun a shining to beat the band and it's cold as ice out there. Well, I guess to be truthful it ain't really cold. But it sure feels it since it's the first bad frost. I knowed I should have brought in the rest of the garden before now, but it slipped my mind. Just a few maters left but they'll be puckered up good now."

Miss Liz turns back around and wraps her hands around the

coffee cup again. "You done set me to thinking on Papa, Ramie. I reckon he's the one person nobody never found fault with but I seen him do things that just fretted me to death. He was a good man, I ain't saying he won't. Me and Papa used to always set by the fire about this time and Papa'd say, 'Well Lizzie, the oats is sowed, got plenty of kindling under the shed, and I done tossed the cat in the crib so I reckon we can rest for a spell.' That's what he'd say, he didn't miss a winter saying that at least one time to me. Only I won't never prone to rest, not a bit of it, and there Papa'd set, just tossing wood on the fire like there won't no end of it while I'd fidget the winter away. Many a time I kicked up the snow to see if the oats were a-coming, and Papa'd poke fun at me. Come the first big snow and 'Lizzie,' he'd say, 'you going out to shovel the snow off your fields?' Then he'd say to me, 'Why you're worse than a youngun, Lizzie. You're just like a youngun opening every present before Christmas and not having a surprise left when it gets here.'"

Miss Liz starts to laugh and tap her fingers on the coffee cup, "But I declare to this day Cecie won't bring the Christmas presents out before we're all here for the opening. I opened every last one of them one year and stuck them back up and then put on like I was surprised when Christmas got here. But she knowed it." Miss Liz's shoulders bounce up and down when she laughs and says, "That really got her goat, it did."

She stops laughing and slides the cup toward her, splashing coffee over the top on her hands. Then she says, "The truth was she was mad as the devil. I declare I'm going to fidget myself to the grave, fretting over this and that. Papa and Cecie's right, I fear. Why I got stuff on the shelf in the pantry I put up ten years ago. It's just foolishness, ain't a soul to eat half of what I've put up. It ain't a few times Cecie made comment to my foolishness and I ain't got no answer to her. But Cecie ain't seen what I seen, she don't know what hard times is. I seen my papa bust up my cedar chest and throw it on the fire one winter like it won't nothing but a burning stump and it was a fine chest my mama give me. And I seen the time my mama had to set stuff on the table I wouldn't throw to the hogs. My mama got me into many a habit, she did. She made some of the fanciest quilts you ever saw. The last one is worn to shreds or I'd show you some fine work; it's out in the pack house, I suspect, where I covered the tobacco, but it was a fine piece of work in its day. I ain't never had her patience when it comes to quilting, working out all them fancy designs. Mine ain't fit to look at but they keeps you warm, I guess. And soap, you should have seen her soap, was so fine to look at you hated to used it, just as white as an onion."

"Mama," I say. "That reminds me. I was going to ask you if you would make me a big piece of soap to take back with me. I saw somebody at school do a carving in some and thought I might make a big carving if I could get some soap large enough. The ones in the grocery store aren't big enough. If you slip and make a mistake, there won't be anything left when you finish."

"I used to watch Papa whittle out little animals for the young-uns in soap, cutest little things you've ever seen, little pigs and cats and such."

"Oh, did he? Do you have any of them?"

"Oh, heavens no. He'd carve them out and then I'd let the younguns go wash with them. He'd have wasted every scrap around if I'd let him. They were cute little things though and I'll have to admit, I reckon, that it was a good way to get the little ones to go wash. He had a fine hand at making things for the younguns. Papa would take my empty thread spools and get him a rubber band and some match sticks and make a cute little thing you could wind up and let scoot across the floor. I won't never able to make one what would work. I declare if the more I don't think about Papa, he was as much a youngun himself as any real youngun I ever saw. I won't even able to allow him to take any extra money when I sent him to the store or he'd come back with a bottle of bubble stuff for one of you or a pack of Old Maid cards. He'd just spend every extra penny he had on foolishness."

"Oh, now I do remember the bubbles. I'd sit on old John and hold out the loop and let the wind blow through it."

"Law me, we going to waste our day away jabbering about this and that, before we know it." She sighs deeply and says, "You go fetch that wreath and a jacket and we'll walk on down at the church and get that done with."

When I go into my room and take the wreath from my suit-case, I think for a moment of the bubbles that I would blow up in the air to keep them from breaking on the ground. In the sun-light they would have different colors in them and they would start to fill with little holes until finally they would pop into little drops and disappear.

The plot that Mama owns at the church is over by the edge of the graveyard. They built an iron fence around the graves, and when Papa was buried there was a lot of room inside but now there are stones almost to the edge. Papa's grave has a big stone with THELTON MARSHALL written on it and with a line cut down the middle with ELIZABETH MARSHALL already carved on the other side, but with only 1884- under her name.

"Mama, I didn't know you already put your name on the stone."

"That's the way it is done proper. I done paid for my box too. I ain't planning to make no trouble for nobody like that sorry thing did."

Miss Liz points at the grave beside her spot where there is only a mound of dirt with a little American flag sticking in it. The flag is almost rotted away from the stick and the colors are pink and light blue from the rain.

"Didn't he have a family too, Mama?"

"He had one all right. They started popping up everywhere when word got here he was dead and the first thing they done was come begging at me to buy him a stone. Papa said they was all at the burying, all boo-hooing and carrying on about what a fine son he was, giving his life to his country. You can bet he wouldn't have been in the army less they made him, and him giving his life to his country. Pshaw! It won't his choice you can believe me because if had been up to him, he would be alive this day. What it all come to was, I had to buy his box. I ain't never been so ashamed in my life when the preacher had to come to me and say his body done come in and nobody had put up the money to lay him away in a proper box. And it won't a week later when I was having to put Maylean in a box too. You can see it won't to my liking. I'm great-minded to have him dug up, them putting him there right beside my place."

I look at the smaller stone by Papa's grave and see the words: MAYLEAN MARSHALL.

"If he didn't have the courtesy and decency to give Maylean his name, I won't giving him no stone."

Beside my mother's grave is a small flat stone and a short grave with the words, GREGORY MARSHALL, written on the stone. I walk closer and read aloud the small print:

> Suffer little children to come unto me,
> and forbid them not: for such is the
> Kingdom of God

"It cost a pretty penny to put all that writing on Gregory's stone, but that was always a favorite verse of mine."

I stoop and stick the prongs of my wreath in the ground at the foot of my mother's grave. Miss Liz dumps out a pot of dead chrysanthemums from Papa's grave and sets the empty pot down behind the stone. When I straighten the flowers on my wreath, they make cracking sounds in my hands. It is strange to think we are standing over rotten people; Papa is all rotten too by now, and the other people are probably just a bunch of bones. I look up at Miss Liz and she is watching me straighten the flowers. Her arms are crossed in front of her with her hands run inside the sleeves of her sweater. She stands right on top of Papa's grave.

I stand up and say to her, "Let's go on back, Mama. I don't like to stay here long, do you?"

"No, honey, I ain't never liked making a fuss over a grave. I declare, when I come down here I get to feeling that I ain't got nothing left but graves to show for myself. It ain't good for a body to let their thoughts start dwelling on such as that."

Miss Liz and I leave the graveyard and cross the highway in front of the station. When she takes my arm, I feel strange for a moment. I always feel like she should be taking my hand and leading me across, but now I'm leading her across.

"Ain't a speck of green left," she says as we walk up by the railroad tracks. "When can I expect you back again? I declare, it seems so long between visits when winter comes."

"I'll be free for Christmas in less than a month. I hope Aunt Cecie will let me come out for at least a week."

"I'll speak to her of it. I been catching myself just a-talking away when there ain't a soul here. Why if anybody saw me they'd think I was loony in the head, just jabbering away. I get real tickled at myself sometimes. I used to sit around and talk to old Smut and he would lay there in front of the fire just moaning and groaning like he knowed every word of what I was saying. I believe he did, too. Papa used to say he was moaning over his rheumatism and didn't know a word of what was said to him, which won't so, not a word of it. I'd say, 'You hungry, Smut?' and he would get up and walk in the kitchen to his plate. But won't he the sorriest dog a body ever had? Somebody could a walked away with the quilt he was sleeping on and he wouldn't of let out a yap. Hee, hee, I reckon he finally passed because he was so heavy with lead he couldn't move. I declare, you could hear it rattling inside him when he barked. It won't a few times that Vernon Stiles filled his rear end full of bird shot for meddling in his chicken house. But never once did he mess in mine, why he'd just as soon sleep with the chickens as not and never lay a tooth on them. I think it was just a tale Vernon was telling about him getting the chickens. He drug up an old hen in the yard one day, and Vernon cut into me about it, and I just set him straight fast. The old hen was one I'd throwed down on the trash pile myself and I was sure she was the one because she had one of my red rings on her leg. She had plopped over dead in the yard and I'd throwed her off down there and old Smut just found her and come dragging her back up. Woo, he could find some of the stinkin'est things. Half of Vernon Stiles's pack of hounds got run down by the train, and Smut come dragging them up in pieces and dumping them in the yard, until he smelled so high I had to throw him in the pond."

"Mama, why don't we run by Mrs. Stiles's on the way home? I sort of promised I'd stop by and see her again before I left. She asked about you when I was over."

"Oh child, I ain't going over there! It's been so long since I set foot over there, that she would carry on so about it I'd just feel the fool. And I've got to get the cooking started for tomorrow. I ain't even begun to cook the turkey and I got hold of a fine bird."

"Well OK. I really don't want to go much, I guess. She just made me feel sort of obligated."

"I was counting on getting you to help me with the fixing and all. Oh, and scoot out there and pull us a medium pumpkin. I'll fix us up a pie."

I go out into the field and find a pumpkin. I hold it against my stomach until I can break the stem away.

"This one the right size, Miss Liz?" I call.

"That's a gracious plenty. That'll make two fine pies. I'll fetch you one to carry back with you."

Miss Liz is in the turnip patch, filling up her apron. I go over to her and she starts pointing to the turnips for me to pull up. They swell above the ground with purple rings around the tops. I set my pumpkin down and pull them out of the ground, snapping away their shriveled greens. Miss Liz shakes her apron and looks up at the sky each time I drop in a turnip. "Whoa now, this ought to make a mess," she says. "I sure wish I had a mess of fresh snaps. I would just love some fresh snaps."

"I like your canned ones just as well," I say.

"Oh, they ain't fitting to eat once they been canned. But I guess I can cook up a pot if you're meaning to like them."

I pick up my pumpkin and we start back toward the house. Miss Liz is saying, "I got a can of them cranberries you like, with the whole ones in them. And I'm certain I got enough old bread stuffed away for the dressing. Wish I had thought of celery, it ain't a fitting dressing what you ain't got celery . . ."

Supper Plate . . .

MISS LIZ has started her cooking for tomorrow. She has everything going at once and runs from one to the other, banging her hips on the corners of the table. I've been in twice to see if I could help her and the last time she almost knocked me down running to the stove. It's like it won't be right if anyone helps her with it, after she told me I could help with the fixing, and she has to do it all herself to please Cecie.

It's getting hazy out and I can see a few lightning bugs down by the edge of the woods; there are not many left. I can remember when the smoke from the tobacco barns would start to settle out flat across the bottomland, like something was pressing it against the ground when the dew would start to fall. There were so many lightning bugs then that you couldn't even count how many would light up at once. And Lyndie Stiles would catch them and put them in a jar so she could take them under the covers with her at night and read comic books after her mother had put her to bed. It seems too early for it to start getting dark, but the days are already getting shorter.

Mrs. Stiles's back screen just went open and she dumped some water; for a minute it looked like fire instead of water when the sun caught it. Soon as it splattered on the ground, all the chickens went running and clucking at it. I can hear Mr. Stiles rattling the barrels down at the barn as he feeds up and the cows are mooing and groaning, waiting for him to throw the feed over to them.

I think it's strange how things go on over there and they go on over here, as close together as they are, and one doesn't know what the other one is doing or thinking, almost like they're just two carloads of people passing each other on the road. And I can hear all the sounds come across the fields, and see Lyndie and her little brother running under the trees, waiting for their mother to call them to supper. And Miss Liz doesn't even speak to Mrs. Stiles; she lives this close and doesn't even speak. Mrs. Stiles has a whole house full of people and Miss Liz doesn't have anybody unless someone comes to visit, yet she's the one who won't speak. I don't guess I've ever seen Miss Liz have anything to do with anyone that wasn't kin to her, like just being kin made them mean more than anyone else in the world, whether they were nice or not.

I see Lyndie now at the top of the steps, her hair in a yellow tuft on top and looking like all the clumps of grass between me and her. She picks up something from the steps, a plate, and starts circling around the trees, skipping and trying to keep from spilling off the dish as she goes. I can't see her now for the fruit trees; there she is, by the barn door. She sits the plate on the sill and I hear her call, "Dummy, the cat's going to get your food!"

She runs back toward the trees and I can hear all the children laughing and singing. Their voices echo back from the woods and I can hardly make out what they are saying since all the farm animals are hungry and are crying out with them. Now the children are all together, calling in one voice, "Dummy, Dummy! The cat's going to get your food; Dummy, Dummy! The cat's done got your tongue."

I look back at the barn door and Dummy is sitting there. He

doesn't look up from his plate and sits in a dark little knot in the shadow of the barn. The red glow of the sun behind the barn makes it so I can only see a white hand moving toward his face. Mrs. Stiles just called the children in to eat and get ready for church, and the screen went back against the outside of the house. Almost as soon as the children went in, Dummy got up and now I see him shuffling toward the house, holding his plate down by his side. For a moment he stops; Dummy is so still he doesn't seem to be a person, just part of all the bushes and sage grass between us. Now I see what happened; he dropped his plate and now he has picked up the halves and is carrying the two pieces toward the steps.

I hear Mrs. Stiles hollering at him but I can't see her. Now I see her hand point from the open door as she tells him just to go throw the plate on the trash pile. She snaps the screen shut and when it slams, Dummy throws his plate against the house and it breaks like a handful of pebbles. He is looking in the grass and picking up the pieces and slinging them at the house and all over the place. I can hear him grunting all the way over here, he sounds like a wild pig caught in the briars.

"Dummy! Dummy, you rotten thing! You show your temper like that once more and it's away from here. Do you hear me? Do you hear me, I say?"

That is Mrs. Stiles and she is at the top of the steps with the broom in her hand.

"You make some sign you understand me, you hear. Biting the hand that feeds you," she yells. "You make some sign before I beat your sorry behind black and blue with this broom."

Dummy drops all the pieces of the plate as she comes toward him and starts running back toward the barn. Mrs. Stiles doesn't say another word, just goes back in the house with the broom and slams the screen. I have never seen her get mad like that. I can see where Lyndie learned how to cuss somebody out, but I hope she never starts sounding mean like her mother does. And she's so big, I really bet she would have beat Dummy bad if she could have run him down.

There goes Dummy out of the barn again, running back up to the house. He is down on his knees picking the glass back up. I see it all hit the screen again, and no sooner than it does, the screen comes open and a flash of water like fire in the light of the sun comes out and hits Dummy. He lets out an awful sound, like he is really hurt and he goes crawling off into the orchard. I can't see or hear him anymore. It was all so fast that it seemed Mrs. Stiles just burned him up and made him disappear.

I walk out under the persimmon trees and feel the air already beginning to chill. The frost last night took what little color there was left in the fields away. All the morning glories look slimy where they've rolled up, and I know they won't be blooming tomorrow morning. You can already see the change in Miss Liz; I bet she won't come out again before dark, even to rock on the porch. She'll keep finding things to do in the kitchen until it's dark and too late to come out. She won't go to revival tonight, either. I see the Stileses already going out across the field toward the railroad tracks. Mrs. Stiles has on a hat now and Mr. Stiles is walking behind her bareheaded. Lyndie and Little Brother are just two little dark specks as they run out again and they are starting to hop down the railroad tracks like two little bouncing balls.

The animals had all quieted down after the feeding, but I can hear the Stileses' mules running around behind the barn. You can tell it's the mules because of the plopping sound their feet make. Even their cows are getting restless again like they do when there's heat lightning filling the sky, but tonight the sky is quiet. It's strange they should be so restless instead of just eating their hay in their stalls.

I bet somebody's chasing them around. I know who is . . .

that Dummy is, I bet, because nobody is paying any attention to him. He probably thinks he's going to get Mrs. Stiles back for wetting him. There's nothing that will put up with his fits but a mule, if the children aren't around. I can even hear him grunting and he's beating on something, like something metal. He must be running a stick down the wire. He's going to get himself hurt in a minute. Something just made a loud clicking sound.

"Miss Liz!"

She didn't answer. I heard the gate open over there, I'm sure of it. Yes, I know I did, and I can hear something going through the corn because the dry stalks are snapping.

"Miss Liz, come here quick!"

One of their animals is heading down the road toward the house. I run up the porch steps just as one of the big sawmill mules comes under the persimmon trees. It stops short when Miss Liz turns on the porch light. The mule starts puffing its nose in the dirt and beating its front foot up and down.

"Land's sake! Is that Betsy broke out?" she says. "Naw, that ain't Betsy, that's the Stileses' big old mule. Ramie, you scoot inside and put the pans off of the stove."

I run in the kitchen and lift the bubbling pans off the burners. When I get back to the front screen, I see Miss Liz at the top of the porch steps with a big wooden spoon in her hand. As she starts down the steps, the mule comes toward her with its ears flopped forward and makes a noise in its nose. Miss Liz hits it in the shoulder with the spoon, sending whatever was in the spoon all up in the air and in her own face.

"Don't you rare back at me, you thick-headed fool!"

The mule falls backward like it was hit with something big, and I see the bottom of all four of its feet in the air as it lies back on its side. It only has on one shoe that flashes when its foot flies up. She raises the spoon again and yells, "Get up, you hear! You get back where you belong. Get!" I hear its shoe clanging against the rocks as it goes back off down the road. Miss Liz comes up the steps, wiping the food she got on her face off in her apron.

"That rattle-headed fool will tear what little else I got left in the garden up." She looks down the road toward their house and says, "Pshaw, not a light on. Off gadding about somewhere and leaving their livestock loose to go tromping all over the countryside. If that had been my mule, I would have gotten a row of sad stories a mile long about how it had tore up this and that and left a footprint here and ripped down this clothesline and stomped into that rose bush. It's always my chicken what pecks the buds off Virginia Stiles's flowers, never would consider it was one of her own."

"They've gone to revival, Mama. I saw them leave."

"I ain't concerned with their reasons. It's a fine thing to let your stock go gallivanting around. Did you see him roll the white of his eyes back at me, snorting like a pig? He'll tromple somebody down, you just wait. He'll go busting into somebody in the dark."

"I think we should have caught hold of him while we had the chance."

"You think so, do you? Goodness alive, child, you don't know what you're saying. You would have changed your way of feeling and you would have known what a pile of meanness he was, if you had grabbed hold of that wild-eyed thing. He'd of slung you around like a shuck of corn. Once they get the taste of being loose, you mark my words now, they don't never have good sense again. I don't claim to explain it but you wait and see if they can keep a fence around him. He'll tear himself up pulling it down and will act like he ain't got a feeling spot in his body."

"I think we could have caught him."

"Don't talk foolishness, Ramie. And it's after dark. You don't go around animals after dark, even if they penned up, you don't mess with animals at night."

Miss Liz stops talking a minute and holds her hand for me to be still. "Hush," she whispers, "listen and see if you don't hear something peculiar." I listen for a moment and above the screaming of the night bugs, I hear the thuds of a lot of feet and the sound of stalks cracking again.

"I declare I believe everything they got is loose! As sure as I'm standing here, everything they got is out. Either they got a fence down or some fool's left a gate open. Look yonder by their garden; see if it don't look like them cows is on the wrong side of the fence. There ain't a doubt left in my mind that their stock is going to be scattered over the whole county before they decide to come home and tend to them."

"Do you think it would do any good if I walked down to the church and told them?"

"You stay right here. Don't go tending to other people's affairs. Mind your own and you'll see there's more than enough to keep you busy."

Miss Liz doesn't go back in the house. She stands at the edge of the porch and almost smiles as she listens to the animals moving in the dark. Suddenly all the chickens at the Stileses' start clucking and flapping and I hear wood breaking.

"Woo, listen at that!"

"Did one of them get in the hen house?"

"Got in it right through the side. That mule just hit it headlong I'm guessing. Papa told Vernon Stiles ten years ago that he better not lean on that house or it'd fall over, and he ain't done better than nail up a slab or two since then. Well, it just went clean over, it did."

Miss Liz starts to laugh and reaches behind her for a porch chair. "The fixing is going to have to wait. I won't be worth a hoot scooting back and forth to watch the goings-on."

I sit on the edge of the porch and see headlights come up from behind the Stileses' house. When the people start getting out,

Miss Liz says, "Got back sooner than I figured. Vernon Stiles was never one for hurrying. Borrowing my hay rake five years ago and didn't offer to bring it back till he seen I bought a new one, since he left it out and let it get no-count with rust. But you wait and see, they'll be up half the night getting them penned up and till daybreak finding where they got out. You and me will be asleep in our beds while they go out stumbling and feeling around, trying to hunt out the hole."

"Mama, listen. Isn't that someone screaming?"

She stops talking a minute and the scream stops then rises again.

"Don't fret. It's just Lyndie. She got whipped, and you listen and you'll hear her whip the other one, so we got to listen to that for a while. Reckon it must have been the gate open then instead of the fence being down."

I don't answer Miss Liz. It couldn't have been that Lyndie or Little Brother left the gate open. It was Dummy. Dummy did it because he was mad at Mrs. Stiles.

"You see how I'm figuring, don't you?" Miss Liz asks.

"What?"

"You see how I'm figuring, I say. I can tell clean over here that Virginia Stiles is blaming it all on the younguns 'cause she had to have somebody to accuse of leaving the gate open, and she just give them a beating for it."

I see lights begin to move through the field until the three lights start moving in a semicircle. Then I can see the dark shapes of the cows, all huddled together.

"They found the cows. They won't be no trouble if they can get them headed in, but you better look out if one of them takes a notion to bust out. The whole bunch will take out running till kingdom come. Ain't got good sense even when it's daylight."

The group of cows begins to move slowly, bumping into each other but going back toward the barn. As the lights come across the ground behind them, I can begin to see the legs of the men. Another car pulls up at the house then turns back and heads down to the highway.

"I'm not going to get a thing done watching this, but ain't it a sight? And would you look out yonder pecking under the trees, two of her white chickens come clean over here."

The two white chickens stand still for a moment, then open their wings and flutter under Miss Liz's house. She starts back down the steps with the wooden spoon still in her hand.

"Get! You get out from under there." She starts to rap on the side of the house with the spoon, but the chickens don't come out. She stops beating the spoon as Lyndie and Little Brother run up to her.

"Miss Liz! Miss Liz, all our animals got loose." Lyndie runs up to face Miss Liz, and I can see tears shining on her face when the porch light reflects on her.

"Now if you aren't a fine one to come breaking your neck to tell me that, after I been setting here watching them tearing up everything I got."

"We done lost Jack Mule, Miss Liz. Papa says the others will wander back but there's just no telling where the mule will go."

"You just go tell your Papa that his fine animal has been over here an age ago and rared back at me and took out again, and he can bet somebody is going to put a bullet in him if he ain't caught up soon."

Lyndie and Little Brother turn to go, but before they're to the edge of the yard, Miss Liz says, "Now you hold up there. You get yourself under my house and catch up them two white chickens."

Lyndie walks slowly back into the yard and says, "They went up under the house?"

"They did, and you can get yourselves under there and catch them before you take off for home."

"Go up under the house?"

"Yes, up under the house, I said."

"I'm scared to go up under there, Miss Liz."

"Scared! Have you forgotten how you used to play back up there?"

"Yes'um, but that was daytime and I could see where the spiders and bugs were, and Mama said if I got up under there, a rat would bite off my nose."

"Well you can tell your mama she might have rats under her house, but that don't mean I have them under mine."

"Can I get the chickens tomorrow, Miss Liz? Sometimes Papa lets them roost out."

"Send that brother of yours under there to run them out. He's no fraidy cat."

Lyndie turns around for Little Brother but he isn't there.

"Now where did he get to?" Miss Liz says.

"Here he comes back. He went and got Dummy to do it for us. We brung him with us but made him wait down at the road."

"Dummy! Now I won't have him rooting around under my house."

When Dummy sees Miss Liz, he starts running and crawls under the house.

"You get out, you hear? Get out from under there."

The chickens start squawking and drown out Miss Liz. Soon Dummy crawls out and has got them both by the legs. Their wings are flapping, and white feathers are coming out.

"Don't you stand there grinning at me, you ugly thing, you get off my place."

Lyndie goes to Dummy and takes one of the chickens, turning it right side up and folding its wings back down. Dummy watches her, then folds his chicken up the same way, and both of them have stopped squawking. Dummy has spider webs all over his head, and I can see streaks of blood on his hands where the chicken scratched him, and you can even see where he rubbed the chicken and got blood on its white feathers. He still doesn't move, just stands there, the front of his shirt still wet from the water Mrs. Stiles threw at him, smiling at Miss Liz and rubbing the white chicken on the back until it starts to peep like a biddie.

"I think he wants you to thank him for catching it, Miss Liz," Lyndie says.

Miss Liz walks back to the bottom of the steps. She is as mad as I've ever seen her. She turns and looks back at Dummy who still stands there with the chicken, but she is so mad she can't even talk, just clutches tighter to that spoon.

"Lyndie."

"Yes'um, Miss Ramie."

"I think you better take Dummy on back home. Don't you reckon you had better put up those two chickens and see if you can help catch the rest of them?"

"I reckon we ought to put them up, only we ain't got no house to put them in no more. It fell down.

"Yes, I saw, Lyndie." I hear the screen slam and turn and see that Miss Liz has gone back inside. "I saw from over here how it happened."

I look at Dummy to see if he understood me. He has stopped grinning and must have loosened up on the chicken, because one of her white wings is stretched out straight and beating him across the face. Now the other wing is loose and flapping, and I can see the chicken's yellow claws scratching his hands.

"Hold her legs, Dummy," I say and walk over and take hold of them myself.

"Here. Put your hand around her legs, then you got one free to hold down her wings."

Dummy's hands are shaking as he wraps them back around the chicken, but she is quiet again and stretches her long neck up and looks at him. Then she starts to peck at the top button on his shirt.

"She's going to eat your shirt right off you, Dummy," Lyndie says, and Dummy starts to laugh.

"We'll be going now, Miss Ramie. Do you reckon you could tell me how the chicken house got knocked down so I could tell my Daddy. He's awful mad about it."

Dummy starts to grunt and shake his head and when his face is still again, I see water beginning to form around the edges of his eyes. "Dummy was trying to tell Mama something when we got back and she said she might as well of asked the cows for all he could tell her."

"It was the mule, Lyndie. You can tell him I heard it go running out through the garden and figured the fence was down, and then it ran right into the chicken house and knocked it over."

"It won't the fence down, Miss Ramie. It was the gate open which is what really made Mama and Papa mad."

"I put the board up!"

That was Little Brother who yelled that.

"Then how come it was down, because I didn't undo it? You was the last one out," Lyndie says.

"I put the board up!" he yells again.

"Well, we done got a whipping that will last a week or more, I reckon, so it don't matter. See."

Lyndie turns the back of her leg around and I see the red switch marks across it. I look up at Dummy and he has started crying. Soon he is sniffing and whimpering so loud that Lyndie and Little Brother notice him.

"Look at old Dummy. He cries every time we get a whipping."

Dummy starts to cry harder and shake his head.

"Hey Dummy, it'll get well before I get married."

Mrs. Stiles calls to the children and Little Brother starts running back down the road.

"We got to go, Miss Ramie. You tell Miss Liz we are awful sorry, and I'll be over to see her and get the butter come next Friday."

"All right, Lyndie, I'll tell her. I hope your animals are all back home now."

"I'm thinking they will be because they weren't done eating when they got loose. They'll all probably come back but that knuckleheaded mule that had to go and knock down the chicken house."

I watch Lyndie and Dummy walk off until all I can see in the dark is the white rear ends of the chickens under their arms. I turn to go back up the steps and see Miss Liz is standing looking out through the screen.

"I didn't know you were there, Mama."

"I have an idea where that mule is. Don't reckon Vernon Stiles has the sense to think of it himself."

"Where, Mama?"

"Sure as I'm standing here, that mule has run back off to the sawmill. He was a sawmill mule not a tobacco mule, and sure as stuffings he'll go right back to the mill."

"Do you want me to run over and tell them, Mama?"

"No, you just wait and see if it occurs to them, and come morning if they ain't got him, you might run over and tell them where he is."

Miss Liz walks out on the porch and sits back down in her iron chair. When I sit on the porch beside her, she starts to swing her feet and I can hear the bottom of her shoes scrape the grit on the floor. "Terrible hot in that kitchen." She is already over being mad.

"It's a pretty night out though, don't you think?"

"It's the last of them that will be bearable. Ain't half the bugs out hollering there was a week ago."

"They're still making a lot of racket. I always think it's going to bother me sleeping, but it never does."

"I used to get so aggravated at them. It would be about this time that Papa would take the tobacco in to sell and you couldn't get him to take no light with him. He'd leave in the daylight and would never think that it was going to be any different on the way home. He'd be coming in after dark, and I would wait out to see if I could hear him whistling up the road, just stomping my feet to keep the life in them, and every stinking bug in the county would start fiddling and squealing, and I bet I would get up and go to the edge of the yard a dozen times thinking it was him. Papa used to say he reckoned they must be the bravest bugs in the world just to get louder when I told them to hush."

Miss Liz laughs to herself and I can hear her scraping her feet to keep them warm.

"I could tell by the whistling. When I could finally make out it was him, then I could tell by the whistling if the tobacco had sold good. You ask Cecie sometime. I would run tell the young-uns, and they would meet him on the road and start a dancing around him to see what he had brought them. Then I would light in beside him just about at the well and say, 'Brought good, didn't it, Thel?' And he would say, 'Lizzie, you're the beatingest thing I ever seen for telling a body what's on their mind before they even had a chance to say it.' I recollect once he said, 'what if I was a mind to hide away most all of the money and tell you it was a bad day?' And I just told him he knowed before he said something, what a batch of foolishness that was. I told him he would just have to take a batch of sodie crackers with him and start popping them in his mouth all the way up the road to keep me from knowing. Well, I tell you that got away with him something terrible, trying to figure what I meant about the sodie crackers, and pretty soon I was sorry I had been so smart, he got on me so much to tell him, and I knowed if I telled him, that it would spoil my way of figuring."

"What did you mean, Miss Liz? I don't think I understand either."

"Well, I finally went and told him anyway, that the sodie crackers was to keep him from whistling, and I declare we laughed till tears run down our faces when Papa went in the front room and sat there with a handful of sodie crackers, trying to see if he could whistle with one in his mouth. Ask Cecie sometimes if she don't remember that foolishness. Papa got himself so tickled he said it made his insides hurt. But I knowed him, I did. I could near about recite to him what he was going to say every time he popped his mouth open. He couldn't say nothing what would make me jump, other than creeping up behind me in the kitchen, making out like he was a screech owl. Papa was as full of foolishness as a man could be. That screech owl sound was as awful a sound as you ever heard made, and when I hear a real one, I will have to think before I'm sure it's not a person out in the barn just hollering for his life."

Swamp Forest . . .

I HAVE ALREADY had to get out of bed once tonight to put my bird
back in the box, and I hear his wings thumping against the cardboard sides again. I should have let him out some today, I guess,
so he'd be sleepy tonight. Miss Liz is still in the kitchen; I hear
her closing drawers and stirring and banging pots together. I
even fixed a thing for the center of the table at the dinner tomorrow. I stuck gumdrops on a briar branch and got some red berries
to put around it. I'm afraid it looks more like Christmas than
Thanksgiving, but Miss Liz liked it. I'm just hoping Aunt Cecie
doesn't come out tomorrow bringing half the dinner with her; I
don't think she knew Miss Liz was going to go to this much trouble. She talks about Miss Liz right to her face, and hurts her
feelings. But I do think the house ought to be clean enough to
suit her. I tried to hit all the places that Aunt Cecie usually finds
to complain about. It's just hard sometimes to make such an old
house look clean.

Early today I went back down by the pond when I was looking
for a briar branch, but I didn't walk back by where the spider had
his web. I sat down by the water for awhile and looked at everything that was there, the cattails, the water, the sky, everything.
And I tried to decide what all their colors would be if I tried to

paint them. Water is not blue in the winter unless the sky is blue, and I tried to see the line of light you always see in pictures between the sky and the water, but it wasn't there. Today everything was gray. But there are many colors of gray; Miss Liz's hair is not at all the same gray as the water, her hair looks warm gray and the water is cold gray. But I guess that's not their color but how they feel when you touch them, or maybe it is their color. I never will paint the water though, I know that I never will. I never paint landscapes, I mean I never want to paint them. Even when I know I should put a background in a picture, I don't. I always start in the middle of the canvas and start painting a face. Sometimes I don't even know who I'm going to paint, but I paint eyes and a nose and a mouth, and work in the paint until I have a good face. When I get the face, I don't care about the rest. If my teacher makes me fill in the background, I just put a color there or try to think of something. Like when I paint Miss Liz, I try to think of something that she would have behind her, but I never can paint it. Not after I already have her face. There are so few faces that I really know. I looked at Miss Liz today when I was working with her, and I noticed a mole by her eye that I never saw before, and the way her wrinkles all go down from her eyes and nose and mouth, the way her bones make her skin stretch smooth, and where the skin falls away from the bones. When she is thinking or mad or laughing, everything changes and moves. And the colors coming over her head, they were from the jar and the tadpoles. Yet at the pond the water is gray, and the tadpoles are just dark spots running into the deep water when they see my shadow. How do I paint Miss Liz, saying, "There is a rainbow on your face."? How do I paint myself with a rainbow, how do I paint myself when I am afraid, when I think the spider is in my hair? Sometimes I make faces at myself in the mirror and try to paint them. One day I read that Rembrandt did that. Then he started painting all the people around him and went out and found more people, but mostly at first he only painted himself and his family. I wish I knew my daddy's face, I want so much to paint him.

My bird is getting quiet again; I hope he's finally getting sleepy or giving up or something because I sure am getting sleepy. When it is dark in the room, I begin to see red light flicker through the cracks in the door. Miss Liz is stirring the fire before she goes to bed, and as the air goes under the wood scraps, they are flaring up again. As I hear Miss Liz walk toward her bed, the light comes across the foot of my bed like red feathers and flies up across my arms, trembling each time her heavy footsteps jar the house. The feathers crisscross until they look like birds flying and I think of the blackbirds at the pond and make the red dots go under their wings until the dots are the only red left. I see the birds going up and down, opening their wings to glide and showing the red spot. Then they are round and not like birds at all, but the red spot is still on each one. They are all starting to fall out of the sky, but when I look down to see them splash into the water, I see them fall into the cattails around the pond and disappear. The cattails burst into yellow fuzz, bursting and bursting from their stalks and spreading their seeds across the water. I hear a creaking and thumping from the stalks; there is someone walking through the reeds. It is Papa. He is walking through the reeds and getting his overalls wet.

"Papa! Papa! You're not dead."

He starts to walk toward me; the legs of his overalls are wet and covered with water weeds. At first I am frightened because he does not speak. Then he looks at me and says, "Have you seen Maylean? Where is Maylean? We have to find Maylean."

We look and look in the water, but we can't find Maylean. Papa takes my hand and we start to walk. We walk across the pond; the water is not even deep, I thought the water was deep. I want to tell Papa not to run through the spider web but he doesn't hear me. Then I see the web, and the spider is not over the path anymore. The spider is on the side of the path, and it is black and on its chest is the red hourglass of the black widow. It is very big, but Papa doesn't look at it. He holds my hand so I am not afraid as we walk by the black spider, and I watch it carving the numbers for Miss Liz's stone instead of letters. Papa is telling me about the swamp forest. He says we are in the swamp forest, though I know we are not, that the swamp forest is down around the mule spring. He says you can tell a swamp forest because of the mushrooms, and we are walking through mushrooms as big as I am. Papa is talking and talking, and I am trying to remember his voice, but though he is talking and talking I cannot hear him. The hill is getting steeper and he is grunting, and I look up and see he is not Papa at all. He is Dummy, and he has on Papa's clothes and Papa's moustache. I pull my hand away and start to run, but my legs won't work, and he grabs my hand again, and I can't get my feet on the ground as Dummy pulls me with him, faster and faster. I stop moving and Dummy is gone. I hear people talking around me everywhere, and Dummy has left me in a line of people and we are inside the barn. There is Miss Robinson, my teacher; and Mrs. Stiles and Aunt Cecie, and Miss Robinson is saying, "Where is Miss Liz, Ramie? Miss Liz ought to know," and I see what they are watching. It is my father and he says, I have come to take her with me. I am looking at me in the straw beside the mule stall, only I am very skinny and my hair is wet and I have no clothes on, and my father is walking toward me and my arms are outstretched to him. Miss Robinson is saying, "Miss Liz ought to know, Ramie." I can't answer Miss Robinson, I can't make my words loud enough for her to hear me. I have my father's hand now but my fingers won't close, I can feel his hand but my hand is getting smaller, it is so tiny, and it is sliding away from him. I am going to fall. The ground starts breaking and crumbling under me and I feel the fire but there is nothing to hold onto and the ground won't stop breaking. I am falling and falling. I see his hand above me and I reach for it again but he doesn't move, he doesn't reach for me, and I am falling faster. It is dark and the fire is hotter but I do not feel the ashes when I hit the bottom and I see the red spot and then it is dark.

Shoddy Product

plane was flown by a pilot with two broken ankles, his legs in casts and his shoes attached to the Hawk's rudder controls with metal clips to hold his feet in place.

Jimmy Doolittle, then a 30-year-old Army Air Corps test pilot, had been injured in a fall from the second story of the officer's club several days before he flew the demonstration mission.

Despite his injuries, Doolittle insisted on demonstrating the Hawk. He won the competition. Chile

force in North A... in England and Schultz said.

He was also a late 1920s and th onstration missio And he was a gineer and test Massachussetts I ing aircraft to w

Jaybirds . . .

WE ARE THROUGH Sunday dinner now, and Miss Liz and Cecie and June are inside talking. I am out on the porch but I know I won't be able to stand it out here long because it has really turned off cold. Cecie was telling Miss Liz how they had the Christmas parade on Thanksgiving and how awful she thought that was. Every year she talks about that and last year they had the parade before Thanksgiving, so she really had something to talk about then. I came out here because it's no good to hear someone talk about a parade, about watching all the little children's faces when they saw Santa Claus, especially when you know it's all over until next year and you've missed it. I always feel that way the day after Christmas, even though I got presents and opened them, sort of like I missed Christmas and it is already gone. I told myself this morning when I was listening to Miss Liz that I was here today on the farm and with my bird to care for, but tomorrow I would just have to remember what it was like, tomorrow I would be back in town and have to go to school at a certain time and the days would all be alike until I was out again for vacation.

All morning I was hoping it would snow and we couldn't leave. Then I would tell my teachers that I couldn't get back into town and that Cecie and June got snowed in and couldn't come after me. It has looked like snow all day, sort of pink-gray, but Miss Liz said it wouldn't snow and even if it did the ground was too warm yet for it to stick. When the snow has been gone in town for days, it will still be white out at the farm, because no one ever goes out driving when there's snow, and just Miss Liz walks on it. You can look out the window and see just what Miss Liz has done since it snowed, her paths to the chicken lot and to the hog lot. I remember how Miss Liz always used to cook an extra pan of biscuits when it snowed, and would take them to the animals, and you could see the mules almost choke trying to swallow them, until they bent down and busted a hole in the ice to drink. I even saw Miss Liz take the ax from the chop block and during one of the bad freezes, chop up the ice at the edge of the pond so the mules could drink. Sometimes I'd just go and watch her from the window, my hands would be so cold, but she wouldn't come in until she had seen to every animal.

Miss Liz would shell off the corn for the chickens. She could just turn the ear in her hand and the grains would all come off. I watched the grains make little holes in the snow, then the chickens would scratch and peck until they found the corn and the brown ground would show through the snow. It would make my hands sore to shell the corn and I would have to push the grains out with my fingers and couldn't get half as many shelled as she could. Then we would go to the wire and wait and see if the red birds were going to come down and eat with the chickens. They usually came when there was snow; all the birds did, but to me the red ones were the prettiest.

We would crumble biscuits for the birds and Miss Liz would say, "Now mush it up small. Them jaybirds will make hogs of themselves." And the jaybirds would drop down and frighten all the others away. As soon as they come in the trees overhead, the little birds would leave and the blue jays would light with their wings spread out, looking all around them, daring anything to show its face.

Miss Liz said once, "I wouldn't give you two cents for every one of them in the trees, but ain't he about the prettiest thing you've ever seen, strutting around like a peacock."

I told her I liked the red birds, and she looked at me and said, "Well that one there is a whole sight prettier than any red bird I've seen." And she threw back her head and said, "Nay!" and the big bird looked at her and said it back and she said it again. He didn't look our way but flew up into the trees.

"Don't even know what an ugly thing he sounds like. The Lord must not have given him ears," she said and went and picked up one of his feathers that had fallen out. "Keep on throwing out your feathers, you fancy thing, and your hiney will get froze before you know it." I still have the feather in my room in my dictionary; it is deep blue with black strips and a white tip.

When we went back to the porch, we could hear the jay up in the cedar tree, fussing at us and knocking snow down in chunks as he went from limb to limb. No sooner than we were back inside the house, he swooped down again and started eating.

"Just look at that meanness. If you was to throw a rock at him, I bet he would catch it in that fancy beak and sling it right back at you. Ain't scared of a thing."

We heard the jays fussing this morning before Cecie and June got here. I guess that's what started me to thinking about the snow since the birds always get noisy before a storm. And Miss Liz started talking about the bad snow, when I was a little girl, and about the time we walked out to measure the drifts with a yardstick. I remember the stick went out of her hand and I thought there was a snow monster in the drift who had pulled it away from her. She tried reaching for it but the snow was too cold. "Biting the stuffings out of my hand. Eat it to the bone," and I had thought the monster was biting at her hand when she reached in the snow.

When Miss Liz was standing over the table this morning, rolling out a pan of biscuits for the dinner, and she was making so many, I thought of all the times she had fixed biscuits for the animals and the people. She puts balls of dough in the pan and presses them out flat, leaving knuckle prints in the top of each one that I know will disappear in the oven. I could remember how her fist always skipped down the pan, mashing each biscuit, and the way her face was drawn up tight, knowing she had done this so many times that she didn't even have to think about it, and that her mind was somewhere else.

She spoke suddenly when she slid her biscuit pan into the oven. "Ain't you ever wondered, Ramie, why the Lord made some things up wrong?"

She went over to the window and I had to ask her what she meant, if she was talking about the pretty bird with the ugly voice, and she said, "Well, I reckon that was what set me to thinking on it but it's been on my mind before today. I was thinking once about ugly people and decided that a pretty one is sent along every now and then so the rest of us won't forget how ugly we are."

Then she went over and put her elbows on the window sill and said, "But what I mean is bad things wrong. Did you know Tessie Allbright had one youngun that never grew a hair on his head or anywhere else for that matter. He was just as slick as a goose egg and you could look at him real close and see he didn't even have peach fuzz on his arms and not a speck of a eyebrow, just as bald-faced as he could be. Though I wouldn't have never said it to Tessie, I was thinking that you couldn't tell that child's face from his hiney if he didn't squint out at you with them little beady eyes. And I remember her carrying on after he was born about how she felt something wrong down inside of her the whole time she was a carrying him, that he was tossing about in her like a ball. Pshaw, I don't believe a word of it is so. She started into that tossing around after she had done seen what a sight he was. I never heard her make mention of it when she was carrying him, and then he gets born and she comes whispering to me like it was a big secret, 'I felt him come loose from me, Lizzie,' she said, 'I felt him come loose before his time.' Some need to whisper since she told every last one of us at one time or the other, told me three times. He won't right in the head neither and didn't live to be grown which was a blessing, I reckon. I told her she'd never raise him."

Miss Liz looked at the biscuits in the stove and when she opened the door, I felt the heat hit my face.

Then she said, "I don't believe one word about that feeling something was wrong all along and knowing he won't going to be right. I carried that Maylean just like the others, won't a bit different, all of them kicked around a little, and I could tell just as good when to quit out in the fields and to tell Papa to go fetch someone. Now if I'd a taken a fall with her, I could have understood it, but to save my life I can't recollect a thing different. She was a pretty little old baby, the curliest head of hair in the bunch, but I took to noticing how it took her twice as long as the others to learn anything and then she would up and forget it. It won't a few times I had to send Cecie out looking for her and she'd turn up somewhere asking folks if they knowed where her house was. I took to telling her the gypsies would steal her if she didn't come straight on home from school just to keep her from poking along and taking up talking to strangers. She was so trifling I was ashamed to death of her. I declare I was plumb sad when she died and in the awfullest way, but I have thought many a time that if she was going to have bright younguns for the Lord knows why, then let them grow up with her out of sight. And the Lord knows I never wished her dead, not for a minute, because though

I hated to know it at the time, she was as much mine as the others, and I was being punished for something I done unknowing. It do seem sometimes that I'm drawn more toward the weak ones than the strong, I declare it does. I'll fiddle around with a weak chicken till I'm certain there ain't no more to be done . . ."

Miss Liz told me that this morning about the weak ones and how she found herself loving them even more, and I know it's true because I have seen how she can't rest until everything is cared for. She will tend to my little bird, I know she will make it live, though it would probably die if I took it with me. But there is one thing I can't understand . . . Why is she so mean to Dummy? I could never ask her. She has gotten mad at me every time I have mentioned his name. And early this morning, when Lyndie and Little Brother and Dummy came walking down the road by the house, leading the mule, Miss Liz called out, "He was down at the sawmill, I reckon." And Lyndie asked her how she knew and she said, "Some people think instead of talking all the time . . ." which wasn't like her because she talks a lot and is the first to say so. But what she said next was really mean. She said, "Some folks ain't got the sense to do neither." Dummy just bowed his head and walked on by, and I thought at the time that she really didn't need to say something mean to Dummy then; he was hurting bad enough because Lyndie and Little Brother had gotten whipped for what he had done. You could still see the red streaks on Lyndie's legs where Mrs. Stiles had switched her. But Miss Liz must have been mad at Dummy still, I guess, because he had the nerve to crawl under her house chasing that chicken after she told him not to. She had stood there watching them until they got back to their house, and then she said without looking at me, "That sorry scrap will outlive us all. Papa was the last of the Marshall boys when he died, and there ain't a one of any of the others that grew up with us left living, least not a one of them any count for anything."

She starts talking about Papa a lot when Dummy is around. He is always reminding her of Papa, like when he made the moustache at church and when he closed his eyes and pretended he was dead. Miss Liz talked all about Papa dying this morning and I could remember little bits of it happening, but not everything; yet after hearing Miss Liz, it's as clear as if it happened yesterday. Papa got sick suddenly, he was in the fields and he came in with his face flushed red. Miss Liz took his wrist and shook it, his breath was coming short like he was burning up with fever. Then she started calling his name, but he just stared across the room like none of us were even there. And all the others started coming in out of the fields, talking and asking questions, but Papa didn't move or say a word.

Miss Liz kept pushing people back from him, then started rubbing his hands between hers. She sent Uncle Buck for a wet rag. I'm trying to think what Papa finally said; Miss Liz said it over this morning. He shut his eyes and dropped into a chair in the front room, I remember his eyelashes were white and they trembled when he tried to talk. Miss Liz made Buck start rubbing Papa's hands, and she wiped his forehead with the rag and kept saying his name over and over, "Thel . . . Thel," like she was calling him back from somewhere. She would whisper it, then she would yell it, until he opened his eyes and shook his head. I remember he said it was screaming inside his head . . . "Lizzie, something is squealing and yelling in my head, I can see you a-talking, but something is screaming, just taking every word you say and making it holler back at me, so loud." And the last thing I heard Papa say was, "The plow blade caught a stone, and the sound come up at me like my head was where the stone was."

From then on he was in his bed and never got out of it, but Miss Liz kept telling people he would come out of it, that he had a lot of years that were due him left. She said the doctor ought to let her walk him every day, keep his insides moving, and she would tell everybody she was going to walk him that night, that he was strong as a bull, never had a sick day in his life. But more and more people kept coming to see him, coming from a long way off, and Miss Liz would tell them all the same thing. "Shouldn't have made the trip," she said, "he'll be up and about . . ." The men would sit on the edge of the porch and hold their hats, and people kept bringing things, jars of pickles and canned stuff, and Miss Liz would nod her head and put them on the shelf.

And she said to me one night on the porch, when almost all the people had gone — "strangers," she called them strangers — "There shouldn't be all these strangers in a man's house when he is not able to defend hisself. Fair-weather friends, just living on other folks' sadness. Come to see a man sick and leaving feeling fine because they are well. I don't take kindly to strangers under my roof."

Then one day when she came from his room and went to the porch and sat down, all the people got up and stood around her.

"He done give up," she said, and all the people went into the house and left her staring across the yard. Old Smut got up from his rug when she spoke, and went and started scratching his back under her chair. It wasn't until he rooted his nose in her hand for her to pet him that she even noticed he was there.

The house was soon full of people, all the ones who had come to visit and more besides, and the house was filled with flowers. Miss Liz hardly talked to any of the people but I remember she counted all the designs; I remember that she kept giving me numbers to keep on my mind for her and saying, "Folks thought high of Thel, I reckon he'll have fifty designs before it's done," then she would start counting them again. Mama lifted me up to see Papa but I didn't want to, and I saw his face wasn't red anymore like when he came in from the field, and his yellow moustache was combed down smooth around his mouth. It looked just like corn silks, only like on white roasting ears instead of feed corn, and I sat all afternoon and thought of how we used to make like Papa with corn silks under our noses and get him tickled at us. I kept wanting to talk to him, it had been a lot of days since I had talked to him; but Mama told me he wouldn't talk anymore, that that was what dying meant, that he was getting to rest from all that screaming. I would just have to remember him, what he talked like and the things he told me. Sometimes I would try to remember him and would see Dummy in my mind instead. I could never tell Miss Liz that.

Maybe that's why Miss Liz hates Dummy so; she hates him because he is still living and Papa is dead. And if Dummy could have been a normal person that could talk back when he came in the store the first time she saw him, when he ate the sodie crackers, then she might have been Dummy's girl friend and married him even. She said she thought he was a fine-looking man at first, he could have been a fine-looking man who told her his name. But she won't even let him come in her yard. I can't ever remember not seeing him when I came out here, even if it was just to see him out playing with the children. And last night when he was holding that chicken, I was really afraid for him; I was afraid he would make like Papa was dead and Miss Liz would hit him with that spoon. Was he there the day they had Papa's service at the church? I couldn't see for all the people; I just saw Miss Liz and she was crying, but Dummy must have walked by the casket, he must have looked before they shut Papa up. Miss Liz must have seen him look at Papa before they locked the coffin and carried him across the road to the graveyard.

Patch in the Dutch Boy's Britches . . .

IT'S SUNDAY NIGHT now and Aunt Cecie and Uncle June have gone downstairs to the living room. Cecie wouldn't let me take my bird in the car and said she was ashamed for me to take something like that back to school. I should have told her it was for biology class too, since she let me bring the tadpoles for Miss Robinson. But what is really true is that I wanted to leave him with Miss Liz because I was afraid I couldn't make him live.

The dinner at the farm went all right. Of course Miss Liz cooked too much food; she cooks the same amount of food for four people as she does for twenty at Christmas, when all the relatives come, and then tries to make us eat after we're already full.

I have got my tadpoles on the window sill and they're smacking at the top of the water like there's no air underneath. I know what's wrong with them; the water got all stirred up when we were riding home and the crawfish kept trying to pinch the tadpoles. I bet the girls at school have never seen a crawfish before except in the pickle jars in the lab. You can stick a pencil in the jar and he will pinch onto it so tight with his claws that you can lift him out of the water. I can hear what my roommate would say if I was still living at school, squealing about how dirty he was, like something living in water could be dirty. She was as bad as Cecie about being neat and not having any animals around. If she was here now, I'd have to keep the tadpoles in the closet. She cried all the time, so they sent her back home; that was the time I liked best, when I didn't have her or Cecie around. I hardly ever got to sleep the whole night when my roommate was there; she would scream and cry at night until the house-mother would come running into our room and talk to her. The housemother would try to make her stop crying, tell her that her mother wasn't far away, that they could call her by telephone, so not to worry about her parents or something like that. She would write them all the time and call and they would come to see her. She was scared to go anywhere without telling them, even the field trips with the teachers, and I told her that was what I always hated about Cecie, how I always had to tell her where I was going and how Miss Liz used to let me do as I pleased as long as it was daylight. And all the time the housemother was in our room, I would pretend I was asleep still, so she wouldn't talk loud; so I wouldn't have to listen to her words as she pretended she was a mother.

Everything I used to do, Cecie would act like she was inter-ested and start asking me questions that I didn't feel like answer-ing. I was catching black ants at the farm one day to put in the doodlebug funnels and Cecie kept telling me all these other things that I could be doing, that she thought would be more fun, until I just told her I was going out in the barn to play in the wagon and then I left. I was sitting down by the edge of the pond when I heard someone calling me. I saw Miss Liz walk up behind the day lilies and she had her hands rolled into her apron. The sun was back of her head and made it look like her hair was standing up in little horns. Then I saw Aunt Cecie come up behind her, her white face almost all in a shadow under her hat.

Miss Liz said, "Ramie youngun, didn't you hear me holler-ing?"

"I thought you were calling the chickens," I said.

"I ain't got no chickens named Ramie." I didn't get up, something made me feel that to get up I would have to try very hard, and I wanted to just stay where I was.

Then Cecie said to me, "Ramie, I wish you would tell us when you're going to wander off, at least tell us the truth where you're going. I didn't know where in the world you were."

I turned back to look at the water and remembered that I had been watching a measuring worm go up my arm when they called me.

"I'm going to get a new dress, Miss Liz."

The little green worm had looped almost to my elbow when Cecie said something and made me lose my count. I started him over again at my wrist.

"Mama, that's your doing," Cecie said sharply.

"Ain't no harm in it."

"There was harm in it when I was a little girl. I don't know how many times you had me sure I would get a new dress if I let an ugly worm crawl all over me. I certainly remember a lot more worms crawling on me than new dresses."

"I want one with little flowers, Miss Liz," I said, "and rickrack braid the same green color as the worm. That was eighteen inches to my elbow, Miss Liz."

"Well, I would say that is a short worm you have there, and I wouldn't bank too much on being able to find your hands once you get it on."

"Mama, don't raise the child on foolishness. She'll believe it's so, that that worm will bring her a new dress."

"It won't be long before we have an empty sack of feed. Got a pretty pattern with flowers if I remember correctly."

Miss Liz never made me the dress. Soon she was sending me to visit Cecie more and more until everything was turned around. I was visiting Miss Liz instead of Cecie, and I had more dresses than I cared about. Cecie would pick things out for me to wear and I would find them laid out for me when I got up in the morning. At first I would pull things on out of the closet, knowing I wasn't matching the colors right, and leave the clothes Cecie put out lying there to make her mad. But then the girls at school started telling me I was wearing the wrong colors together and I felt ashamed to take off my coat every day because I knew they were waiting to laugh at what I had on.

When fall came there was no school bus anymore, Cecie made me go live at St. Anne's and only came to get me for vacations. She told me my new name, it was not Marshall as I had told them in the country school but Hopkins, the same as hers and June's. Then Thanksgiving vacation I went through all my comic books and filled in the coupons; I put Ramie Bastard in all of them in the space by "name" and Cecie found out. She didn't whip me like Miss Liz would have done. She just stood at my door and said, "Ramie, please don't ever use an ugly word like that again." I wanted her to be mad but she wasn't and she just shut my door. I asked her later if it wasn't true, if I wasn't a bastard because that's what I heard at school in the country and she said no, I was an orphan and she had adopted me. Now I know she was lying to me because Miss Liz told me the truth. Cecie would try to get me to tell her about things when I was crying and I wouldn't; she always wanted me to tell her about things Miss Liz had said when she wasn't there, like tonight even, when we were driving back, but I will never tell her what Miss Liz told me this time, about Maylean and my real father.

Even if I were to wake up scared, I wouldn't let Cecie know it. I remember when I did wake up at night when my roommate was screaming in the bed next to me — first I would look for the window and since the trees were bare, I could see the moonlight come through the shades. As soon as I found the window, I knew where I was and the screaming wouldn't bother me. It did scare me the first few times; I heard my own heart start beating faster when I had my ear against the pillow. But the reason I was scared was because it really sounded like something was wrong with her, like she was hurting. But after I knew it was silly, that she wanted her mother to be in the house, I tried to sleep through it. I never could though; as hard as I would try, the scream would wake me, and I would have to wind my head in the pillow to make it sound a long way off. Then it would sound like a screech owl, out in the barn at night, and I would think I heard Miss Liz moan in the other room, because she thought a screech owl at night meant someone nearby had died. When the screech owl would holler, I would hear Miss Liz get up and walk at night, sometimes even come to see if I was in my bed. But she would tell me in the morning why she had checked on me, that a screech owl cry meant an unnatural death and might well mean a little child.

Sometimes just before I would wake up from my roommate's screaming, I would have a funny feeling that I was here, at Aunt Cecie's where the window is on the left side. Cecie never would let me move the bed the other way when I told her I wanted the window on the right side like at school and at Miss Liz's. Then as I would wake up, the bed would spin in a circle and the window would be on the other side and I would know I was at school. I am always sort of frightened here at Cecie's, though I know it's supposed to be my home. I told my roommate that; I told her I felt safer at school and in the country at Miss Liz's than I did at home. She wouldn't believe me but it's true. When I was first here I had nightmares and Cecie would run in and shake me awake. I could see Cecie's face; I could feel I was talking to that face that was blank like white paper, could feel I was talking but I was too sleepy to hear and know what I was saying. I always thought that I must have said a lot of things to Cecie, things that I didn't remember; I was always afraid that I told her that I wanted to live with Miss Liz instead of her, things that she hated me for.

The day my roommate left school, she was sniffing and crying. It seems like she was always sniffing, even when she didn't have tears in her eyes, and for awhile I got the whole room to myself. I couldn't talk to her or help her because everytime I would ask her what she was afraid of, she would get mad or say something dumb like "things, mean scary things." She told me she saw things coming up out of graves when the lights were turned off in the room. I don't think she had ever even seen a real grave. I didn't tell her I'd seen a lot of graves, and that what was really scary was that people *didn't* come out of graves. Once they were there, you never saw them again, and you just had to try to remember them, what they did when they were alive, going places with you, things that weren't important then; they only became important when they were dead. Dead people are in little bits in your mind and the longer time goes on, the more you forget their voices or their faces. Sometimes I think if I don't try real hard to remember people right now that they will disappear forever. Even away from Miss Liz for just a few months, though I know she is alive, this happens to my memory of her unless I paint her. I don't see how anyone could be afraid of what's in graves, dead and rotten things. The people never really come back, even in thoughts and paintings, good or bad people, not really. I have this thought at night sometimes, that what would really be better, better than any of the faces and voices that I try to remember and to paint, would be a rabbit or a puppy like I had once. They died too, but with animals you can get another one and get used to it and love it just as much; it's different than with people. Cecie would say I was too old to talk like that, if I told her what I wanted, but I bet Miss Liz would have something in a box for me by the time I woke up the next morning.

Before we left the farm Miss Liz handed me a package

wrapped in newspaper, and all the way back Aunt Cecie was waiting for me to open it, so she could see what it was, but I didn't have to open it because I knew what it was. Miss Liz had made me a big piece of soap like I asked for, to do a carving with, and until we got ready to leave I thought she had forgotten.

I get my wood carving tools and a nail file and put them on the floor of my closet. My flashlight is already in there, where I read at night, and now all I need is a towel to put under the door crack. I stick my pillow under the covers and cut off the lights, just in case Cecie looks in the door. After I get in the closet and close the door, I stuff the towel in the crack and then flick on my flashlight. I had better wad up the newspaper and put it out of the way so there won't be any noise.

The soap is almost completely smooth and white. There are only a few dark spots that show in here, though there may be more in the light outside. Miss Liz said she never could make a perfect piece of soap. I usually worry a lot about the first cut I make into something like this; it's so different from clay where you can stick it back on if you slip. But I already see the little white slivers start to fall on the floor, small, like cut fingernails as I carve at first, but larger soon as I get more nerve. I am going to work only on one side, so if I mess up I can always turn the soap around. Pretty soon I have the little round shape that I wanted. It is the shape of my little bird and though I haven't carved hands for it to sit in yet, there seem to be hands under it. Rough ugly hands though, as rough as the real little bird's feathers were. But I am going to make him smooth like a grown bird, only the size of a little baby, make him like he could tuck and fold all his feathers down smooth just like Mrs. Stiles's white chickens. When I smooth the soap, making little grooves for feathers, it gets warm and sticky in my hands.

My hands stop moving as I hear my door crack open. Cecie is looking in my room to see if I'm in my bed. I feel my heart start going fast, because I don't know if I really made it look like I was in the bed. If she looks and sees it is only my pillow, then I'll have to tell her I'm in here and why. I watch the door to the closet. Oh, how awful if the light is showing under the door. But I can't cut off the flashlight because if she should hear the clicking sound and open the closet door, I would have no place to go. I do not move and make no noise, yet I cannot hear any noise on the outside. Cecie would think it was foolish to be in here and not to wait until tomorrow to do it. Then the door to my room shuts, and I wait a moment until I hear her footsteps in the hall and the door to her room opening.

I look back at the soap, and it doesn't seem so white now. My flashlight is getting weak, that's why. It fades almost out, and glows and fades again. I shake the batteries in the case and the light seems to get a little brighter. As I look at my own hands in the light, I try to make the hands under the bird match them, but my own hands are covered with the dark ridges of my veins, and they get darker and tighter as I work on the soap. I would like to carve my little bird in the soap and keep him to sit on my dresser beside my statue of Miss Liz. If I can carve him good, then I'll always be able to remember him even after he grows up and Miss Liz has to turn him loose.

It is quiet outside now. I look at the hands in the soap under the little bird a long time; I look at them until I see they are like an old man's hands, like Dummy's hands drawing a tear on his face, making a moustache, hiding his eyes and peeping through his fingers, his hands with the bright yellow fingernails. It's Dummy who wants to hold the little bird, so soft and little, and he is afraid to close his hands around it to feel it, afraid he might hurt it. He is afraid someone will take it away from him. I start to carve Dummy's face in the soap that is above the bird. I will make it look the same as his face, only it will be in the white soap. And I will look at his face in white and know where the dark speckles are and will know the color of the shag of his hair.

Soon I have the face. It is his face but with his eyes hollow and white, like a Greek statue, staring at me like eyes but just as white as the rest of his face. I put the soap in the corner of the closet and look at it for a long time with the light of the flashlight moving over the surface. In the hands is the little bird, the little bird is still there below the face of Dummy, and Dummy's old hands are holding the bird up. But I have done something all wrong, something is the matter, there was not enough soap for that. I have ruined the soap. I have carved it too soon and ruined it. The little bird is smooth and the face is jagged like flint rock and they do not go together and the hands should not be there. I have ruined the soap and will not get another piece like it for a long time. I should have waited. I shouldn't have carved it when I was tired. I remember Dummy, that isn't what is wrong. I can see him, eyes like blue flowers when Miss Liz said "died," hair yellow like broom straw only dull yellow, persimmon stains, blood, and Dummy playing dead in the field — all colors and the soap is white. I wanted him to see how pretty the bird was, to let him hold it. His blue eyes aren't there and he is afraid, afraid to hold the bird in Miss Liz's soap.

It was Cecie's fault, coming to my door. I don't want to see it in the morning when there is light; Cecie ought to leave me alone. I put my head down on the floor of the closet for I am getting very sleepy, and pull my furry bedroom slippers under my face. I cut out the flashlight and for a moment the white soap glows in the dark. Miss Liz would use it to wash with. She used all of Papa's little animals to wash with. If she were here now, she would. She wouldn't believe me if I said it was ruined because she cared nothing about the little animals Papa made; to her it would still be soap and just as good as ever because it could be used to wash with. And I could never tell her I carved Dummy's face; if I told her that, she would be glad I ruined it.

Suddenly my closet door pops and starts to move open. I jump to my feet and a coat hanger crashes to the floor behind me. But there is no one opening the door; I am alone in the room. I hear footsteps in the hall and I run to my bed and get under the covers. The footsteps go by my door when I slide between the cold slick sheets of a fresh-made bed, and I hear Cecie shut the window at the end of the hall.

On the edge of my bureau across the room, I see my statue that I made a long time ago, the one of Miss Liz carved in wood. The wood was dark and smooth and I could see the grain run through it and feel it with my fingers. I remember the knife, how I was afraid to touch it with the knife the first time, and I waited and tried three times before I could make myself cut it. And tonight I ruined my white soap. So stupid to do it in my closet the first day I had the soap. I ruined it trying to carve Dummy, trying to carve that dirty Dummy, Dummy of all different colors, in a white piece of soap. And the little bird — making my bird all smooth with feathers instead of the rough and prickly little thing I left with Miss Liz — my bird was ugly, not smooth and white. Miss Liz, she made the soap for me, and I tried to carve Dummy in it. I tried to carve Dummy's face as it would be if he was holding a warm little bird, and Miss Liz helped me ruin it. She would take it and wash with it until the big piece of white soap was nothing but foam and bubbles. She would be so angry with me if she knew I had carved him, and let him hold the little bird, like he held the chicken. She would have beat him with that wooden spoon.

Across the room I see the square of light, the window shade over the street lamp and moonlight outside, and as the sheets begin to get warm with me, I can slide my feet down further. I hear the tadpoles still smacking slowly at the top of the water, and before I close my eyes, I look at the window. It is almost a warm feeling, the square of light like the sun, breaking through the clouds after a rain, or is it the first patch of blue on a gray day, and Papa says:

"Yonder it is! Yonder's the patch in the Dutch boy's britches!"

And I hear the wind outside hitting the tree, thumping the branches on my window, sucking them away and thumping again, and the wind will slowly break the gray sky away until it will all be blue, as blue as the patch in the Dutch boy's britches, and the wind will blow the water in and crash the waves and spread white foam along the sand.

I saw Papa last night. And it wasn't just a dream, I am sure that part of it was real. Before, when I remembered Papa alive, I saw mainly his clothes, the denim of his overalls, wet when he was holding Maylean, or I saw his hands nailing up the sign on the crib, or his feet stomping the copperhead. This time I saw a face, a real face on Papa that was more than just a moustache the color of straw. In fact I saw two faces — I will explain it.

When I have seen him before, it always seemed that someone was laughing at him, always Miss Liz was laughing; and Papa's face was way up above me where I couldn't see it. Once when Miss Liz moved the bed and didn't tell Papa, he went in the room in the dark and jumped in it like he always did, and it wasn't there. They'd poke fun at him about it, and I thought he might get mad because he had knocked his breath out bad and had broken his false teeth, but he just laughed instead. I guess Papa never really got mad and said anything cross to anyone. At least I didn't think I remembered him being mad, that is until last night in the dream. I remember his face that time. It was when we were at the ocean, so I know it really happened. Papa was already an old man and had never seen the ocean. Miss Liz and I hadn't seen it either but I remember way back then having to beg her to lock up the house and leave, to please let us all go just for one afternoon, when Aunt Cecie and Uncle June said they would drive us down one Sunday.

When we got there I walked out with Papa, up over the high

banks of sand. I had never seen the ground glare so brightly, and the sand was hot as it rose around my feet. That was when Papa said to me, "That's a poor-looking dirt to have all them oats a growing in it. Look at them seeds on them, Ramie. Twice as big as a rye pod."

The sea oats scratched and thumped against his pants when he walked across the sand, like they were trying to beat his thin legs from under him. Papa was walking so fast I couldn't keep up. Finally he stopped and lifted me up on his shoulders when I got a spur in my toe, up where I could see his face in the white glare of the sun, as shiny as my cake of soap with his eyes behind his white lashes. The sky got bluer as the wind blew the clouds further into the land, and Papa's eyes behind the white lashes were like the blue sky behind the clouds, the patch in the Dutch boy's britches. Soon I was up where I could see over the hills of sand, and when I was looking at the blue water and the blue sky out in front of me, Papa stopped walking and said,

"I declare. I declare, Ramie, there ain't no end to be seen. There is water clean to the sky with no other side there a'tall." He said that over and over, "no other side there a'tall."

I don't know if he stopped talking then or if I just couldn't hear him for the sound of the water coming in. He walked down to the edge with me still on his shoulders and he got closer and closer to the water until the waves were breaking and hitting his shoes and getting his pants legs wet. He wobbled in the water like a skinny tree in the wind, and I held to the top of his head for fear I would fall. I guess it would have been Papa who would have fallen, not me, but I felt like someone had tossed me into the air and if he forgot to snatch me back, I would be sucked away in the wind.

Then I heard them hollering, Aunt Cecie and Uncle June and most of all, Miss Liz, and I turned to see them dark against the white sand, swirling and looking almost like tops where the heat rose around them. Papa went walking back until soon only a thin little shoot of water reached out and sucked at his wet shoes, and I moved with him, still on his shoulders.

"Just look at you," Miss Liz said, "soaking wet and with your shoes on to boot. Acting like you ain't got good sense." Papa set me down then. As I felt the ground under my feet again, I saw that his Sunday pants were dark and wet and his shoes all stuck up with sand.

"Look at that, Lizzie," he said from above me. "Look at that water just sucking in and out and bubbling whitelike. Why it looks like it could just reach out and grab you."

"I see it and I ain't going near it. You taking that child out there! Why it could just snatch her away from you in a minute!"

Papa acted like he didn't even hear her. "And look at them little birds just running in and out and a-pecking up grubs like they could outrun the devil? Water right over their heads, just a smashing down, meaning to get them . . . and zip . . . they ain't there no more!"

As we watched the little birds run in and out with the waves, Papa laughed and said to me, "You see them, Ramie? I declare I ain't even seen one of them get wet; just teasing that water to beat the band."

He stooped and picked up a tiny little pair of shells that was opened like a lavender butterfly. He said, "Ramie, do you reckon that there is two of every one of these on the ground, that here somewhere everyone of these little covers has got another side, but only the Lord above knows for sure where it is?"

And he spoke more of the shell in his hand; he closed the butterfly up into a little empty case and said how pretty it was just to be a dead thing . . . that is when it happened, when he was speaking of the shell and how many of them must have died for that many shells to be on the beach.

"We are going home. I'm not a mind to stay another minute.

We have seen it and we are going home," Miss Liz said and turned her back. I saw the shell Papa was holding fall from his hand in little pieces and hit the ground beside me. I looked upward at his face. It was bowed down, and in the sun Papa who always looked golden and shiny like ripe grain had turned dark. He did not move when Miss Liz started across the sand with Cecie and June. He just stood with his face in that shadow, until this strange feeling had drained away from his hands and face, and he could follow them back across the sand.

I think that what I saw in Papa's face, though I never saw it again, had to be put away somewhere inside of him and kept with him until he was dead, because he never had any way to put it outside. And what he said, the words I could not understand then, but could feel go cold inside me when I heard them: "There is some things you can't whip, Lizzie. There is some things in this world that won't stand for you to whip them and they will wait, Lizzie. They will wait and take you in time."

When I was walking with Papa back to the car, I saw in my mind then, when I was a little girl, Miss Liz beating on a lion, which was the biggest animal I could think of; Miss Liz with a stick beating on a lion and it was growing bigger each time she hit it, but she wouldn't stop beating. Her face drew up tight and the three pins in her hair came loose and it all fell down, gray and stringy and wet looking. Her hair got wilder and wilder until I could barely see her eyes shining through it, getting wider each time she hit the lion. Soon the lion was so big her stick was just a twig and she seemed as tiny as my wood statue of her. Then the lion smiled and ate her. I started crying on Papa's lap when the lion ate her, and though they thought I was crying because we left the ocean so soon, I never told them different.

But the funny thing is, this part of my dream last night was different, different from what really happened that day at the beach. In the dream I didn't think of the lion, in the dream we never went to the car. The water came a long way up the shore, sucking at our feet and pulling the sand from under us, making us wobble a little each time. I turned and saw one of the little birds running from the water. But it fell, it fell and rolled over and over as the foam pulled it into the ocean. And I saw it rolling and rolling and getting larger, until I saw it wasn't really a bird after all. It was a person. Just before I woke up, I saw the face of the person rolling in the white foam, the face of Miss Liz as she was pulled out into the water, and I turned to look beside me on the sand and Miss Liz was gone.

Spring Lizards . . .

DEAR RAMIE

IT IS FINE HEAR. I HOPE IT IS FINE THERE.
SET YOUR BIRD OUT TODAY. HE WAS GET-
ING TO MUCH TO KEEP IN AND BUMPING
OFF HIS FETHERS ON THE GLAS. RECKIN I
SEE HIM AGIN BEING ALL THE OTHERS IS
GONE SOUTH I AM THINKING. HE MIGHT
TAKE A NOTION TO CATCH UP WITH THEM.
GOT TO DO THE WASH TODAY. LYNDIE
STILES IS SETING HEAR WITH ME HER MAMA
SENT HER I AM THINKING. SHE WILL BOX
THIS FOR ME DOWN BY THE ROAD. SOON AS
I HUNT A STAMP. WANTED TO SAY YOUR
BIRD WAS FINE. WANTED TO SAY WHEN
YOU COMING BACK.

LOVE — MAMA

IT's SATURDAY and Miss Robinson and I are on the way out to
Miss Liz's to collect some animals for class. I got this letter from
Miss Liz this week, and it is the first letter I have ever gotten
from her. She asked me to address an envelope for her when I
was there, so she could let me know if my bird lived or not. I

have read the letter over and over today, and am reading it again because it seems so strange to think of Miss Liz talking to me when we are in two different places.

Miss Liz writes all in capital letters and spells some things wrong. She won't write unless she has lined paper, then she draws her letters all the way up to the line like a first-grader. The only other time I can remember seeing something she wrote was a grocery list she sent me to the store with. I had to go over in the corner and read it out loud to myself first before I knew what she meant: SUP, LOF BRED, CELRY, FAT BACK, CABAGE 2. Even then I remember Mr. Allbright making awful fun of me when I asked for two ca-BA-ges. Reason Miss Liz writes like that is she had to learn how to write in Sunday School, since there wasn't a regular school when she was a little girl. I can't think Miss Liz ever was a little girl; she has never been anything but an old woman since I have known her. Out in the smokehouse once I found a picture of her when she was young, a brown picture with tight hard skin on her face and her chin sticking out. She was not pretty even then, and she took the picture away from me and scratched out her face with a hatpin. In most every picture of her in Cecie's scrapbook, her face has been scratched out, even in the little snapshots where there are long rows of people, there'll be one person with a white face and if you look good, you know it was Miss Liz. When I got my camera for Christmas last year, I tried and tried to take her picture, but she would turn her head.

The only time she ever let me take a good picture of her was when she had on Cecie's hat and fur coat. Miss Liz always wants to act like she doesn't care about feminine things like powder and jewelry and fur coats, but I know that's not true. You start to take a picture of her in her apron, and she'll run take it off and grab something that belongs to someone else and put on that rhinestone pin. Getting ready to have Cecie for dinner, she's the same way, changing her way of fixing the table and all, which is really silly because if anybody knows what she's really like, it's Cecie. Sometimes I wonder what Miss Liz feels inside, if she really thinks she's fooling anyone. And the picture of her in Cecie's tall hat and fur coat — she didn't scratch her face off that one. I put it in the album and showed it to her; Miss Liz was combing out her hair and she took three hairpins from her mouth and said, "Now who's that elegant lady?"

I remember Cecie didn't catch on to her kidding at first and said, "Well, who do you *think* it is?" That really tickled Miss Liz, and Cecie got a little mad and said, "You could have a decent-looking coat and hat yourself if you weren't so stingy."

Miss Liz said, "You keep all your fineness. It ain't for me to go strutting around in."

"Honestly, Mama, I was so ashamed of you the other day when you took off that old gabardine coat and half the lining was hanging out. And your nightshirt sticking out the sleeves of your dress. There's just no excuse for that, Mama."

I remember Miss Liz started to frown then, and the two creases between her eyebrows deepened. She had her gray hair spread out across one shoulder, and it was thin and fine with ripples all the way down where it had been plaited. She put the three pins back in her mouth and tightened her lips around them as she pulled the last tangle from her hair.

"Would you wear a new coat if I bought it for you?" Cecie said.

"One I got suits me fine," Miss Liz mumbled, then I watched her start to braid her hair. Cecie was quiet now, and we both watched Miss Liz plait her hair all the way down to the very end, until it was just a tiny string. Then she pulled the hair from the comb and wound it around the end, and the long braid was rolled up and stuck on the back of her head with the three pins before Cecie and I could even breathe.

And on the way home, Cecie had said, "I've watched her do her hair a thousand times. I've watched her pull that hair out of her comb to tie it with and wondered since I was a child if it was the same hair she had tied it with every day, because her hair is always the same, a little whiter all the time but always the same. I guess I wouldn't feel right, Ramie, if I didn't see that little bun on the back of her head with those same three pins."

I guess Miss Liz wrote to me because she's so lonesome now. Lyndie can go see her but Mrs. Stiles can't, since they had that falling out over Dummy. Though she is awful hard to get along with, I do feel sorry for her living there all by herself. I think it's hard on her, though I don't guess she'd admit it. Once all the children were there and Papa was there; I bet there were as many as ten people living in that house at one time, and even though she would get fretted with them, she was never mad long at the family. I bet she will be happy to see me today and to tell me all about caring for the little bird. I had forgotten she was caring for the little bird, that every day she was feeding it and it was growing. I know it must have changed a lot since the time it fell down the chimney. I just wish I could have seen him before she set him loose because now I'll always have to remember him as a little baby; I won't ever get to see his new feathers.

I used to think that nothing went on at the farm when I wasn't there, that everything started living and growing when I got there and stopped when I left. When I used to go back after the seasons had changed, I found it really hard to believe that things were different since I didn't get to see them happen. But with the seasons you always know what will happen. Every fall the living things change but the same trees are always the same color. Winter will be the same dead grass when I get to the farm today, the same snow patches and dark fence posts. And if I think hard I can remember spring, the frail grass when the snow patches in the shade start to disappear, and the honeysuckle around the dark fence posts, bright green on the black, until you can't see the black at all.

When spring gets here, the windows in Miss Liz's house will

come open; she'll unstick them where she painted them shut on the inside and she'll pull out all the stuffing she put in the cracks. As the wind starts to blow in March, the curtains will suck in and out of the windows; I can remember seeing the colored curtains flap against the outside of the house when I was out in the field getting broomsticks for a kite. And all the smells change then too. You can smell the wet ground where the fruit tree petals have fallen in the rain and smell the white foam in the ditch beside the dike — it burns in your head the same as when you get caught in fertilizer dust. But there aren't many smells and colors now, nothing to make you want to go outside and be doing something. Mostly you just stay inside and talk, go out when you have to, and Miss Liz keeps the house so closed up the kitchen smells like food even when she's not cooking and the living room smells of wood smoke from the fireplace. She makes you slip through a little crack in the door if you want to go outside, then she stuffs a rag in the crack under the door, making so much to do of it that you had just as soon stay put. The windows stay so steamed up on the inside that it's hard to see out anyway; Miss Liz always let me draw pictures in the fog on the windows. I remember helping her carry out the ashes when the wind started blowing down the chimney in spring and scattered ashes all across the rug. When I would fill the scuttle with the ashes, I could hear the sweeps already starting their nests up above, and their noises were so happy and busy I could feel sure winter was over.

My little bird surely didn't sound happy when he came down the chimney screaming and crying. Miss Liz said he was bumping his feathers off on the glass. I guess he hit the glass because he could see through it to the outside and couldn't understand there was something there between it and him. I hope he's not sorry now that he wanted to get out of Miss Liz's warm house so much. I used to think I wanted to go out when I would look through a clear place in the glass and see the train go by, or see the beagle hounds running through the bushes; but then I would get outside and get so cold, and I couldn't find anything to do to keep warm, until I would have to beg Miss Liz to let me back in. She used to say, "You just won't stay put a minute," but she was always glad to have me back inside because she always had a lot of stories ready to tell me. But my little bird didn't get to come back in because he couldn't tell her even if he wanted to. If he had been born at the right time of the year, I guess he would be down south now. I sure hope he doesn't freeze to death.

I wonder if he'll know what happened to the others, why he is alone out there and why the air suddenly got cold. I wonder if he'll fly into a tree and listen to hear the whistling sound of the others, and if he'll know why it's quiet. Will he be able to sing? I'll have to remember to ask Miss Liz if she hears him singing outside, because all the noise I ever heard him make was that fussing when he was hungry. Maybe he'll be like Dummy. He'll look like the others, like Dummy did when he came in the store for the first time, but he won't be able to make any sound. I think maybe what is wrong with Dummy is that no one talked around him when he was little, that there was no one saying words for him to copy. He can copy the things people do, so maybe if he had heard words he could have copied them too.

My bird can fly away, he can disappear in the trees and the fields, and Miss Liz and I will never get to see him again. We won't know if he just fell out of the sky and died the first day he was free or if he will live a long time. If he can't sing, he has the whole world to hide in and no one will ever know. I could ask Miss Robinson if he could sing, but it might be a real stupid question. She would say he could, I bet, that instinct would take care of him and he wouldn't be helpless like a human. But Miss Liz said my little bird was like a human baby when it was crying for food, like me and Gregory and even Maylean; we were all little babies once for Miss Liz to care for. It must be so hard for Miss Liz to tell when babies don't need to be cared for anymore and watched over, whether they just want to get out by themselves or whether they really should. And Gregory, she left him alone and he died because he didn't know about the spider.

I remember one day in lab when Miss Robinson put a spider in formaldehyde and it turned out to be a mother spider that had had all her little babies sitting on her back. They all went swimming out from her, but she reached out and tucked them under her even though she was dying. Though I could never stand for her to touch me, and she was awful with her legs moving in the liquid, I am sorry that she had to die, and she is not evil, not meaning to be really. She just doesn't have any way to think like I do, and they were her little babies; she tucked them just like a mother hen tucks all hers under her wings. And even my mother, Maylean, in the closet, holding me against her with her skinny little arms; she was trying to protect me. Miss Liz was hiding us from my daddy, not letting us see him.

I have thought before that even the black widow that bit Gregory didn't mean to be evil. She was just not meant to be touched by people, and she bit Gregory because she was afraid, because she was afraid he was going to kill her. The only reason that Gregory had to die was that he was a little child and didn't know not to touch black widows. That is why Miss Liz blames herself. She did know not to touch them and should not have left Gregory out there alone; it is her guilty feeling that bothers her. She wasn't caring for Gregory like she should have been, like the chimney swift that let her baby fall down into the fireplace. Miss Liz should have taught Gregory to be afraid. But she hides things, she thinks that she can always hide things from me. I remember one day Papa hid my face, he held my head against him while I was screaming to see, and I could hear Miss Liz asking, "What is to be done? What is to be done?"

Before she had come out to the field, I was with Papa, helping him chop. He was saying, "Mama is going to make me plumb wear this bean patch out. I have chopped it till I'm going to have to start whacking down the beans in order to have something to chop. Ain't a half dozen sprigs of wild grass in the whole row."

I was coming behind Papa with the little hoe he had given me and I was picking up the grass he chopped and shaking it on my hoe until all the dirt was off, then I would get on my knees and turn the roots up toward the sun.

Papa was still talking, about Mama, then he stopped and put his hand on my head, "Little one, little Ramie, you listen to what I tell you and try your best to remember it and take note of it when you're grown. That is a hard-headed woman. There is only one way around her and you can mark my word, that way would be the same if she was right or wrong and knew it. Now, I ain't saying she's not a good woman, because that would be a fib. She's got many a fine quality, a harder worker I never saw and not a word of complaining. But because she said to chop, I will have to chop until it suits her."

"Papa, what would happen to you if you just said you won't going to chop no more," I asked.

Then he laughed and said that Miss Liz would get so mad she would explode in a thousand little pieces and he wouldn't have any one to cook his supper.

And I was trying to remember what he told me to, about Miss Liz's one way even if it was wrong. That was when something happened; I couldn't see up to his face, but his hoe dropped and fell and broke some of the little purple bean flowers off. It scared me at first and by the time I had seen it was only his hoe, he was running off, jumping through the rows and just stepping all over everything. I started behind him but he was so far away I stopped, and I pulled a yellow bean leaf from my skirt; it stuck like it was glued and was so full of holes from the beetles that it

looked like lace. I started up the hill to Papa to show him the
leaf. That was when I saw Miss Liz for the first time; he must
have seen her come out across the field and she had something
wrapped up in a blanket.

When I got to the top of the hill, I held my hand open to show
Papa the leaf, but he closed my hand shut in his; he held my
hand so hard it hurt, and when I cried out, he picked me up
quick. He pressed my face against his chest until it was hard for
me to breathe. I was saying right or wrong over to myself, trying
to remember, and trying not to think that it was hard to breathe.
That was the day. I didn't know it before, but that was the day it
happened.

"What is to be done, Thel? What is to be done?" Miss Liz was
saying.

"Don't be asking me now, Lizzie. What is done is done."

Papa's voice was soft, like someone who was tired, yet he held
my face tighter. I started to cry and tried to pull my face up so I
could see, but he wouldn't let me, and I was mad and beat my
fists on him.

"You should have knowed better, Lizzie. It was wrong to leave
such a little one out by himself." Papa's hand was still strong
against the back of my head, but his body was trembling.

"I couldn't have knowed, Thel. You know as good as I that I
couldn't have knowed he was there. I didn't know no wrong
would come for just setting him out to play."

Papa was holding me to keep me from seeing Gregory. Gregory was dead in Miss Liz's arms and swollen from the spider bite.
She had carried him across the fields to find Papa and he had
died in her arms.

Papa thought it was her fault; it was her fault because she
knew about black widows. She knew to look for the red mark on
them. The spider tells you not to touch her by having a red mark
on her.

"Miss Robinson?"

She turns to look at me and raises her eyebrows in that way she has to tell you that she is listening. "Since a black widow has a mark on her that says she's poisonous, doesn't that make her innocent really? I mean she doesn't try to hide her poison."

Miss Robinson is silent a moment then says, "I don't quite understand your question, Ramie. You want to know if a spider is innocent if it bites you?"

"Well, sort of. No, not really. I mean like a black widow has a red spot on it to tell you it can kill you."

"Lots of things can kill you, Ramie. Things that you think of as innocent . . . water, snow, the sun even . . . you just have to learn to live safely with them. Everyone knows not to walk out in the desert without water, but a lot of people don't know where black widows are, so they get bitten because of their own carelessness. On the other hand, some harmless animals, like snakes for instance, look poisonous and get killed because of it. Remember, you can't judge the things of nature like you do human beings."

"Then why is a black widow called a widow?"

She laughs and says, "Because she destroys her mate when she has no more use for him, and that makes her a widow. And she's black, you know, in mourning clothes, and she always lives alone in a dark secluded place."

"Where is that?"

"Well, more specifically, in tin cans, on the bottom sides of boards, in any dry, dark sheltered place." Then she stops talking and looks ahead at the road, and I see her smile and know she is going to try to talk to me without sounding like a teacher now.

"You know I heard once that mailmen became afraid to deliver mail in rural areas because of them. It seems they were nesting in the mailboxes and a few postmen were suffering bites on the hands and arms from them. I think they really throw a false scare into people myself. The way the newspapers talked about the mailman thing, you would think there was a black widow waiting in every mailbox in the country. They would know how few there are if they ever had to go out and search for specimens. Why, I must have picked up a thousand boards one summer, and you know I only found one! One black widow!"

Sometimes when Miss Robinson talks, she just gets louder and louder, then when she quits and you have to say something natural, it sounds funny.

"I've only seen two in my whole life," I say. "I mean loose ones. One on the tobacco stems Aunt Cecie bought for the lawn, and one Miss Liz turned up with a hoe and beat to death before she knew what kind of spider he was. I was mad at her for killing it because I thought it was just a plain old spider. It was all dusty and looked just like any grass spider before she squashed it and its legs drew up under it. And sure as everything, there was that red spot on its stomach."

Miss Robinson is talking again, she's still talking about how hard it is to collect specimens. She talks a lot really, and you can just nod your head and look at her every now and then, but you don't really have to listen to what she says because she always answers her own questions before you can say anything. I'm almost always sorry when I ask her something, like when she said the writing spider wasn't really writing, that he was a hedge spider and was reinforcing the center of his web so he could catch flying insects. Miss Liz would know that too, she knows he catches bugs, but she has a story for everything. She could teach Miss Robinson that some things are more important than she thinks they are, but I'd never tell Miss Robinson that. I bet she wouldn't even listen to Miss Liz. I told Miss Robinson how Miss Liz could tell how far the lightning was away, about the time she knew it was getting a mile closer each time it struck, and she was running across the fields to the house, carrying the knife she was using to cut the tobacco stalks. The lightning was coming faster than she could run; she felt it flare up only a mile away and the next time it struck, it hit the knife she was running with and singed the hair on her head. Miss Robinson said it was certainly foolish for a farm person not to know better than to attract lightning, that Miss Liz was lucky she wasn't killed, it was foolish not to know that metal would draw lightning. I didn't like that, her calling Miss Liz foolish.

I hope she'll do all her collecting herself really. I don't like to catch things, like she does anyway; just scooping them up and never making a special pet of any of them. I especially don't like to know they're going to be put in a bunch of jars and just dumped in the trash when they die. When I catch something like she does, I can't help but say to myself, 'If it hadn't been for me, you'd still be running loose.' And she is going to catch bugs and worms, things you can't touch and I can't even stand to watch. I love to touch soft animals with fur and feathers and all, and don't really mind frogs and turtles either. I just don't like creepy things that make your skin crawl; even if I know they can't hurt me, things with a lot of skinny legs and feelers, I still don't like them; I think they were meant to be left alone. Miss Robinson and I can talk about the same things and it's more than just calling them different names — we see them so different that soon they are not even the same things.

Maybe I can just go up and sit with Miss Liz while we're there, and I know Miss Liz wants to see me since I got the letter. She is lonely there now, by herself in winter. I can see how she'll be when we get there; I can see her in my mind. She'll hear the car a mile before it gets to the house, and she'll know every bump and curve in the road by the sound of it and will be able to tell you just at what spots you can see the car. Before we turn into the yard, she will have gone down the color list of every car in the family in her mind. She just can't wait to see who gets out; she has to figure out who's coming before they get there, and then she asks about the children, why all of them didn't come, before she even pays any attention to who is there. She won't know this car; that'll bring her out on the porch before time. The old house that looks so dead and dark will swing its door open, and Miss Liz will walk across the porch and stand at the top of the steps, setting everything to shaking, and maybe she'll be standing there in that red dress, with her arms crossed. Maybe it's silly to remember everything somebody does, but it seems like with Miss Liz every move she makes has been thought out and should mean something, and she means for you to take notice when she walks out of the house or when she points at something. And most important, you always know ahead of time what to expect her to do.

"Miss Robinson, you better slow down a little. The turn-off is on the other side of that mailbox."

"Which mailbox?" Miss Robinson steps on the brakes and I have to grab the dashboard to keep from bumping my head.

"That one, see the dirt road? That goes right on in."

As soon as we turned down the road, everything begins to become familiar. Even though it is colder than it was when I left Thanksgiving, and more things have died since then, there seems to be the same gray and green there was then — dark green. There is a winter green here that is almost black. I am so glad for winter green; it makes things not look so dead as I thought they would. When we pass the swamp forest, the clump of trees that are richer and taller than the others, I see Miss Robinson turn her head.

"That's a healthy looking spot. I imagine there are springs down there?"

She looks at me with her eyebrows raised and I hear myself answering her, though I don't really want to tell her. "Yes the old mule spring is there, the freshest and best spring on the whole farm. It never goes dry, and all sorts of things grow there that don't live anywhere else . . ." I hear myself answering, and I know I shouldn't tell her.

"Well, we'll have to go down there. A fresh spring means salamanders."

Salamanders, the spring lizards. Papa said they keep the water fresh. Papa said that everywhere else on the farm there was either too much or too little of everything, too little wild grass where the banks washed away, and too much wild grass in the garden. But in the swamp forest, if you were to touch a single flower or kill a bug, it would never be the same. And when there are too many greenflies, they go up over the trees and are eaten by the swifts. Also another mushroom will grow to fill an empty space if the fairy ring is broken. Papa said he would never bother the swamp forest; he would never cut the trees or plow there. He said he would go there to be reminded of his place. Reminded of his place; that's what he said and I can hear him saying it sort of low and fuzzy and high up.

Miss Robinson stops the car on the edge of the road, and I see that she is not going up to the house.

"Miss Robinson, do you mind if I go say hello to my grandmother. I'm sure she's seen the car and will be wondering who is here."

"Of course, of course. Stay as long as you like." Her voice is muffled as she bends over the seat, stringing wire baskets up her arms and pulling her seine up from the floor.

I get out of the car and start up the road to the house. Miss Liz didn't come out on the porch as I expected, but I've never seen her miss a car coming onto the place yet. She'll be at the window, looking through a clean place in the glass to make sure the car is planning to stop at her house. Then she'll come outside and stand at the top of the steps. I am at the edge of the yard and still she hasn't come out.

The steps to the house are clogged with dead leaves but Miss Liz has swept the porch clean. I see her sage broom by the door. When I look through the window in the door, the house is strangely dark. There are only a few red coals glowing in the fireplace. In a shaft of white light coming from the other end of the house, I see the table, filled with bowls, each covered as always by a flat dish. The white light ripples and slides across the furniture, and then I see where it is coming from — the back door is open and is swinging open and shut with the wind. A chill goes through my body when I hear the door slam hard then creak open slowly again, its latch not catching.

Where is Miss Liz?

I start around the house, brushing through the dead hydrangeas that make a death rattle behind me. Miss Liz would never leave the house open in the winter, not for any reason. When I come around the edge of the back porch, the corner of my eye catches the red peppers by the porch post, bright red against the gray wood. In front of me I see more red. Lying in the grass by the iron pot is Miss Liz.

Washday . . .

I RUN DOWN the path, and when I am beside her, her head snaps around at me. She is reaching at the pot with one hand but her fingers are opening and closing in the air. She stares at me like she doesn't know me.

"Mama!"

She turns her face to the ground and pushes her weight upward until she is on her knees. She still hasn't spoken and acts like I'm not even here.

"Mama, can I help you up?"

"No! No . . ." Her voice is hoarse and she begins to cough as soon as she speaks, her back jolting up and down. "All swimmy-headed. Was washing the clothes . . . dogs was tearing them off the line."

There are no clothes in the pot. There is even a little square of frost that hasn't melted in the shade under the pot. Miss Liz hasn't had a fire there. She hasn't even washed. She turns her head and I look where she looks, down at the broom sage field where two brown-and-white beagles run in and out, the white tips of their tails showing over the top of the sage.

"Sorry dogs . . . bad enough got to run down every rabbit on the place . . . getting in the hen house . . . ripping down the

clothes . . . I'm a mind to just walk over and tell Vernon Stiles
if he doesn't pen them up, I'm getting Papa to shoot them . . ."

Miss Liz stops talking and her head begins to shake; her eyes
look like she is trying to hold her head still but can't. "It's a
shame when an animal has to suffer for people's wrongs," she
says. "Mind you, I ain't got a bit of hate in me for them dogs
. . . dogs is dogs and like as not to be like the folks that tends
them . . . Vernon Stiles starves them and sends them over here
to feed on my rabbits and chickens . . . I fear Papa is going to
have to shoot them . . . not a doubt in my mind they're going
to have to be shot."

She is crawling toward the pot now and is pulling herself up
on it. Her dress is all dark and wet in spots from the ground.
Her body is bunched up over her feet now as she gets her balance, her weight bending her ankles outward. She raises her arm
and I watch her square finger point down toward the pasture. I
look where she points and hear her say, "He got the post in . . .
you get on somebody enough, things'll get done . . . see yonder, that post there's been rotted out for three winters and Papa's
just now getting it done . . . no way to run a farm . . ."

Miss Liz pants behind me and I hear the grass crackle under
her feet as she wobbles back and forth. I look at the post a moment, Papa's Christmas present to her, years ago, and Miss Liz is
talking like he is still alive.

"Won't catch me letting my stock run all over the countryside
. . . having to account for a melon that got trampled five miles
down the road . . . no cow of mine . . . not one post, it's another . . . never no end to the work we got to get done."

I hear Miss Liz now, making whispering sounds but not like
she's telling me about something. It is so soft and far away, I
can't hear it.

"Mama, don't you think you'd better go in where it's warm?"

She looks at me hard, then she smiles and says, "Ramie, I declare, Ramie. You change so much every time you go I hardly

know you. I declare." She acts like she's recognizing me for the first time.

She's smiling now but something is still all wrong. She doesn't look like herself. She's all bent looking, and like she'll fall if she tries to move, and like her mind isn't working all the time, just in little spurts.

"Mama, let's go in the house." I walk to her side and take her arm. It goes stiff when I touch it but she doesn't pull away. I have never helped her walk before. She has never seemed an old woman really, at least not like most old people. Something is wrong; I'll have to ask Aunt Cecie, but something is wrong.

When we go up the steps of the house, Miss Liz almost pushes me down leaning on me. I am really scared until we are on the level porch, because if she were to start falling I would never be able to hold her up, she is so much heavier than me. She stands looking at the screen but doesn't reach out to open it, and waits till I open it for her. The house is already cold from the door left standing open, and is hardly much warmer than outside. I leave her with her hands resting on the table, and go to the front room and start stirring the fire. I hear Miss Liz shuffling slowly across the kitchen. The curtains aren't open, and it is almost like night in here.

"Mama, come get in front of the fire and warm up." I see her come into the room, and it seems an age before she has walked across to her chair in front of the fireplace. She has no wood in the house, just a few scraps of kindling and I see where she has been tossing it on without even putting in a log. When I get up and go toward the door, she looks up at me, her eyes shiny and her breath making clouds in the air.

"No, Ramie! Don't go, don't go yet! You can stay for a while . . ." Her voice is very loud for the first time.

"I'm not going yet, Miss Liz. I've got to bring you in some wood so we can get a fire going."

"Ain't nary scrap left. What we didn't burn, folks around here stole out from under us, try as we may to watch out for it. Can't trust your own neighbor . . . trust your blood . . . all a body can do. Been a longer winter than I've ever seen." She stops talking and shakes her head.

"Long winter? Mama, it's just December. You know it doesn't get really cold until January and February." She turns back to face the fireplace and her only movement is the thumping of her fingers up and down on her lap. I go outside and to the woodshed by the smokehouse. The logs are stacked high up the wall where Uncle Buck put them last summer, and the kindling is covered by ragged bed quilts. I fill the scuttle with kindling and put two of the logs over my other arm after I cover the kindling back over with the quilt. It is Miss Liz's mother's quilt; I can tell it's not Miss Liz's because all of the bits of material have been cut exactly the right size and they are all the same kind of material. Miss Liz uses corduroy or wool or satin; she doesn't care what kind. The only pattern I've ever seen her make was a wagon wheel, either a lot of little ones or one big one that looks like a huge spider web. A chill goes up my back as I start up the steps with the wood.

"Mama, open up!"

I wait but no one comes so I have to put down the logs and open the door myself. Miss Liz is just as I left her, still looking at the hot coals in the fireplace.

I start to build the fire, wadding paper and putting kindling on it the way I saw Miss Liz do it so many times, but she doesn't say anything to me like she usually does about how I'm doing it wrong. The paper begins to glow from the hot coals, then blazes up and the yellow kindling starts to turn black.

"Mama, you've got plenty of wood. You've got enough out there to last two winters."

"Pshaw . . . pshaw."

"You do. Really you do, Mama, and if you do run out, you know you can get some more."

"It's a-going. But it won't matter none. It won't matter. I won't last two winters, not two winters more." She rocks a minute in her chair, patting her hands in her lap again. "Ramie, fetch me that quilt over there. I need to busy my hands."

I go where she points and pick up the quilt and take it to her, spreading it in her lap.

"When I get done," she says, "when I get done working it, it'll make a cover . . . little bits and snatches good for nothing but when I get done working it . . ."

I get her shawl and warm it in front of the fire then put it over her shoulders.

"That feels good, doesn't it?" I say.

She pats my hand that is still on her shoulder and says, "That's fine, Ramie." She smiles and starts to rock quickly in her chair as I sit down on the hearth. I feel warmer now too, and Miss Liz seems to be all right again.

"I keep losing track," she says, "with this day and that. I was thinking it was wash day . . ."

"That's right. Today's Saturday. That's why I'm out of school."

"Oh, it is then." She is silent for a moment then she says, "Ramie, I would like to ask you not to make mention to Cecie about me going sprawling out back. She wouldn't think well of it."

"Think well of it?" I ask. "Mama, you couldn't help falling. It's not like doing something wrong."

"Just keep it to yourself is all I ask," she says quickly.

"I will. I promise. I don't tell Cecie when I fall down. I don't have to tell her anything I don't want to."

She is staring at the fire again and acts like she doesn't hear me.

"I wish I could stay on over tonight with you, but I'll have to go back when Miss Robinson goes, since she brought me. That's how I got here; she's out yonder collecting things."

"What . . . what?"

"My teacher from school. You remember, I told you that she wanted to come out here and collect some stuff for class. And it gave me an excuse to come see you anyway."

"Lets snakes bite her, that's the one?" Miss Liz looks almost mad at me.

"Well, she just said that once. What she wanted to get out here was little animals, snails and grasshoppers and all, you know. And you know she won't find much either, not in the winter." Miss Liz is acting strange, one minute I think she doesn't hear me and the next minute I think everything I say makes her mad. She must have hit her head when she fell. Maybe she got dizzy bending over.

"Dead . . ." The word whispers through her lips, almost not a word, just air. Then she lifts her chin and says, "Time will be soon that every living thing is frozen to its spot, won't be no burrowing in the ground or hiding in the barn. Screech owl won't even yell. Devil is going to freeze us, not fire like is said. Freeze us, mind you."

Her voice is far away again, like a preacher at a funeral. The fire has warmed one side of me but the side away from the fire is cold. As I stand and turn, Miss Liz looks up at me.

"Losing ground, soon as you quit fighting, things start getting the best of you."

I wish she would stop; she is scaring me like she used to do at night when she tried to make me think someone was prowling in the yard. It's so dark in here and so cold unless I get all the way on the hearth. The fire is cracking and poping out sparks because the wood was damp. A spark hits my hand and I hear my voice cry out as the spark dies. It burned a little red spot and made tears come in my eyes. Miss Liz didn't even see it or look up like she heard me.

"I burned my hand," I say. "Guess I better put up the screen, don't you, until the wood dries out. I guess it will cut off most of the heat though." I put the screen up and say, "It hurts a little but I don't guess it's a deep enough burn to put soda on. Maybe it won't blister up."

Miss Liz doesn't speak and her hands still haven't started to move on the quilt in her lap. The only sound is her chair creaking back and forth and the fire popping. Big sparks are hitting the screen and glowing a long time on the hearth before they burn out. I feel like talking to her, but it bothers me not to know if she is listening or whether she understands or what. What is wrong with her? Why doesn't she talk to me? I see the firelight moving in her eyes when she rocks but her eyes don't follow me, even when I stand up or when the logs pop. Something has happened inside her, she looks almost asleep with her eyes open.

"Mama, I got your letter." She doesn't answer me again and keeps rocking and staring at the fire. "I wondered about the bird, if he would be able to sing, even though he didn't have a mother to teach him how. And he doesn't have others around him singing either, so I was wondering if it was just natural for them to sing, whether they were taught or not, if they didn't have to be taught like people are taught to talk. What do you think?"

She still doesn't answer. I hear a horn blowing down the road and when I go to the window, I see Miss Robinson waving her hand at the house. Then she turns and walks back toward the swamp forest.

"Mama, I got to go now."

She jumped when I spoke, almost as though I woke her up from a dream.

"You got to go already?" she asks.

"Miss Robinson is calling me. It won't be long at all now until I'm out for Christmas and I'll be back."

Miss Liz starts to pick the mud off her dress that she got when she fell down and she tosses the little chunks over the screen into the fire. "Now, Ramie," she says, "I'm going to ask you not to make mention to Cecie that I took a spill out back."

"You already asked me not to, Mama. I won't tell her, I promise."

"Well, I can tell you that it wouldn't do for Cecie to think I couldn't manage for myself. It wouldn't do a'tall."

Miss Liz holds her hands up to me and I see her eyes blink as I take it and the horn blows again. She squeezes my hand once and says, "You take care, you hear? Take care now and hurry back out. Don't you be so long next time."

I hear myself say goodbye and I turn at the door to wave but she is looking back at the fire. When I shut the door behind me, I hear the rattle of the wind through the dead flowers, the flowers that won't shatter away and will have to be cut from the plant with shears, so the new flowers can bloom. Mama didn't cut them and the steps are slick with wet leaves as I walk down them. The light hurts my eyes out here, because it was so dark in Miss Liz's house. I shouldn't have worn my coat inside because it feels like I don't have it on. I stand where the sun is a moment and feel my skin get a little warmer on the outside. The sun comes out stronger from behind the clouds and I feel the wind stop for a second and the trees quit rattling. I don't want to go back inside to get warm. Miss Liz wouldn't get up and come to the door and she won't talk to me. I don't want to go back inside, it was like being by myself in her house.

Nubbins . . .

I WALK OUT under the persimmon trees and their leaves are wet and soggy under my feet, brown, and the ones on top that just fell are yellow-speckled. There are only a few tiny leaves left now and the tree is all twisted together with the tent caterpillar webs. They look all battered up now too, like dirty cloth, where the birds have stopped when they were migrating and fed on the worms. But up through the tree limbs I can see that the sky is bright blue, the kind of blue in early winter that is almost too deep to look real. It's like the sky is making fun of the earth, it's new and fresh-looking up there, it never gets old, and everything down here is battered apart. The wind picks up again and the corn fodder crackles together like it's on fire.

Everything is just before being dead completely and I will like it better when it is, it looks so pitiful now, being almost dead, because you know there won't be anything green until spring. I would like for the snow to come and cover it all over, smooth and white, but it's too soon for that, the dead things will have to show for a while yet. I could go and find something to carry in to Miss Liz, some flower or something that might make her happy, but I don't much want to go in the fields, they're so scratchy and full of briars.

I can hear the Stiles children laughing in the corn field. The tassels are shaking when they pull the corn, so I know where they are even though I can't see them. At the end of the rows I see all the bushel baskets they've filled, little ears almost round they're so short. They must be getting the last of the nubbins so the rats won't get them. Every time I hear one of them yell, I get chills on my arms. I wonder if Miss Liz hears them. She is just sitting there, she is usually out watching them at this time to see they don't get into her field.

"Dummy! Hey Dummie, come here and carry it out."

I stand in the road and wait a moment as Dummy comes down the row with the basket of corn. When he sees me he sets the basket down and the top part of the corn goes sliding off. Then he starts jumping up and down and smiling like he's real glad to see me. He comes up to me and starts to shake my hand, then stops and points at the ground where I'm standing, wanting me to wait while he goes back into the field, to get Lyndie and Little Brother, I guess.

"Dummy, wait. I can't stay and talk. I have to go home now." He stops very still and looks sad, really sad instead of like he usually does when he is pouting or pretending. He smiles suddenly and holds his finger up for me to wait. He reaches in his back pocket and gets out a long ear of corn and when he pulls the shuck back, I see it is Indian corn, and is dark red with yellow-and-white speckled grains.

"Thank you, Dummy," I say when he hands it to me, "it's very pretty."

"Hey, who you talking to, Dummy?" Lyndie runs up beside him. "It's Miss Ramie!"

"Hey Lyndie, look what Dummy gave me." I hold up the corn and she frowns.

"Well, you Dummy, what you are is an Indian giver. You said I could have it."

"Oh Lyndie, you can have it if you want it."

"We'll find another one, Miss Ramie. There's a whole row of it by the house. I was just picking at old Dummy. Besides he's already snitched three of Miss Liz's gourds for me. You won't tell Miss Liz, will you, Miss Ramie?" she whispers.

"Miss Liz would have a fit if she knew that, Lyndie."

"I know, Miss Ramie, but she just left them. They won't twined on the corn no more and was likely to rot on one side."

I hear a rattle and see that Dummy is shaking one of the gourds he took from the baskets.

"What's that, Lyndie? The seeds?"

"I reckon. They near about always rattle. I know that, you Dummy. Now put that back under the corn before Miss Liz sees you out of the window and comes out and chops your head off."

Dummy stuffs the gourd back under the corn and looks at Miss Liz's house. There is nothing moving there, not even any animals in the yard, and I can see the dark shape of her washing pot out back. Dummy starts running back into the corn field, and Lyndie and I hear him rattling all the way to the other side of the field.

Lyndie starts laughing and says, "That Dummy is scared crazy of Miss Liz. She can make him run quicker than my Mama. He ain't gone nowhere near her since she got so mad at him when he went up under her house after that chicken." She looks up at me and asks, "You going to stay awhile out here, Miss Ramie?"

"No, Lyndie. I have to go back to school but I'll be here for Christmas."

I wonder if I should tell Lyndie about Miss Liz, to have her check on her every day and see if she is all right. No, I can't do that. Miss Liz said not to tell anyone, not to let anyone know she had fallen. Lyndie would tell her mother and not be meaning to do anything wrong. I look back at Miss Liz's house and it still looks like it is frozen.

"Bye, Lyndie," I say, "I really have to go."

"Bye, me and Dummy and Little Brother are going to cut across and beat you to the mailboxes to wave goodbye."

I hear Dummy running back up the row toward us, and Lyndie and Little Brother laugh as they spin him around and the three of them start dodging through the field to get to the mailboxes before we get there with the car.

I start down the road to the car but I can't seem to make myself hurry. Miss Robinson has gone back out in the field anyway after all that horn blowing for me to hurry, and I can see her rear end sticking up in the sage where she bent over to catch something. I feel tired, like I did when I was in the house with Miss Liz and it didn't really do much good to come back outside. I get in the car and look back at the porch to the house. It's just not right, she should be over by the post watching until we leave but she's not. She's in the house in front of the fireplace just staring at the fire. I bet she won't even keep the wood on it, just sit and watch it burn out. It's almost like I didn't even come to see her. She told me to come back but it didn't sound like she meant it; it didn't even sound like she was thinking about what she was saying. All that talk about dying and freezing, and nothing making any sound. I guess I have time to take her this Indian corn before we go. No, I don't really want to. I don't want to go back inside. I'm almost afraid to go back again and see she hasn't gotten up from that chair. And I don't want her to ask me who I got it from.

I see all the baskets of nubbins that Dummy has carried to the end of the rows and under one of them are the gourds he took from Miss Liz's field. I guess they'll shuck the nubbins this afternoon and put them in the crib. Papa used to let me throw them in the crib and I would watch the ear I threw roll down the stack, then when it would stop moving, I couldn't tell which one it was that I had thrown. I can remember when there were the big corn shuckings, when the best of the crop was pulled. The mules dragged the corn up in sleds and Papa put wire baskets over the mules' noses so they wouldn't be tempted to get into the corn and so they would pull the sleds down the row without snatching at the stalks. That was always a big day for Papa, when all the children would come back home and help shuck, even Aunt Cecie and Uncle June would help; I remember Cecie always wore gloves. It was like a reunion because of the long table full of food and seeing all the cousins and all. Papa always said if enough people would come then it wouldn't be work at all. You wouldn't even be thinking that you were husking, you were just getting to see everybody and were talking and laughing.

It was really Papa's day because everyone would see what pretty ears of corn he grew, long and yellow, so many ears just perfect without a grain missing. And the day he had the bushels all lined up, counting to see if he had a hundred off the best acre, he said to me, "Rather have them than a hundred pots of gold."

But I remember Miss Liz. She would get hold of an ear that had had a worm and would hold it up and let the corn sift down in powder, or spread one open in front of everybody that a rat had gotten into. She never would brag on Papa in front of him and he wanted her to, she'd just keep finding bad ears and saying, "It's ruint. Ain't that a ugly sight . . ." and the ear would have gray-and-black swollen grains where the smut had gotten it and would smell rank like it was rotten.

"Ain't fitting for the pigs. Hate to even touch it, smells up your hands." Or she'd say, "You can't expect to make a crop with it all going to husks. Look at that stack of husks. Reckon the cows will have something to trample on, but don't know if they'll have anything to put in their bellies."

She would complain so much that after awhile no one would pay any attention to her; they would start making fun of her fussing so, and she would mumble and go off and work by herself for awhile. She'd always come back though, because even though she didn't like to admit it, Miss Liz loved the shuckings. She loved to talk and have all the people there. And she was proud too. She was really something husking that corn, twice as fast as anyone else. When I was too little to break the corn out of the shuck by myself, and would just open them up for the boys, I used to watch Miss Liz's hands. She would split the shuck away and snap it off across her knee and make it look so easy. Everybody else would have red hands and be complaining at the end of the day and rubbing cream on their hands, but not Miss Liz. Her hands were white hard skin, as calloused as the bottoms of her feet. They looked like hands that wouldn't even bend and move, yet they were faster than anyone else's. She could stick them down in hot water and pick a chicken, water I couldn't even stand to stick my finger in, and then turn around and run little rows of fine stitches across a quilt.

But not today. I don't think she even felt the needle in her fingers. I have seen her get a little older before, but it was slow. The only way I could tell would be to think about her hair and how much more gray was in it when she combed it out. But today it happened fast, like in the little bit of time that I was away, she got old. Her hair didn't seem whiter, it's not that. She just is not doing anything with her hands. She fell too and she didn't even want to walk any, even to come to the door with me. And she's afraid, more than I've ever seen her, though I do remember that she was afraid of some things, of nighttime and people stealing things. She always thought people stole things from her garden and out of her shed. I remember at night, when she couldn't see because there were no outside lights, she would make every sound into something.

She would whisper to Papa, "Thel, did you hear that, hear that whining? Reckon somebody caught his neck on the clothesline trying to slip across the yard into the woodshed?" Or the

crib, she was always hearing something in the crib — "I heard
them shuffle down, Thel," — and he would say, "You're imagining things, Lizzie. There's more things than you could dream of
moving around at night. Why I bet there are ten or more possums rooting around the hog lot that you won't never catch sight
of in the day. You take a light out there sometime to shut up and
you'll see them flipping up on their backs and slipping into the
bushes everywhere you look."

And Miss Liz, every time he spoke of taking a light out at
night, she would say, "Won't catch me poking around out there
at night. Got no business out there."

She would keep on him about something being in the barn or
in the crib until he would say, "Lizzie, are you meaning for me to
take a light out and see, so you can rest easy." But he would
never move from his chair when he said that, he knew how she
would fret if he left her there watching out for him to come back.
She would say, "You stay put, Thel. It's probably the cat." And
she would ask him where the gun was. Papa hated the gun, especially after what happened one night, back when I was living
there.

Papa had been working late, and it was after dark before he
got in for supper. I remember it was dark because Miss Liz kept
going to the door and cracking the screen. For a while I could
watch the red stripe of the sun behind the tobacco field, each time
she opened the door making the tobacco look blacker and getting
dimmer itself, until all the light was gone but the lightning bugs.
I wasn't talking to Mama, because she was fussing about Papa
not coming in for supper and how it wasn't going to be fit to
eat.

When he finally came through the door, he was tired and bent
over. It was summer and had been hot; he was so bent over, the
tops of his shoulders were forward and I could see where the sun
had made his shirt light there.

Miss Liz said, "You can wash up but it ain't fit for the hogs."

Papa had started to sit down in the front room beside me, but she yelled at him, "Now don't get settled down in there or I'll never get out of the kitchen. Nine o'clock and still not done supper."

Papa went to the kitchen and sat down; I didn't see him but heard him drop in his chair.

"I washed in the barrel, Lizzie. Give me my plate and let me be done with it."

Then Mama came into the front room and sat down with her mending. The only noise was Papa eating, and Miss Liz stopped working and shushed me.

"Shush, Ramie. Sit real still a minute," she whispered.

I didn't move at all and listened.

"Did you hear that, Ramie? There is something out there."

I told her I didn't hear anything because I really didn't hear any more than the usual night sounds and she had done this so many times. But then she shushed me again. This time I heard it too. There was something thumping.

"Thel, get the gun," Miss Liz whispered. "Just stay put, Ramie, and don't make like you've taken notice of anything." She told Papa to get the gun again and she pretended to sew in her lap but I could see that the needle wasn't going through the cloth. Papa still didn't get up in the kitchen. I heard the thump again, and Miss Liz and I both jumped, though we were trying not to show we heard it.

She was getting mad at Papa, and I heard him get up from the table and sigh as he went in the back room for the gun. Just as he got to the door to the front room, something scraped down the side of the house, and we all heard it. Miss Liz didn't talk any-more. I wanted to run to her, but when I saw her face, I saw she was as afraid as I was. Papa let the gun down by his side so whoever it was wouldn't see it, and we watched the window. It was open and I felt chills come on my skin each time a bug bounced off the screen.

Then it happened. Something scraped hard across the screen, and Miss Liz yelled, "Shoot, Thel!" and he did. The gun went off and made a big tear in the screen, and there was an awful sound outside. I heard hoofbeats, and Miss Liz started yelling at Papa, and there was so much confusion I can't remember all that happened. But Papa had shot the mule.

Papa was so tired, he sat down and put his face in his hands. He told Miss Liz how tired he was, how he wanted to rest, but she wouldn't let him. And she had stirred him all up inside and made him shoot the mule, but he hadn't wanted to, he never would have shot the mule.

The mule didn't die, I remember that. It wasn't hurt so bad that Papa would have to kill it. He had been afraid he would, but every day he rubbed the mule's shoulder with black oil and pine tar, and finally was able to work him again if he put a pad under the collar. Papa didn't mention it again to Miss Liz, at least I never heard him. I heard him tell Mr. Stiles that the mule had sores, reason he had him padded. But Papa knew Mama was wrong and she made him do it. She always makes you do what she says, you can't help it. Papa would do like me, he wouldn't tell Aunt Cecie he thought Mama was sick, not if she told him not to. I think Papa would not say anything about it.

Miss Robinson slams the trunk shut, and I feel the car rock before she opens the door and gets in beside me. She hands me a big jar to hold between my feet on the way home. I put my Indian corn Dummy gave me on the dashboard, and the grains light up in the sun where Dummy has peeled away some of the shuck, thinking it was just going to be another old twisted nubbin with worm holes in it and finding it was colored. I bet he went running to show it to Lyndie and told her she could have it. Then he turned right around and gave it to me. Miss Robinson backs the car up and starts back down the road. At the end of the last row of corn where the water has been standing, I see a stalk with two burst ears, covered with black smut and swollen grains. She stops the car and goes to get the ears and when she puts them behind the seat, I smell the rotten grains. I don't want to look at the corn but I can see Miss Liz in my mind, pulling away the shuck and sticking the ear out for everyone to see . . . "Ain't it a hating sight."

The Boy . . .

THE ROOM SMELLS of formaldehyde, so strong that I can smell nothing else, even though the walls are lined with plants that have flowers. The sound in here, the slow gurgling and bubbling of all the air pumps in the tanks, is mechanical like the tick of a clock. I watch the animals in the tanks rise up and down, but none of them seems to be really moving. They'll swim if you thump on the glass or if you frighten them; but they'll only move if you make them move, sort of like they don't care whether they live or not if they have to be in a bowl. A hamster is chewing the metal bars of his cage, pushing his nose between them, spreading the bars apart, trying to get his head through so he can flatten his body and slide out.

Miss Robinson has all her new animals in the storage room and is preparing them for class. She is making slides for class from the pond water and has called me in several times to look through the microscope at what she's found, but now she thinks I've gone on home. I can hear the scratchy sounds of her new animals in the storage room, like the rats that used to run on the inside of the wall at Miss Liz's. The rats would run around and tear up paper for their nests; always I would hear them at night and sometimes get frightened because their crackling noise sounded like flames and I thought the house was burning down. After I left Miss Liz's today, left behind the fire noise and the wind noise and walked across the field to the car, I listened hard to hear my bird, wondering if he could be flying nearby, but the air was silent.

I watched Miss Robinson go back to the spring. She had green loops of running cedar wound around her arms and was bending over, grasping the tips of the runners of cedar. The cedar reaches up through the pine straw in green sprays, and when she snatched it up, it ripped from the ground like a thousand stitches being broken, like pulling the loose corner of a piece of thread in Miss Liz's quilts and pulling until the squares are ripped apart.

When the car got to the end of the dirt road to the highway, I saw Lyndie Stiles jumping up and trying to reach the mailbox flag. Before I could get the window down to call to her, we were already back on the highway, and I turned to see the red flag swing up. Then all three of them ran and lined up, Dummy and Lyndie and Little Brother, and they stuck corn silks under their noses. When I waved at them, they all raised their hands to wave back, and Dummy's corn silks broke loose and spread down his front.

I had a jar between my feet coming back, and each time we would hit a bump, a slosh of water would float over the block of water in it and I would feel the water seep through my socks. Behind me I could hear all the scratching sounds of the bugs, the bright-green bodies climbing up glass sides and screen wire, thumping and slipping and landing on their backs in the bottom with their feet kicking in the air. The back of my neck kept itching because of the sound, and I felt my skin crawl under my clothes. Miss Robinson just drove on, faster and faster, across the railroad tracks, until I had to watch ahead and hold the jar with both hands when we hit a bump.

In the jar at my feet the spring lizards moved so fast they

looked like one long snake. The water was all astir, like a fight was going on, and a crawfish reached and pinched at the spring lizards from the bottom. There wasn't enough water; they had nowhere to swim and couldn't get away from him, but Miss Robinson kept saying we would separate them soon and told me what a pretty "swamp robin" she saw in the swamp forest.

Papa kept the lizards in the spring; he would never have let her take them out. He said they kept the water fresh and he was right. The spring was always clear, even after the mules would drink and after a hard rain. You could scoop the foam the mules left on the water and the pollen or dead moths or whatever off the water, and look all the way to the bottom of the spring. You could see the lizards race through the mica chips in the sand and send the chips sparkling into the water. Papa called them a "poor man's diamonds" and he would hold my shirttail so I could bend way over and not fall in when I watched them. I could see my face and see my skin sparkle and I asked Papa once if that was what was in Miss Liz's rhinestone pin and he said no, that what was in the spring was real. But now the lizards are in Miss Robinson's storage room.

I would like to set everything she caught free, open all the doors and dump out all the jars and stand and watch them run across the floor and up the walls and fly in the air until they could find their way out.

Cecie made me bring my tadpoles over here and one of them is swimming on its side. Its thin tail trembles in the water, and its legs reach for something that is not there. Each time it drifts to its side, the tail moves and sets it upright, then it topples to its side again. The water pushes it to the top and the pale white stomach sticks out of the water, throbbing up and down, but the legs and tail do not move. I put my fingers around the cold wet body and set it upright, and for a moment I can feel its insides moving through the thin skin. It darts to the bottom of the bowl, wiggling away from my fingers and rests stunned a moment before drifting back to the top, upside down again.

If I leave and come back tomorrow for class, the throbbing in the white stomach will have stopped, the others will have picked at him until he will be frayed and pulpy and dead. If I had just left him alone, he would be in the pond at the farm, in the cold gray water, but I brought him here and he is in the aquarium with the air pump and he is dying. No matter where he is, the legs would have come, and the tail would have started to go away. From the time that he was an egg, there was a certain time that that would take place and Miss Robinson could tell me what would happen and it would all happen on schedule until finally he was a frog.

I am like that, like all the babies in the jars, one month, two months, then I am a baby, then five years old, ten years old. Because I am thirteen now, I can't still be a little child, but Gregory is eight and he is still a little baby, in a baby casket at the graveyard. Gregory will not get any older than a little baby; he will never be any older than he was when his finger picked up the spider, because he is dead. And he was like the tadpole who has weak little legs and a tail, and will be dead tomorrow and will never be a frog. But I will be alive tomorrow and next year, and each year I will be bigger until I am grown, then I will get wrinkles and get older and older until I am as old as Miss Liz, and I will die an old woman. Gregory is my brother and only five years younger than me, but he will still be a little baby in a short grave beside me when I am buried an old woman. Someday I will be older than my mother. I am almost as old as she is now and she is dead and will always be a young girl.

It's hard to think that I will be like Miss Liz, that I will get older and older until I can't walk by myself and will be tired like she was today, leaning on me going up the steps. She was talking about Papa who has been dead a long time. Though I think of

things he said, the swamp forest and the salamanders, it has been
a long time since he stood by the spring and talked of them, since
I was a little child and long before Miss Liz was an old woman.

I get a jar, and scoop the tadpole out of the water and put the
jar in my pocket. I go out the back way from the building. The
sky is pink-orange with the sunset and I can see the yellow smoke
from the factories getting caught under the trees. I sit down beside the pool behind the building and when my coat brushes
against the rock wall around the edge of the pool, I hear the
clunk of my bottle in my pocket. I look to see my face in the
water but the sky burns red behind my head and my image is only
a black shape with no face. I turn my head to the side and can
see white patches appear on the black shape I make in the water,
on my cheeks and my chin and above my eyes, and a face is there
now. The white patches tell me where my eyes are and my
mouth, though I can't see them. That is the face of my mother
almost, of Maylean as she looked into the water before she fell in
and drowned herself.

I touch the water, and the cold makes my hand jerk from it.
Maylean had no mind, she did not think, she was crazy. She
didn't have any sense, Miss Liz said that, that Maylean "didn't
have a smart bone in her body, not a lick of sense, couldn't remember a thing one day to the next, was like as not to lose her
way home." Maylean looked at the water and could not think;
she did not think that she would be dead and that Ramie who
was a little girl would someday be older than her. She just felt
the water cold against her and felt it go in her lungs until she
could not breathe.

I hear a ball bouncing, a boy bouncing a basketball, and I hear
it hit the garage and rattle against the goal. Over and over since
I've been here, I've heard the same sound and the grit under his
feet as he runs in the driveway. Every time he gets a basket he
yells, "Yeah two!"

I open the jar and let the tadpole slide out into the water. It wiggles along the top until it hits one of the lily leaves then it is still again. My face is black in the water with no patches of light on my cheeks and behind my head the sky is almost gray. The tadpole starts wiggling and disappears and I wait for it to float to the top. There it it, its white stomach still throbbing.

The air hurts me inside when I breathe; it's so cold and all that factory smoke makes me want to cough, but I know if I do, I'll hurt even worse in my throat. I think so much now of how I hate being cold, not having enough clothes on and not being able to warm up. I remember the cold days at the farm, especially the mornings. There was a sort of white light across everything, and though the air looked like it was full of white smoke, I could breathe deep and smell only the sharp, cold wetness that hurts your chest, and knew it was mist not smoke. The frost stayed on the ground until the sun was directly overhead and the grass was matted and frozen, breaking like it was made of glass as we walked across it. I walked with Papa, walking behind him and listening to the crackling under his feet and looking at the big dark footprints he made in the frost. I was so cold and tried to keep up with him but couldn't move fast enough; he was warm and was melting the ground where he stepped, but I couldn't catch up to him.

Papa had put me into my coat and hadn't made me hold my sleeves, so I was twisted and tangled inside it. I tried to bend to pick a flower; it was blue and sort of like a bachelor's button and its petals were going limp as its frost coating melted, but I could not bend low enough to pick it before Papa was way ahead of me and I had to leave it and run to catch up with him.

"Scoot up, Ramie. You and me want to get there before anyone even has a chance to think of it."

Papa had set out a gum the night before. I didn't go with him to set it, but I remember he had carried with him a piece of fat

meat that Miss Liz had cooked the cabbage with, to bait the gum.
When she took it from the pan the fat meat wiggled like it was
alive. I had wanted to go with Papa, I thought, and had begged
him to let me, but now I kept wanting to slow down; I was afraid
of what we would find there when I thought of some animal
from the woods smelling that lump of fat meat and coming to get
it.

"Ramie honey, you purposely poking?"

Just as Papa said that to me I stopped. He had started down-
hill and I could look over his head. Then in an instant he was
beside me and towered above me. I only felt his tallness for a
moment before he scooped me up and began to carry me but I
was no warmer, his hands were cold on my bare legs.

"What you shying off from? Don't tell me you're scared I done
caught a grizzly bear in my gum, or a wild cat . . . or a polecat,"
he said and laughed. His voice was bumpy when he talked and
walked across the rows of dead stalks and soon his hands were
warm against my legs.

"Does it catch him by his paw, Papa, or just bust him in two
like Miss Liz's mousetrap did?"

"Now did she go and tell you that?"

"She told me you were going to kill it and eat it and have a
rabbit stew."

"Well, I don't know what makes her so sure it's going to be a
rabbit. Likely as not, it's a possum and likely as not, he done got
himself caught before I was even back to the house last night. If
I had enough gums to catch every possum in the woods and pen
them up somewhere, a rabbit might get a chance to get caught.
Don't you be feeling sorry for the rabbits. They're too smart for
the likes of me and it don't hurt him when you catch him. I have
turned loose three possums this week and twice it was the same
one, that white rascal. All's he's doing is using me for a meal."

When Papa talked I thought of all the things that must be loose

in the woods and how many you could see if you could lift away
all the trees and grass.

We got to the gum and I saw it was a little wooden box. Its
door that Papa had propped open had shut and when we got close
I could hear whatever it was bumping around inside. Papa
tipped it up on end and cracked the door. When he did, an
ugly pink-and-gray tail came poking out the crack.

"Durnit, I am going to have to bust this one's head on a tree to
keep him out of here."

I could see the animal back up tight against the door, a tuft of
white hair caught in the crack. It was the white one that Papa
had spoken of, with fur almost as white as Miss Liz's chickens.
Papa took this burlap bag and wrapped it around the gum, then
he lifted the door and the possum fell like a rock into the bag.

"If I had any sense, I'd just drop him in the pond," Papa said,
"though it do seem a shame. Don't know of a way in the world to
learn him a lesson. Ought to let Lizzie tan his hide good one
time. Reckon I can coop him up somewhere until I get me a
rabbit. Ain't it a shame, Ramie, when a body lets a little old, ugly
beady-eyes thing like that get the best of him."

"Get the best of him . . . ," that was what Papa said though I
didn't know what it was. When we got to the house we knew
Miss Liz had been watching us from the window, because she
came running out to meet us and hurried across the yard with her
hands in her apron.

"Look at Lizzie come busting out thinking I got something fine
kicking in this bag."

"You got a fat one, Thel?" she called.

"Yeah, I got me a fat one all right," Papa said and laughed but
Miss Liz didn't know he was joking. When she got to us, he
didn't let on that it wasn't a rabbit.

"What did you bring him up here live for? I ain't doing nothing but the cooking. If you are wanting so for a rabbit, then you
can mighty well plan on doing your own skinning and dressing.

I'll cook it up fine for you but you won't catch me skinning it if my life depends on it."

"Why, this one is so thick and bristly, you could make you a fur wrap out of him."

"Pshaw, you could trap from now to doomsday and never get enough of them to cover me up."

"But you ain't seen what a rabbit this is," Papa said.

"Well, let me take a peek at it." She took the bag from Papa and looked down in it.

"Theldon Marshall! Theldon Marshall, that is a stinking possum!" she yelled. "You get it away from me. Here you was getting my hopes up and then come fooling around and hand me a filthy stinking possum."

Papa was tickled now as he took the bag back and Miss Liz wiped her hands on her apron like the bag had gotten them dirty.

"And if you think," Miss Liz went on, "if you think that was funny, then I'm as good as telling you that it wasn't. And that child probably thinks that you ain't got no better sense and can't tell a possum from a rabbit."

"It ain't got ears like a rabbit," I said, "and it's got an ugly tail."

Miss Liz looked at me funny when I spoke and I knew she knew I already could tell a possum from a rabbit. Then she pointed at me and said, "Have you ever wondered why the Lord didn't put ears on your grandpa like a jackass?"

Papa said, "What I'm meaning to do, Lizzie, is to coop him up so I can keep him out of my box long enough to catch me a real rabbit if you want the truth of it."

"Do as you please, but I ain't cooping him up. All I bargained for is the cooking." Then Miss Liz started back toward the house.

Papa started laughing and said to me, "Now you watch old Lizzie."

"Lizzie, you say you bargained for the cooking?" he called.

She stopped and looked at him for a moment then she said, "I always bargain for the cooking if you had a mind about you."

"Well, let's have us a possum stew." When he held the bag up in the air, I could see where the possum had rolled into a ball in one corner and was as still as though he really was a rock.

Miss Liz slammed the door so hard, some old dirt dauber nests fell down off the porch ceiling and broke in little dust clouds on the floor. Papa was still chuckling to himself when we went into the hen house to find an empty coop for the possum. He held back the wire door and let the possum run down the bag into the cage. It kept running until it hit the other side of the cage and fell down, then it bunched up into a little ball.

The possum was in the chicken house a long while, I remember that, until his fur had gotten all yellowed from living in the cage. He wasn't white like Miss Liz's chickens anymore because she never took him out to clean his cage. He was always scared and would run and try to hide every time I came in but there was nowhere to hide so he just rooted under the straw. I never could make friends with him and I was afraid he would bite me if I touched him. I don't remember if Papa ever caught his rabbit or not, but I do remember how mad Miss Liz stayed about that possum being in her house, because as soon as anything went into the hen house it became hers to look after. But one day when I was walking in to get some chicken grain, the possum was lying still. I walked around the cage and saw that his feet stuck straight out and his eyes were all crusted over. His feet had curled around like the claws on a dead bird and already there seemed to be a dead stink coming from him. I ran for Miss Liz, but it was a long time before she would come out. She just nodded her head when I told her and didn't say anything back to me. She pulled my wagon out of the barn down to the chicken house and went in and carried out the cage, setting it in the wagon. She never looked at the possum, and he just rolled back and forth a little, never moving his stiff legs. I was so sad that he had died there; if we had turned him loose maybe he would be alive.

I walked behind her as she pulled the wagon down toward the trash pile. We got to the edge of the ditch where Miss Liz always dumps the garbage over, and I saw a rat disappear behind a can, only its tail showing and sweeping back and forth. Vines would grow over the old garbage, but then Miss Liz would come and dump again and cover up the vines. She lifted the cage and pulled open the door; then with a quick snap she sent the possum out the door. He rolled over and over down the side of the ditch. I watched his white body as it got closer and closer to the bottom of the ravine, snagging and almost catching, then rolling again until his fur was blacked. Then he stopped moving and didn't roll anymore.

But a strange thing happened; it happened almost as soon as he stopped rolling. I saw the ugly pink tail start to swing from side to side, then he ran. The dead possum was running down the gully. He stumbled through the garbage, but he kept running out where we could see him until he scrambled to the top of the ditch. There he started down the road and in a moment he was gone into the trees and everything was quiet. He had come back to life; as soon as we set him free, he came back to life. I turned to ask Miss Liz what had happened, what was this dead thing that had come back to life again and I had seen his legs curl up like he was dead, but I didn't ask her. I saw her face and I have never seen Miss Liz look so confused; she looked down the road and back at the cage and then to the bottom of the trash pile. When she looked down in the ravine, I could see in my mind again that dead white thing rolling over and over and I was waiting for it to stop and lie there and be a dead thing, but it had stopped rolling and come to life. When we started walking back, Miss Liz stopped pulling the wagon and looked up in the sky. I looked up and saw a buzzard glide over the treetops.

"Did he tomfool you too?" she said, looking up at the buzzard.

I thought she was talking to me and I said, "I thought he was dead, Mama, now he's going to run and get back in Papa's gum again."

"There is going to be no more gumming. No more. Now you are not to tell Papa that possum went scooting off alive, you hear? No more gumming. If that white rascal turns up again, just turns around and gets himself caught again and don't learn no better, then I'm going to fix his tomfoolery."

And Miss Liz fussed all the way back to the house about the possum and told me over and over not to tell Papa. I remembered soon after that, when I was sitting in front of the fire, I watched Miss Liz splitting up kindling to stick under the logs. I saw something I had seen before, I knew what she had done. She had busted up Papa's gum, and she was splitting the door up with her hatchet, the door that I had seen the pink tail come under, and piling it under the logs to start a fire. Miss Liz stood back and watched the fire burn and smiled as the dry wood of the gum disappeared. I watched a little flame go down the string that had held the door up, and behind the flame the string turned into a thin ash and broke. When the little flame reached the end of the string, it flared once and vanished, and I turned to Miss Liz and saw the fire moving in her eyes. Not like today, so different from the way she was today. Today there was no life inside of her, just the fire could move. I wonder if she let the fire go out again, she can't bust up kindling, she can't seem to even move her hands. It's getting so much colder. Already the sky is looking like snow.

I jump up quickly and feel my heart start beating fast. Something hit my leg. It is hard to see what it was, it is so much darker now. I know it wasn't anything alive, a bat or anything. Now I see what it was, over the curb by the pool, a basketball spinning. When I pick it up and turn around, I hear footsteps and see it is so dark I cannot make out the person who is making the noise.

"Gary . . . Gareee! Supper!" A voice calls, then a door slams on the other side of the dark garage. I see the white rag of a t-shirt, then the boy sticking the shirt in the front of his jeans as he walks toward me.

"Hey, did you see . . . Oh, you got it," he says, talking in spurts. His chest is moving under the white shirt when I feel him pull the cold leather of the basketball through my hands. "Thanks. I figured with my luck, it'd be in the pool."

He is gone and I hear the ball bounce from the sidewalk to the grass and his feet bang up the steps of the house. I stand for a moment in the dark and I see his face in my mind, red and wet, and his knuckles red then white when they closed on the ball. There are sounds all around now, a lot of cars, people going home from work. I start to walk toward my house and can see lights on in all the windows and see the street lights come on. As I walk through the circles of light from the street lights, I find myself running through the dark spaces between until I'm in the next patch of light.

"Step on a crack, break your mother's back . . ." then I am in the dark again and running until I am stepping on the sidewalk cracks in front of my house.

I turn to walk to my house. By the walkway is a stack of leaves Aunt Cecie raked up with bunches of dead hydrangeas piled on top. I see the stubbles of the bushes by the house, and remember that Aunt Cecie said that today she was going to cut them back so they'd come out in the spring. Miss Liz told her that, but she didn't even cut her own back, just let them stay dead on the bush. They were already dead Thanksgiving; I remember them then and Dummy going through after that chicken, but that seems like a long time ago.

I see Cecie through the window, she is putting the plates

around in the dining room. Then she comes to the window and I see her breath on the glass, blurring her face so I can't tell if she sees me or not. She leaves the window and I see the door open, but I cannot move.

"Ramie dear, why are you standing out in the cold? You know it's time to eat. I thought you were coming straight home from Mama's. I was just about ready to call Miss Robinson and see if you had had an accident."

"I've been over at school." When I spoke my lips stung, and I realize how long it has been since I have said anything to anyone.

"How is she?"

"Ma'am?"

"How is Mama?"

I can't say anything. I can't talk. Cecie is taking my arm. She's pulling me into the house where she can see my face. I feel the heat of the house hit my face and the cold behind me as Cecie shuts the door, like something hit me on the backs of my legs. I can't lie, Miss Liz. I can't, I told Papa you chopped up his gum, and I told him the possum didn't die, I did. I turn my face but Cecie walks around me.

"Ramie. Ramie, something's wrong. Something has happened to Mama."

She knows, she is not mad at me, I can tell that, she knows. I couldn't not tell her, Miss Liz. What if you die?

"She's sick, Aunt Cecie. She didn't have a fire and she fell down in the yard . . . and couldn't get up. She's sick."

Cecie leads me to the dining room and starts to tell me about the food and where it is. I hear her get her coat and call to Uncle June in the den. I start to drink my milk, but it's hot and as I leave the table to go upstairs, I hear the garage door go up and the car go out the driveway, flashing its headlights through the house.

The Porgy . . .

It is cold today and not many people are on the sidewalk. Aunt Cecie is in the kitchen making mints for Christmas presents. I watched her for awhile, cooking up the mint and pouring it onto her marble slab. I found the marble for her. She was always saying that you couldn't make mints right without it, that she had seen Miss Liz just dump out the batter on a piece of tin and that they would bite down on grit in the candy. I told Cecie that they gave me the marble over at the old library when they tore it down, but really they didn't, I just took it and dragged it all the way home because I didn't see how I would get it on the bus. I think it was the heaviest thing I've ever tried to carry and I almost gave up and left it. I would have left it if they had just given it to me, but since I took it, I felt like I had to get it home and hide it. Cecie would put it in the car and take it back if she thought I had taken it. She's like that; she'd walk up to the workmen, who couldn't care less if someone took everything there away, and she would make me apologize and give it back to them.

I am at the corner of my street now where the bus stop is to go downtown. Cecie doesn't like for me to go downtown by myself, but as long as I get back before dark she doesn't worry, so I don't tell her where I go until I get back. I already thought of my excuse; I can tell her I was shopping for her Christmas present and make her feel bad for asking me. I want to go to find a fish market and get a fish with pretty scales. I saw where this woman made prints with apples cut in half by rolling ink on them and pressing them on paper. I thought I could take a fish and do the same thing and it would certainly be better than apples if each scale would make an outline. I haven't told my art teacher yet; I just want to see if it works first.

The bus just passed to go turn around, so I sit on the bench to wait for it. A cat is walking under the bench and rubbing against my legs, then ducking back under again. She has left her hair all over my black stockings. An awful lot of her hair seems to be coming out. The hair sits in loose tuffs on her back, like she's got mange. She's skinny too and I can see her bones moving when she walks, showing through her skin on the pink spots where she hasn't any hair. She jumps up on the bench beside me and starts rubbing her back against my hand. Her eyes have got dirt in the corners and one of them is almost shut with only a little of the black slit in it showing. I take her into my lap and start to rub her, but I can't feel her fur because I have on gloves. Her legs stiffen against my lap and she gets her claws caught in my coat, wiggling and tugging until she pulls the threads loose, then she cries and jumps to the ground like she didn't want me to pet her. She sounded like it must have hurt for me to touch her. She doesn't turn and look at me, just stands there a moment, leaning sideways on one leg.

I push the thread she pulled up on my coat back down and watch her while she starts walking toward the curb, stretching her leg with each step. She stops there, still staring straight ahead as the cars go by. Suddenly she darts into the street, paws at a gray lump on the pavement, runs back to the curb and watches the lump while the cars pass over it. When the cars move over the lump, it ruffles a little in the wind then settles back down. There she goes again; the lump is beginning to loosen a little. Now she's back on the curb. The cars are lifting the lump from the ground now and it flops around in the wind, moving a little from the spot it was stuck to. The cat is out again and as she gets the lump into her mouth and runs to the curb, I see what it is. It is a dead bird, run over by a car.

"Put that down!" I call. "You dirty old cat. Put it down." She runs from me, carrying it by one wing. Now she watches back from the edge of the bushes, one eye wide and yellow and the other dropped shut, the bird still in her mouth.

I hear the hissing sound of my bus as it comes to a stop. The doors fold open and when I turn back to the cat, she is gone. I get on the bus and sit behind the driver. This isn't the same bus I take home from school, the advertisements are different. Even the driver, he's not my regular driver that lets me off in front of my house.

"Do you go anywhere near a fish market downtown?"

"A fish market?"

"Yes, sir."

"There's one in nigger town."

"OK. Just tell me when we get there."

I have never been to nigger town before, but we go by there on the way to church; you can always smell the fish. When one of us would catch a catfish at the farm, we'd always give it to Mattie Ruth to take to her mother. In a little while the bus stops and the colored people all start going out the back door.

"It's over there on the corner," the driver says.

"Thank you. And when will you be back by?"

"Takes about ten minutes to go to the end and turn around."

"Thank you."

"Now you watch yourself," he says. I turn and look at him and he is shaking his head. I get off the bus and cross the street to the market. On all the windows are price signs, so large you have to stop walking to read them, all painted in red-and-white paint. Those signs are the only colors I see, the people's clothes are so dark, and all look too big for them. Colored people hate winter, Mattie Ruth's mother told us that, but I knew it already just after seeing them on Easter morning when they get to wear their pink and yellow dresses with a lot of starch and they hold their faces up instead of walking bent over.

Inside the market are rows and rows of fish on ice, but most of them are slick and shiny and not very pretty. I don't see a single one without broken scales. I come to a tray marked "Porgies" and see rows and rows of fat wide fish with nice scales but with their fins all pressed down. When I touch one and spread the fins in my fingers, the fins fold back down again like a fan closing up. I take off one of my gloves and touch the side of a fat wide one. When I touch it, its scales feel like little flakes of metal, almost sharp enough to cut me. After I lift it up from the others, I see that it is much prettier; there are even rainbow colors caught where each scale joins to the fish. I hand it to the man behind the counter and he slaps it in the scale and says, "Twenty-five cents. It'll be ready in a minute."

I pay him and while I wait the smell becomes almost unbearable. I hadn't noticed how bad the smell was until I stopped looking. I wonder if that man even notices it anymore, working in here all the time. It seems a long time just to wrap up a fish. I see a little square package come over the counter and he says, "Here you go!" No one else reaches for it.

"That's mine?"

"One fish don't make much of a package."

"But I'm sure he was bigger than that."

"After you bone a porgy, there ain't much left, if you're careful to pull all the bones. I left you the head in there in case you might be wanting it."

"You cut it up!" When I spoke I realized what I had done. He

thought I was going to eat it. "Thank you," I say and take my
package and go out the door.

When I look out, I see my bus go by and the driver didn't even
look around. He should have waited or stopped, but he's not my
usual driver. I start to run to see if I can catch him at the next
stop, but there is no one there so he doesn't stop there either. It is
even colder now and I can feel the frozen fish all the way through
my glove. I start walking back to the bus stop across the street
from the fish market and when I stop and lean against the pole, I
have a strange feeling. I feel afraid, yet not afraid of the colored
people that are on the street around me, not afraid of them at all,
because they either don't pay any attention to me or look like
they're scared of me. Some of them smile at me, especially the
big fat women, like they're my maid or something. And on the
farm they all look alike, they're the same family and Mattie
Ruth's mama is mother to all of them, and here there are so many
different kinds, so many families all mixed up in one place. I
don't know anybody and can't speak to any of them. I know I'm
not scared to speak to them, but I still feel empty inside, like
when I've heard a noise at night and don't know what it is but am
scared to go find out and will always wonder. When I reach out
and touch the post that is the bus stop, for a moment I feel like I
did when I was on the end of the diving board. I remember I was
scared to jump but even more scared to have to climb back down.

I don't know why I have to be like that. He would have given
me another fish if I had asked him or anyway he would have sold
me another fish. But I don't want him to feel bad and I guess he
will remember me.

"Shame-faced and chicken-hearted." That's Miss Liz, that's
what she said when old man Allbright didn't give me enough
change and I was ashamed to tell him.

I step off the curb and start back across the street. The store is
crowded now and the porgy counter is surrounded by women
flipping over the silver fish and ripping them loose where they are

frozen stuck. I look through the people, trying to pick out another fish, but I think I will just reach in and take one. They all
look pretty much alike anyway, I guess.

"Honey, you trying to get through?"

"Yes, Ma'am. I just want to get one fish."

"You picking or just grabbing?"

"Just any one will do."

She hands me a fish and turns back to the counter. "Thank
you," I say and hear her tell the woman beside her, "Ain't she
something, yes-ma'aming me." She smiles at me when I get in
line at the counter and I think to go ask her if the man will mind
letting me have the fish uncut-up. I hear him say, "Yes, Ma'am,"
to me and look up at him.

"Will you just wrap this like it is? Don't cut it up or anything," I say.

"Boning comes in the price."

"But I want the fish whole, just like he is now."

He slaps the fish on a white sheet of paper and quickly rolls it
up and tapes it, handing it over the top with the pink palm of his
other hand turned up.

"Twenty cents," he says.

I'm glad he didn't remember me, because now he won't feel
bad about cutting it up. I put the money in his hand and start
weaving through the people to the door. I nod at a man who
steps back from the door as I go through and I see how dark he
appears, no color on his clothes anywhere; I couldn't even see if
he had a face. The cars have their lights on now as I run across
the street. The bus schedule on the pole is so worn I can't read it,
but I don't know what time it is anyway. I bet I'm late for supper, I better be ready to tell Cecie a story. Down the street I can
see the light on the front of the bus. The bus pulls slowly up and
stops, the door hissing open just as the street lights come on. It's
the same driver.

"I missed you last time," I say, then I feel sort of stupid because he probably doesn't even remember me.

"I didn't go right past you, did I?" he says, almost like he's concerned about me.

"No, I didn't get to the stop in time," I say.

"This is no place to be standing around this late."

When he says that, I look down the bus to see if there are any colored people on it that might have heard him, but they all got off. That's the second time he's said something like that.

The bus seems strange, yes, the inside lights are on. I've never seen them on before and it makes the outside look much darker. The days are short now; I will tell Cecie I was shopping for her present and forgot the days were so short now.

In the back of the bus I see a boy and he looks up. His mouth moves to speak but he doesn't make any noise, just wrinkles his nose and looks like he's trying to think. I feel like I know him from somewhere too. I turn away and look at the advertisements over the cord and try to think of who he is. Gary . . . Gary, that's who he is. The boy who plays basketball and lives near the school. I see him get up and start up to the long front seat where I am, but I don't turn around when he sits down on the end of my seat.

"Hey, you're at St. Anne's, aren't you?"

I feel my heart start beating fast when he speaks.

"Yes," I say and then he is silent. "I caught your basketball for you one day." I hear my words and am surprised that I spoke. Aunt Cecie would be mad if she knew I was talking to someone I didn't know. I wonder if his parents are teachers.

"Yeah, I thought I remembered you from somewhere. My father teaches there; my mother's in the office."

"Oh," I say. Then he is silent again and the bus stops to let some people on, so I have an excuse to turn away.

"Phew!" he says loudly.

"What?" I say and feel my body jump.

"I smell a fish. Phew!"

I feel the heat go into my cheeks and I see he is looking at the two packages in my lap.

"You got a fish in there?" he asks.

"Yes," I say. "I got one that's cut up and one that's not and I guess the cut-up one is smelling."

"What have you got them for? Fish makes me sick." He pinches his nose up; I don't know if from the smell or because he thinks I'm crazy or something.

"I'm going to take it to art lab. I'm not going to eat it, because I don't even know if it's a good kind of fish for eating. Well, it's hard to explain the reason I've got it, but I want to make a print with it. I mean I want to put ink on it, you know like on a wood cut and print it on paper. Anyhow it should make a print of the scales and all and I thought it might be sort of pretty."

I know my face is awful red now. I wish we would hurry up and get there.

"Yeah?" he says, "I used to have this old ratty parakeet and I'd stick her feet in ink and make her walk across paper. It was pretty cool-looking, then she flew off across the room one day and walked across Mother's pink sofa." He wrinkles his nose again and looks back at my packages. "What you got one cut up for? You going to print his guts too?"

"Oh, no! I — I'm going to feed my cat. Well, it's not my cat really. It's this cat I saw today when I was waiting for the bus. It was about starved, it hurt its sides for me to pet it even, and you know what I saw it doing? There was this little bird that was dead and stuck to the road where the cars ran over it and the cat was trying to sneak out between the cars to get the bird to eat it."

"I think I just might skip supper tonight. Ugh!"

I didn't mean to say something that made him sick. I bet he's kidding anyway, but I feel embarrassed because I don't think he understood what I meant.

"I mean it was pitiful," I say. "The cat was, though I thought I would feel sorry for the bird because it was dead, but I felt sorry for the cat because he was looking for something to eat and that was all he could find and the cat was still alive."

I don't know why I had to go and say all of that. I heard myself and I don't even know if I could understand me if I hadn't seen the cat.

"It's probably that old cat my father has shot about fifty times with my BB for getting the birds in the yard. My old man is a nut about birds. He keeps these feeders on the window and goes crazy until he finds out the name of every bird he sees in these books he has. He stands there and cusses out all the blue jays and squirrels like they really know what he's saying, if they scare away a bird before he gets it looked up in his bird book. He's a real nut about it." He is quiet a moment then he starts talking again, "You should hear him, 'Peculiar,' he'll say, 'most peculiar, in fact, strange. The yellow-bellied beetle-snatcher is not a native bird,' not native, he always says, 'in fact, they have only been seen in northeast Alaska,' and he gets all ready to report it to the bird watcher's club and Mother will read, 'actual size, two feet tall,' and it'll be a little old tiny bird on the feeder and Mother will turn the page and find one that looks just like it, actual size, two inches high. And every time it'll be a native. A native, that really kills him."

"I had a wild bird before I came to school this year. A baby chimney swift that fell down in the fireplace and I raised it, well, mostly my grandmother raised it."

"Yeah, the old man is always doing that. He gives them booze."

"What?"

"Booze. Liquor. That's what he feeds them to make them

perk up. I told you he was a nut. And he's got a whole file cabinet full of stuffed birds. They call him from the radio station every time a bunch of them gets electrocuted and he gets them and stuffs them, even puts little teeny glass eyes in them. He's pretty good at that, though."

He stops talking like he's waiting for me to say something, but I don't know anything else to say. I see he has his basketball with him and a pair of black tennis shoes with the strings tied together over his shoulder.

"Have you been playing basketball?" That was a dumb question.

"Yeah," he says and his eyes open wide. "I'm on the Y-team, the Midgets, and next year I get to play with the Juniors if I'm good enough, even if I'm not as old as the other guys." He stares at me and asks, "Do you play basketball?"

"We play in gym sometimes but it's girl's basketball and you can't cross the line. I always have to be a guard so I never get to shoot."

"You don't get to shoot?"

"No, not unless you're a forward. You can shoot if you get fouled but that doesn't happen much."

"Well, that's a pretty stupid way to play basketball. Can you play Horse?"

"I can ride a horse."

"No, I mean the game with a basketball. Well, anybody can play it. You just have to shoot the shot like the guy before you did, and if you miss you get a letter, like an H, and the one who spells HORSE loses. Anyway it's easy. If we have someone there who can spell, we play Hippopotamus or Rhinoceros, so it lasts longer. We play everyday for a while till everyone gets there, then we play suicide basketball until someone gets hurt and goes home."

"Do you play in your backyard?"

"Yeah, you can come if you want to. I mean I could show you

how to shoot before the others get there. What's your name?"

"Ramie."

"Ramie what?"

"Ramie Hopkins."

"I'm Gary Livingston. We had a girl played with us once. She was about ten times bigger than the rest of us. I told Mother that the horse played Horse with us. She said that she had gland trouble, anyway, we'd play suicide basketball and she'd have to get close to the goal to even hit it and when she'd get the ball, she'd hold it over her head and kick us if we'd try to keep her from shooting. One day she beat me in the head about ten times with the ball. Boy, she was lousy at basketball, but she'd kill you if you didn't let her win, even had to count the ones she threw up through the bottom of the basket."

He stops talking and looks at me. I want to look away but he would notice. I don't know what to say to him, he talks so much.

"You're real little," he says. "You probably can't get the ball up to the basket."

"I bet I can too. I could hit a baseball further than the boys last summer."

Then he laughs, but I'm not sorry I said that. I think he believed me. He should have because it's true.

"Where do you live, Ramie?"

"Seven blocks up from school. I walk it home sometimes."

"My stop," he says and swings around the pole at the door. "I'll meet you after school," and the door folds shut behind him. "Tell your cat friend I hope he enjoys his fish."

I see the top of his head light up under the street light, then he starts to run and is soon in the dark. As the bus starts to move, I see him appear in the light again, a porch light, before he swings around the railing and disappears through the door.

I am the only person left on the bus. The bus driver looks straight ahead and when I look into his mirror, he doesn't smile back at me like the afternoon one does. And it's so dark out now

I think if I count street lights, I won't miss my street. What if I miss the cord and pull it too late or too soon? Cecie is going to be mad with me anyway.

"Excuse me."

He doesn't answer me but does lean his head over to hear me better.

"Will you let me off at the corner of Malery and Main? It is so dark I can't see to pull the cord right."

He nods his head and I lean back in my seat. He forgot me before, when I was downtown. But he is stopping the bus. As the door folds open, I see the outline of the bench I waited on earlier.

"Thank you."

He doesn't answer and I watch him pull away, all alone in the bus with the lights on inside. Now he has to drive all the way to the end of the line, even though he hasn't anyone on the bus.

I go to the bench and put down my packages, pulling loose the tape on the little one. As I pull away the paper, I see there are dark spots on it, the fish's blood. I never think of them as having blood inside, just bones and white meat. I never knew the smell was so awful before it was cooked. There are shadows around the bottom of the hedge where the cat went to hide and eat the bird. Setting the fish by the hedge, I start to call the kitty. When I hear my voice, I stop. That cat probably doesn't even know what it means to be called. If she doesn't belong to anyone, she doesn't even know she's a kitty. She jumped away from me so fast when I tried to hold her, I guess she was afraid I would hurt her. Like Gary's daddy, shooting her with his gun. Gary called the cat "my friend," but it's not really my friend, but I can leave the fish for her, though it was an accident I got it.

I put the fish down and walk away, the smell following me all the way to the bench where I pick up my whole fish. I start running down the sidewalk to our walkway and when I stop, the air smells cold and clean again. As I go up the walk, I can smell

Cecie's cooking, the mint candy. When I open the screen, I see the candy spread out on trays where she has put it outside to cream.

I go in the kitchen and see Cecie still standing over the marble. She has a long string of candy draped like green knitting yarn between her hands.

"Ramie, is that you?"

"Yes, Ma'am. I missed my bus."

"I'm sorry supper's not done. I got myself started on something and couldn't stop. I had a whole batch turn to sugar because I couldn't get it pulled fast enough, so I'm afraid we'll have to wait supper. I'd hate to spoil the candy after going to this much trouble."

I go over to the cabinet just as she slaps the candy down. She presses her hands against the marble to cool them and I see they are very red from the hot candy. Then she picks the candy string up and begins to pull again, the green color getting lighter each time she stretches it out.

"Honestly, I've put a year's wear on my hands in one afternoon. And I've seen Mama pull candy and act like she doesn't even feel the heat. Here, you want to pull a little strip. Feel how hot it is."

"I better not. My hands are dirty."

"Well, wash them. You'll have to soon anyway for supper. I'll let you make some candy for yourself."

"Miss Liz let me do it once and mine just got lumpy, then it crumbled up."

"You can try again, you know, and it is certainly easier to keep it going if you have the marble."

I go to the sink and turn on the water and Cecie is still talking. "I have almost enough now for you to give all the girls in your class some for Christmas. I know I have enough to give your teachers . . . if only it'll cream right . . . this mint has almost ruined my eyes. Can you feel it?"

I start to pull a little strip that she hands me and I do feel the mint. "It makes tears in my eyes, like peeling onions." The candy is too hot to hold long and I drop it and press my hands against the greasy marble to cool them.

When I pick it up and start pulling again, Cecie laughs and says, "Well, I hope everybody appreciates the agony I've gone through. I think next time I'll go to the candy shop."

I look at Cecie's face and all around her white cheeks I see red spots like she's windburned.

"Oh, I don't really mean that," she says, "I think it's so much nicer to make it yourself and goodness knows, there's no comparison in the way it tastes . . . that bought kind is just so flat . . . Now don't stop pulling."

I feel my strip of candy begin to get gritty. Cecie looks down at it and says, "See, yours is turning to sugar, pull harder." The bright-green candy in my hands is starting to fade in color; I see that Cecie's is too, but mine isn't smooth like hers is. She slaps it on the marble and begins to cut it up in pieces with her big shears. Everywhere the scissors cut, the candy puckers into little squares. She slides all of the candy onto a tray and hurries out to the front porch to set it out. The palms of my hands sting, and they have begun to turn red like Cecie's. She comes back across the kitchen with a bottle of lotion and says, "Hold out your hands." She dumps the lotion in my hands and rubs mine together with hers until the stinging is gone and the cold lotion makes them feel wet and soft.

"We'll know by bedtime if I could just as well have stood in bed today. They should cream right away if they're ever going to. If they don't, we'll cook them again and dump in some chocolate and pretend we meant to make fudge in the first place."

She opens the refrigerator and pulls out a carton of eggs. "If it's all right with you, we'll just have ham and eggs for supper. I didn't think I needed to stop and fix anything special just for you and me, and June is out on business tonight."

"It's OK with me. I'm not real hungry anyway."

"What did you buy uptown?" Then she looks at my package, "That's a meat package, isn't it?"

"Oh. Yes, it's a fish, from the fish market. I had forgotten about it because you can't smell it for the candy."

"Well, maybe *you* can't smell it . . ." Cecie takes the package and slides it into the meat tray. "What on earth did you buy a fish for? You don't even like fish."

"I didn't buy it to eat. It's for school, for art class." Cecie still looks puzzled as she breaks the eggs into a bowl. "It's sort of a surprise. I can explain it to you better after I find out if it's going to work, OK?"

"Honestly, Ramie, what next?" She laughs at me as she starts to stir the eggs in the pan. "Your reports came today, by the way. I haven't a thing to complain about this time. So much better than last year when you stayed at the school; and two of your teachers said you were the best in their class — Miss Robinson, of course, and your art teacher. Her comment was: 'Ramie is not afraid to try something different. Very imaginative and she is improving technically,' so I assume she means you are learning how to use those oils properly that you said were giving you so much trouble. Maybe someone will give you a nice set of your own for Christmas. I was told by the lady at the art store that oils could be discouraging to beginners and were also very messy, but I don't see how any kind of paints could be worse than whatever you're going to do with that fish. I'll just talk to your teacher and see if she thinks you should have oil paints and what kind, all right?"

I am watching the window and it looks like it is starting to snow but maybe it is just the moonlight coming through the trees. "Yes," I say to Cecie.

"Now if you would rather I didn't bother or you want something else, just tell me."

"Oh no, I would rather have my own paints than anything

else. Then I would be able to work on things here and any time I wanted to."

Cecie puts my plate in front of me and sits down at the other end of the table. It seems strange to be eating in the kitchen at night instead of in the dining room. It's not snowing, I can see that now, just the wind in the bushes by the window making shadows. When I start to eat the eggs, I realize I'm hungry after all. Cecie put cheese in them, I didn't even see her do it.

"I checked on Mama again, today, Ramie."

"Oh, is she any better?"

"Now, you stop worrying. She's somewhat improved but she's an old woman, I'm afraid. We all have to start accepting the fact that she is getting old. I wonder if she knows it yet. Since she's been sick, she's started talking about things that happened a long time ago. She has just turned everything around to suit herself. But you don't need to worry about her; the lady is living in with her now, so if she needs anyone at night, there will be someone within hearing distance and someone who knows best what to do. Mama doesn't hurt anywhere, I asked her that. She just gets dizzy and needs someone to lean on if she moves around much."

"I bet Miss Liz doesn't like that, having somebody who's not family in the house with her. She always told me that; the house was for family only."

"You certainly know Mama well to remember that. She doesn't like it one bit. She was whispering to me today where she has everything hidden. She said, 'Now you mention to Ramie where I hid my music box, it's shut up tight in the old wood stove in the back room where that woman can't find it.' That's what she calls her, 'that woman.' I know it's no pleasant job staying with Mama. She hasn't said a civil word yet to the poor lady and I feel it's my duty to apologize for Mama being so hateful to her. It seems she's used to old people and having them act like that, so I guess we can let it go at that. It's my own mother, and some-

times I feel as though her nurse understands her ways better than
I do."

"It's still Miss Liz's house and if she asked that woman to leave
her things alone and she didn't, I think she should hide them."

"Ramie dear, you didn't understand. The woman hasn't
touched a thing of hers. She's just imagining things. Her mind
is not as strong as it was and she is letting her imagination get
away from her."

I finish my plate and carry it to the sink. Cecie turns to me
and says, "Just leave it, Ramie. I'll do the dishes tonight, since I
have to clean up all this candy mess. You can go start your home-
work."

I go to the refrigerator and take out my fish. "Are you going to
do that here!" I turn to Cecie and see her eyes wide open, still
red from the mint.

"I'll be careful not to make a mess. I promise, Aunt Cecie."

Cecie goes to the basement stairway. I know what she's doing,
getting newspapers. Everything I do, I have to spread out newspapers in my room. I take the papers from her as she comes back
through and start upstairs to my room.

"Ramie?"

I turn on the stairway and look down at Cecie. "If you
straighten up your room before you go to bed, I'll bring you a
sample of each color, all right?"

"All right. I'll straighten up."

"And keep your fingers crossed they'll be fit to eat."

Green Fish . . .

I MUST HAVE about fifty fish prints, a whole roll of rice paper across the floor. I did some prints with the fins and some where I left them flattened. I even printed eyes in them with a bottle cap. And every little scale came out in the print, even more fine than some of the wood engravings my teacher showed me and more perfect. Over by my palette glass with all my colors rolled on it, is the fish, smelling up my room and my hands so bad the smell will probably be here for weeks. I stand over the fish and look down at the paint colors still on him, caught under the edges of his scales and when I look back at my prints, I see what is the matter. The fish is much prettier than the prints. The prints are more detailed and prettier than anything I've ever carved in wood, but even then the fish is prettier than any of the prints I made with him. But I can't keep him; he'll just rot.

All the colors caught in his scales if he were alive would wash away and he would be a pale green light darting through the dark water at the pond. I remember feeding the fish, the big ones at the pond, and watching the bread come apart on the top of the water. When the fish would bite at the bread, it would come apart and dissolve into colors where the sun hit it, spreading out oil in a skim that made a rainbow. The fish would come up and nibble at the bread, the biggest ones striking at it hard and making it sink while the little ones would catch the bits that floated down through the water. We could see through their green fins when they came up top and see each little spine that made the fan open up. Lyndie and I fed them, and Miss Liz would always tell us we were ruining the pond for fishing, spoiling all the fish that way, not making them get used to looking hard for food, but she never fished anyway. The water was so clear you could see the bottom if no one had been swimming lately, even see the shiny worm cans on the bottom that people had thrown off into the water.

That's what I had wanted my prints to do, to look like those fish that are so transparent you can watch the food go through them if you catch them up in a bowl. I always want my pictures to make me think of things, to help me remember, so I can put all I know about one thing into the same picture. I want to paint a picture I can look into just like looking at the fields out of a window, but I want it to be one picture instead of so many little snatches like the way memories are in my mind. My statue of Miss Liz is like that, it makes me think of her and it makes me remember what she was like, just as hard as that wood statue, working so hard and burning in the sun and never getting tired, never even feeling the hot water when she picked a chicken, just pulling out his feathers in handfuls like the feathers were meant to come out so easy. Her hands are always grabbing and touching things and never feeling them, like shucking the corn. While Cecie's hands burn red, even mine do, Miss Liz just pulls at the candy and the shucks as she has done a thousand times, so many times that she doesn't feel it anymore.

I never did my picture of her in church, with the songbook in her hands and not singing. I never do her hands, because they don't change like her face. They are hidden behind her hard yellow skin, but her face changes, her eyes and mouth sink deeper and the wrinkles close up tighter and tighter around them until her eyes seem tiny and they drop in the corners. But hands, I remember hands, carving Dummy's in the soap, and they held the soft little bird, held the little soap bird like they were afraid they would hurt him, afraid to close around him because he was so little. But really I never saw my bird in his hands, only in Miss Liz's when she caught it, and in my own. At first I thought it would have made Dummy happy to hold the bird, but then when I carved him, I saw he wasn't happy but afraid, so afraid of Miss Liz.

And Miss Liz, my bird tried to get out of her house. I can remember the last time I was there, when she fell in the yard. When I was outside, I didn't want to go back inside. It was so good to see the sun shine and to hear the children working with Dummy in the field. I wonder if my bird was glad to be outside too. I can see her chasing him around, bumping her legs against the furniture, and each time he would light, trying to catch him in her hands, but he wasn't a little baby and could get away from her now. Too much for her to handle, that little bird, too much for her to keep inside and she watched him hit the glass trying to break out of her house. She couldn't catch me now, if I were to start running from her, she couldn't catch me either, not anymore. She would fall and stumble.

It is strange that I can't remember the first day I left her house for good. I can remember things changing, getting more dresses and eating from different dishes and going to a different school, not having to wait for the yellow bus and watch for the flashing lights as it stopped to get me, not trying to keep warm at the bus stop with my hands inside my sleeves but living at the school and just walking to my classes. But I don't remember leaving Miss Liz's house; I don't remember getting all my things together and going to Cecie's. I don't know why she wanted me to go, why she didn't want to keep me with her all the time but just to let me visit. There was a different bed at night but it seems I was visiting so much that I never really could forget sleeping at Miss Liz's and hearing the noises outside and the fire snapping and her snoring if she got to sleep first. I wonder if I was like the bird and she wanted me to go because she couldn't handle me, because she felt she was getting old and I didn't even notice it.

I can't remember all that I want to and get it put together in my mind. I can start to paint a picture and sometimes more than I could remember inside comes out on the paper and yet sometimes it doesn't work at all. And my daddy, I am scared to paint my daddy because he has never had a face in my mind. Even Cecie has more face than him with her eyes getting red tonight and her cheeks burned. If I were to paint him, what if I were to get no face at all, just a blank circle. I would be sorry I tried to paint him, I know that. All I can remember is the closet, not being able to use my eyes at all, just feeling my mother's heart beat and hearing that man say, "I have come to take her with me," and he would have taken my mother and she would have carried me, carried me out of Miss Liz's house, and nothing would have been the same at all. I don't know where I would have gone, to a strange house somewhere. And my mother Maylean would have grown old and never have died in the fish pond.

I hear Cecie coming up the steps. She will take the dead fish out, and I will be glad to have it gone, so soon the smell will leave. She knocks at my door and it starts to come open.

"Come in."

"Ramie? Oh, the mints are just lovely. Only the green ones are too chewy, but we can keep them and use the pretty ones for gifts."

She is breathing hard from coming up the steps, and she sets a plate full of colored candy on my desk.

"Goodness, Ramie! Your room isn't fit to live in. The next time you decide to do such a thing, I should ask you to use the basement. And it's much too cold to open a window; what an awful odor that fish made!"

She bends over with a groan and rolls my colored fish up in the newspaper. "You better wash your hands before you try to eat any candy."

Her eyes aren't red anymore and there are only a few tiny spots left on her face that look almost like freckles.

"Aunt Cecie? Miss Liz said I could ask you something," I say quickly, "that you could tell me better than she could."

"Well, I'm surprised to hear that. She certainly wouldn't say that to me. What was it?"

"She said you knew my daddy. That you saw him more than she did and that you could describe him to me. Enough so I could do a picture."

"Oh, for goodness' sake. Now how in the world could she say something like that. I certainly couldn't tell you about that man. He was as ordinary a looking person as ever lived. His face was just as common as I've ever seen. I couldn't even tell you the color of his eyes. He just wore the cheapest-looking clothes and walked as if he thought they looked expensive, you know what I mean, with silver metal threads running through them and two-toned shoes, wore a fake handkerchief on cardboard, terrible clothes."

"Miss Liz said he came for us, my mother and me, and she sent him away."

"When did she say all of this?"

"Thanksgiving. When I was out there."

Cecie looked very surprised when I said that. She stops talking and walks over to the door with the fish wrapped up in her hands. For a moment I am afraid that she is going to leave, like she always does, and not tell me anything.

"Ramie, you have never been accustomed to old people." She stops and puts her hand on my door. "You probably don't know what I mean, but I can remember my own grandmother, trying to tell me everything she could remember as if she didn't want to steal a thing from me and she was afraid to take them to the grave with her. She acted as if I would gather up all she said and give it to the next children in the family, and never seemed to realize that all she knew about farming and dressing and making quilts wasn't going to be worth a feather to the next generation. She never understood that her old-fashioned ways were just no good for living, just things to put in school books for young peple and honestly, just to laugh at and say how silly people were."

"But he could be alive, my daddy could be alive and not be old-fashioned at all. He and Maylean could be here just like you and June."

"But he's not. Neither of them, and you know that June and I have done our best these last two years to make things nice for you, so much better than you ever could have had. I don't begrudge you a thing we've given you, I was happy to take you . . ." Her voice starts to shake. It always does when she talks of doing things for me. I feel sad when she does that because I don't know what to tell her.

"I like my room. It's very nice and the school in town is much better." Her eyes start to get red again, but I just can't say the right things around her. I don't know what she would rather have me say.

"Mama has asked me a thousand times if I ever told you she sent your daddy away, a thousand times — she asked me twice today even — and I never knew if she was afraid I would tell you or if she wanted me to do it for her. Now don't you glorify him. No good will come of that because it's not true. If I could tell you good of him, I would be the first to do it, just so you would get it off your mind but you'll just have to grow up and forget him. The truth doesn't always make us happy, but you're too old to believe in things that aren't true. Not when worrying about them doesn't do you one bit of good. You're going to grow up right here in this house and nothing that he ever did is going to make any difference at all."

"I know he's dead, Aunt Cecie, and can't ever change things, but I want to know what he was like when he was alive." She is making me mad; she thinks she can just tell me what to think about and then I'll do it.

"If you will make me the promise never to mention him again, I will tell you everything about him that I remember, which isn't much, I can assure you, but is the most you'll ever find out."

"I won't mention him again. I promise," I say.

"I tried my best to like him — I always try to think the best of someone and not the worst — so that if he did decide to marry Maylean, I wouldn't be sorry for anything I said. I saw him walking home with Maylean one day from school, well, I wasn't sure if it was he and Maylean at first. They were going across the field, he had his coat off and over his shoulder and his sleeves rolled up and Maylean was walking beside him holding his hand. Then I recognized it was them because of the way Maylean always carried her head, tilted to the side. I remember thinking that Maylean had a boy friend and weren't they just pretty as a picture, like in a movie I saw once. Well, I cut through the woods and was on the porch long before they ever started down the road and Mama had started worrying about Maylean the way she always did when she was late getting home and was about to send me off looking for her. I watched them come into the yard and when I saw Maylean up close, she had this cheap pink lipstick he had given her on her face and it was smeared on her cheeks for rouge, just caked. And it was all over his shirt, and I looked at his face, it was filled with pockmarks, just white holes in his face where he had had a terrible case of pimples, and his hair was dirty. I remember he never looked like he had scrubbed himself, so unclean-looking. And I thought that first time I saw him how pretty they had looked from far off, how pretty it was to see them holding hands, which just made me think later how much worse he was. And he had this ugly look on his face that made me want to go hide. I was three years older than Maylean and certainly used to men by then, but he just made me want to hide. Well, I went in the kitchen and told Mama what an ugly thing I thought he was. She had been watching them come up the road by the window. I worried I might be responsible for making her dislike him, and one day that silly Maylean called me jealous, and I just wasn't a bit sorry after that, I never was afraid I had judged him wrong. Never!"

"He died in the war," I say.

"He died overseas. That's all we know, but his family never mentioned that fancy citation they said he was going to get. And with that family you can be sure they would have waved it under our noses if it had ever come from the government. It just didn't, that's all." Tears start to come down Cecie's face, but she turns her head and brushes them away and makes her face red again.

"Maylean was just a little child. She was as simple as a little child and would make me so mad I would want to whip her. Wouldn't listen to a word I tried to tell her, so trying, but I never lifted a hand to her."

"Mama hit her. She said she hit her."

"Yes, she did. But Mama was right and she was the one to do it. I've seen Mama wrong about a lot of things, she's stubborn and too hard on people, but she was right about Maylean. Mama couldn't help herself and I would be the first to understand why she couldn't. Mama wanted a good man for Maylean, she told me so herself. She wanted a good man to come along and marry Maylean and be kind to her, to look after her when she couldn't figure things for herself. Mama had her faults but it was a sight better for you to grow up around her than with Maylean."

"What did she say? What did she say about Maylean walking with the man?"

"Well, it just wasn't proper. It's not like you would think of walking home from school. Not where there are sidewalks and a lot of people around; it was just woods, just woods and trees, and it just wasn't proper for a young girl to go off alone with a man. And Mama asked me to walk with them, just kept asking me, and Maylean would say mean things to me and I got so I just couldn't stand that man, even the sight of him at school. He was such a big talker at school, I just knew what he was bragging about, and I was so ashamed. Mama told me, that very day that I saw them walking across the field, that they were misbehaving. Mama knew they were, and she was right." Cecie's voice has gotten hoarse.

"Ramie, just put it out of your mind. You don't want to know a thing about it. And there is nothing more to know, nothing at all. I never thought you looked a bit like either one of them."

"Miss Liz said I looked like my mother."

"Mama even thinks I looked like Maylean. You know how Mama is about that, then she'll turn around and say the only one she ever looked like was her dog Smut."

She starts to smile and sounds like herself again, but she has said all I wanted, all I have asked to hear so many times. She has already said it and can't hide it from me anymore.

"Please make me believe I've done the right thing . . ." Cecie says suddenly then stops. It didn't sound like she was saying that to me.

"Thank you, Cecie." I start to stack my fish prints up as she walks back to the door. I look up at her and her face is streaked but she's not crying anymore. She looks like she wants to smile but she can't. Then she sighs and says, "I'll take this thing out back to the trash can. He comes tomorrow so we won't have to bother with it anymore. I certainly hope your teacher thinks all these fish are worth the trouble. They are right cute, I think. I like the one where you printed it twice on one sheet, that one." She points at the big sheet where I printed an orange fish with one side of the fish and a blue one with the other. "That looks like you had two different fish."

"She'll probably give me a good grade just because I experimented. She likes that, even though I don't really think they turned out near so good as I thought they would."

"Pick out a nice one and maybe we can have it framed for June's office for Christmas." She smiles and leaves, and I hear her going back down the stairs. I hear her open the back door and go outside, rattling the lid on the trash can, and I hear the fish hit with a thump. I look at the print with two fish and I see that it really didn't come out right after all, one of the fish is upside down. He has the wrong fins on top, like someone flipped him over. I remember seeing the water churn up, watching the fish come up and flip upside down on the water. I saw a live fish turn upside down like that once. It was that Dummy; Dummy dropped a big rock off the end of the pier when Lyndie and I were watching the fish eat and churned them all up and scared them away. Lyndie got so mad at him.

She said, "You Dummy. Now you've scared them all off. Why didn't you throw your old rock in some place else." The water was spreading out in big circle ripples and the sun flickered on top where it was roughed up so we couldn't see through it anymore, couldn't even see the rock where it had hit bottom. Dummy had started to grunt, almost like a laugh, then he sat down beside Lyndie and his face got sad.

"You see," she said. "Now you've scared them all away for good. We were just beginning to make friends with them and you went and acted ugly."

The ripples began to slow down and we could see through the water again, but there were no fish there. We sat there for a long time waiting and I watched the water and looked back and forth at Dummy. He balled up in a knot and drew his feet up against him, his old shoes untied and spreading out on the sides.

Then I saw a shadow and Lyndie said, "One's back. Look! One come back."

Then the fish came slowly up toward the top until we could

see him again; he was one of the little ones, because they are always braver. There was no food on the top, so Lyndie broke off a piece of bread and started to throw it in. She stopped and said, "You do it, Dummy. You throw the bread out. Here, throw it."

Dummy tossed the bread quickly out of his hand like it was hot and the fish disappeared when the shadow of his arm went over the water. Then it came back up again and snatched the whole piece of bread under. It had the bread in its mouth and we watched as all the other fish came back in and started to take it away from him. Then they were all back and I couldn't even find the little one anymore.

"See, Dummy," Lyndie said. "That's how you make friends with them. It's not nice to scare them away and that rock might hit one and hurt him." Dummy sat there all afternoon and tossed bread to the fish. Lyndie and I left him and he must have stayed down there until he ran out of bread because I didn't see him anymore that day. And Dummy would never throw a rock again, I bet. He could learn something, he could learn to be kind and not scare them again. Miss Liz should have watched him; she wouldn't even look at him but if she had she would have known he wasn't bad. He didn't know that he wasn't a little child; he almost seemed a littler child than Lyndie because she taught him what to do, and it was only Miss Liz who thought he wasn't a child.

I put my fish prints in my book sack and take my pajamas from under my pillow. It is so warm in here that I don't get cold at all when I take off my clothes. I put on my pajamas and go to the window, cracking it a little so that dead fish smell will go out. I get in my bed and feel the cold air from the window hit my face. I want to think tonight, before I go to sleep, about my daddy; I want to see him in my mind, to see his face. He was ugly. Cecie said he was ugly and not special at all. And Miss Liz wouldn't even talk about him. I don't want to do an ugly picture, but that's all I know, all that anyone who could tell me knows.

I don't want him here now, looking at me, looking at me ugly like he did at Cecie. I thought I wanted him to look out of a picture, but I don't. I wanted him to be a different sort of man, not just like anybody walking on the street. Cecie said he was ordinary, not a special man at all and that she wasn't jealous of Maylean. But they were beautiful once, when she saw him and Maylean walking through the field, they were pretty from a long way off. I won't paint them close but way out in the fields, and I'll paint the grass and the sky.

I see the picture that Cecie put up on the other side of my room. It's one of those pictures of the ocean, the kind that's too pretty, with the sun setting on the water. She said she wanted it there to keep my mind off all "those awful faces" that I paint. I would like to paint the ocean but it wouldn't look like that; I would put people there, maybe I'll even put my mother and daddy walking by the ocean.

As I look at the picture, I try to do what I have done a lot of times, I try to make it move. I want to see what would happen if the waves were to really break and the water come rolling forward. And all those birds in the air, if they really were to fly through the colors in the sunset. Instead they are just little black v's all in a perfect formation over the water. I want the formation to break apart and for the little black v's to go through the sunset and have orange and pink shine on their feathers. And to make noise, the sounds I heard the gulls make as they flew over me at the ocean. The picture is at that time of day, right before dark, when the water is a mirror of the sky, the wind is getting still and the ground turns black. It is like someone has stopped the ocean with its waves cresting and turned it to ice.

I can think of the real ocean — that picture is not like it. I can see the real ocean and remember walking down the beach and saying to myself, "I am here now. I will be back home tomorrow but I am here now where everything is different." That always made the ocean special, a place I would never want to be all the time. You can't change it, you can't change the ocean and make it like you want it. Flowers won't live and if you wanted to have flowers, you would have to bring dirt from the farm and put it there for them to grow in. There are only the red-and-black daisies, the only flowers I have ever seen at the ocean, that grow in the sand and bloom turning away from the wind.

I remember tossing rocks and watching the little crabs run and jump on them. Instead of running away like the fish at the pond, they were brave and ran at the rock. I was always a little afraid of the crabs, running sideways across the sand, almost transparent and sometimes hiding right on top of the sand because you couldn't see them until they moved. I would hate to step on one in the water, all those sand fiddlers running across my feet under the water where I can't see them to tell if they're shells or really alive.

I cut out my light and think of standing in the warm salt water; in July it is very warm and easy to float on top. But as soon as I feel something touch me under water, I get scared and come out. It wouldn't be so bad if someone were in with me. I feel ashamed when I come out of the water scared, like a frightened girl, but I'm not silly about them like some of the girls at school, not like my roommate was. I bet a boy would be scared too, but he'd never say so. Like Gary, I wonder what he would do? I wonder if he has ever thrown rocks and watched the crabs. He would like to do that. I bet he would know of something at the ocean that I've never seen. I would like to walk down the beach with him and ask him if he has ever seen the little birds run in and out with the water, does his daddy know what they are called. I bet he doesn't know what they are eating, and I could dig up the little clams and show him how they burrow back under when the waves go back out, trying to get under the sand before the little birds grab them.

I can see him in my mind, throwing rocks at the crabs and

watching them run from him all over the beach. And going on
out to swim with the fiddlers running across his feet and making
me go with him, telling me that they can't hurt me, that the
ocean won't hurt me.

Miss Liz was afraid of the water. She wouldn't pay any attention to the little birds. She can't watch the ocean from her window and she will never go to the beach again. She'll sit and
watch the fire and she won't even know I'm there. She would
scream at me to get out of the water, that it will snatch me away,
but I won't listen. Papa wouldn't tell me to go home, to come out
of the water; Papa would tell me to go on out, that Gary would
keep me from drowning.

I can see Gary, and I come out of the water and start to walk
down the beach again. He picks up one of the butterfly shells
and holds it in his hand, walking to me with it, very carefully
carrying it in the palm of his hand so the little center won't snap
and it won't come apart and not be a butterfly anymore. And he
gives it to me, and I feel his hand touch mine as he slides the
shell into my hand, and we walk down the beach with the water
coming around our feet and going back out again. I am carrying
the shell he gave me very gently so it won't break, and I can
bring it home with me to keep.

Flower . . .

THE GROUND IS FROZEN hard and is powdery gray from the wild grass of last summer. The wild grass grips the clods in Miss Liz's oat field like a thousand little claws at my feet, little hands not letting go of the earth even though they are dead. They seem determined to hold Miss Liz's thin green oats under the ground as long as they can while she frets away inside, waiting for spring to come. There are a few red shoots bursting up and slanting under the clods but the green of their stalks will be a long time coming.

It is drab and sad here in winter, but I would much rather see winter here on the farm than see it at home. The cold, dead things spread more here; I can see so far when I am out in the fields. Yet always somewhere I can find a flash of the sun on the water or a bird over by the swamp forest, a black rag of a crow ducking into the trees, maybe screaming in flight, maybe not, but always seeming to be hidden in the trees before you can point your finger at him. Somewhere I can hear the rattling voice of an animal. Is it wild or tame? Its sound is still and lonely, so it must be locked in a pen.

When the vines die on the buildings at school and all the leaves are gone, the world there seems to be as dead as the sidewalk; like all of it is concrete and would freeze your fingers if you were to touch anything. But out here there are always things you can touch, not the water now, because it will make your fingers numb and you can't hold your toes in it at the end of the pier to see if you can draw the fish. Yet in the chicken lot you can pick up the warm birds or even touch their nesting hollows in the ground and feel where they left the warmth of their feathers.

I remember once Miss Liz told me that when it was below freezing, I would turn my tongue inside out and have to yank it out of my mouth if I stuck it on the lock on the chicken gate. She should have known that would make me go do it, though I would never have thought of doing it myself in a million years. And my tongue got stuck on the lock and I thought it would never come loose; I couldn't yell or anything. I was about to yank it away and pull all my skin off when it finally came loose. I didn't tell anybody about it for shame, but it was sore and prickly for a week.

Even though it is cold now, and the wind hurts my face when I walk, I could never stand to stay inside like Miss Liz does. I know there are a lot of things dead now, but to be out here makes you feel that things are all around you alive but having to wait a little while for spring. Then they can run out of the woods or burst up out of the ground. They are all here somewhere, not really like being dead; Miss Liz should know that better than anyone. She always hated the cold so, and now since she has been sick, she hardly moves from her chair and looks at the fire like she has to keep her eyes on it or it will run out of the fireplace and melt the house down around her.

Over by the Stiles house I can see Lyndie Stiles in a bright blue coat. She is hiding behind the trees, one by one, until she is at the edge of the road. Then she darts down the road and doesn't stop running until she is past their pasture. I hear her yelling at their two mules who are standing so close to each other, they look like one creature with two heads. They flop their ears forward and walk to the fence, but Lyndie has darted off again. I watch her cut across the broken tobacco stalks in Miss Liz's field, almost disappearing except for the top of her head as she walks between the rows. When she gets closer to me, coming out of the field, I see she has something in her hands, carrying it out in front of her. It is a pansy, I think, yes, with two purple blooms, the kind of flower they give the little kids in Sunday school. She sees me now.

"Hey, Miss Ramie."

"Hey, Lyndie. Is that a Christmas coat you're wearing? It sure is pretty."

"Uh-un. Least it's not *my* Christmas coat, it was my cousin's Christmas coat last year and I got it for to wear when she out-growed it, though it don't fit right." When Lyndie says a long sentence like that, she stops and pants like someone who's been running.

"And that's a nice flower. Did you grow it?"

She stands in front of me now, her tangled hair falling in her face where her nose and cheeks glow like three red circles. Instead of looking older than she did in the fall, Lyndie looks younger squeezed in her tight-fitting coat.

"It come from Sunday school. They give us all one." Then she stomps her foot and says, "Miss Ramie, can you wipe my nose for me, please? I can't reach my sleeve and it's dripping all over the place."

I see a shiny film of mucus under her nose that's running onto her lip. She squints and says, "It tickles something awful."

"Here, I'll hold your flower for you." I take the flower and she begins to rub her nose on the sleeve of the blue coat. Then she starts reaching into the pocket of the coat and pulls out a piece of candy. The wind pulls the wrapper from her hand when she opens it and the colored paper tumbles across the ground behind her. She reaches in the pocket again and looks up at me. "You want some candy too?"

"No, thank you."

When I hand her back the flower, she looks up at me and I know she is about to ask a favor.

"Miss Ramie, will you walk down to the church with me? I ain't supposed to cross the highway when I ain't got a grown-up with me and my Mama don't even know I'm headed that way and she would count you as a grown-up if I had to tell her." Lyndie is panting again and jumping up and down trying to warm her feet.

"Sure, I'll walk with you, Lyndie. How are you going to get back though?"

"Oh, I ain't planning on staying. I was just wanting to give Dummy his flower."

"Oh, the flower is for Dummy. I bet he'll like that, especially since you're giving him a present. I bet he doesn't get many presents at Christmas."

"He give me the candy. At least he used to and I still got some left 'cause I saved mine. He would give us candy all the time but we had to sneak to eat it." She looks up at me as we cross the railroad tracks and says, "You know what Mama said?"

"What did she say?" I ask.

"She said he stealed it, that he stealed the candy he give us because he didn't have no money and was stealing it from the Allbrights' store, and we was bad as he was to eat what was stolen."

"Now I don't think so, Lyndie, though don't tell your mama I said so. She wouldn't think well of me for saying it. It wasn't right of Dummy to steal, it's never right to steal, but he didn't know any better and it wasn't like he was stealing for himself. He was stealing to make you happy, so it wasn't really mean stealing like most people do."

"It ain't a sin to eat it?"

"Well, I don't think it's a sin to eat it, Lyndie, though I don't know what the Bible would say. I think it would say there are people that do a lot worse things than that and that it would say

Dummy was like a little child, only he couldn't even be taught right and wrong as good as a child, and I think God would forgive him too."

"I think he's gone to heaven but Mama wouldn't say whether he has or not. But I think he's in heaven and that Jesus will let him look down at my flower."

I stop walking and my body feels stiff and frozen. For a moment everything is clear in front of me; then I see Lyndie walk a little ahead and I see only the blur of her blue coat. There is no noise anywhere but her words, "he's in heaven." She looks up at me and I see her face again with her mouth open. I have to get her to wait. I can feel what she said but she has to wait; I have to think.

"Lyndie. Lyndie. Please wait. Wait!"

Lyndie walks closer to me and I can see her face now, little flecks of light in her eyes. The pansy blossoms wobble on their skinny stems and are shaking in her hands as she trembles from the cold.

"Lyndie, I didn't know that Dummy was dead."

"He has gone to heaven," she says quickly. "He won't be back to play anymore, but he can play where the trees are made out of gold and he will get to wear a clean white dress like an angel. I seen him already in a dream in a white dress and he looked funny."

"Lyndie, why did he die? Did they tell you why he died?"

"He took sick. He just took sick. I knowed something was wrong when he went to making this sound like a cough, and he fell all around like he was coughing bad, but he weren't really making much of a sound for it. Like this."

Lyndie opens her mouth and starts making an awful sound in her throat that makes chills run all through my body.

"Stop! Stop it!"

She becomes silent and looks up at me, her bottom lip sticking out and white showing beneath her eyes.

"I'm sorry, Lyndie," I say. "I didn't mean to yell at you. It just frightened me. I mean, I didn't know he was dead."

We start walking again and Lyndie is silent. I want her to talk to me but she is just so little. I can't ask her anything. I'll ask Miss Liz. No, no. I can't do that either. She is not like before, she can't tell me things like before, and she would even be glad he is dead. Everybody is glad he is dead. But the little children, they miss him. It is like he just died when Lyndie told me; that he wasn't dead before.

"Lyndie," I ask. "Did he have a funeral?"

"Uh-huh. There was a few flowers then, but they is all gone now. I seen at church today that they was all gone and turned over and that somebody had took all the ribbons, but they was cut flowers you know. I was thinking a rooted flower might be lasting in the weather till springtime, is the reason I'm carrying this one. Don't you think it might, Miss Ramie?"

"I think it might, seeing as it's got a root and all." I hear my words but I can't really think about the flower in Lyndie's hands.

"Mama give him a wreath 'cause she said she feared there wouldn't be no flowers and she buyed him a box but she didn't see how she could let it sit in the house for a viewing. She was the one who found him, out in the barn when he didn't come to eat, but she locked us out and wouldn't let us look at him when they come to get him. I ain't seen Dummy since he give me this candy, well except when I seen him in a dream in a white dress, and it was as like him as he ever was except his clothes was clean-like."

Lyndie looks up and down and skips across the highway, waiting for me on the other side. I haven't been to the graveyard since Miss Liz and I put out my mother's wreath last fall, and I see that the leaves have all been raked away from the graves, left in stacks against the fence. I see a broken stack of flowers — no one has cleaned them away — three wreaths, by a grave at the edge, and one long wreath down the mound. The wreaths have cards, but as I walk closer I see the ink has been washed from them by the rain. The flowers are not old, even the ground on the grave is still fresh, but the flowers are slick and limp from the rain, their blossoms scattered on the ground like wet paper, smelling up the air like flowers left in a vase too long. Hothouse flowers, in the cold, they couldn't last one night even, I bet. Dummy, living in the barn, nothing but a bed quilt in the winter, no fire, died of the cold while everyone else was inside.

"Miss Ramie, do you reckon this is where to put it?"

Lyndie's voice cracks through the air, much too strong it seems for such a little person, and she sets the flower at the end of the dirt mound. There is no stone — when he was born, where — like he's not a person like everyone else.

"Yes, that will be fine," I say. Lyndie stares at the ground and begins to wrinkle her nose. Then she looks up at me like she is going to speak, but she is too little to have words for what she is thinking. I can't say them for her either; I can't tell her.

Lyndie still stares at me and she sniffs, I don't know if from the cold or because she is crying. Then a smile goes over her face, and I hear a short laugh in her throat.

"He was funny," she says loudly. "Know what he did, Miss Ramie? He was running after us in the yard and run right out of his shoes and he didn't even know it till we told him. Cold as all get out, but he just run right off and left his shoes behind . . . Miss Ramie?" Lyndie's words seem to be caught in her throat and she runs over and takes my hand, squeezing the ends of my fingers. "Miss Ramie, let's go home, huh? I get scared down here real quick, and Mama don't know where I am. Can we go home now?"

We start walking toward the highway, and I feel Lyndie trying to tug me faster until she pulls her hand from mine and I have to call to her to get her to stop and wait by the highway. She sticks her hands in her pockets and jumps up and down to warm her feet. As we cross the highway, I feel her hand in mine again, almost too small to hold onto, but warmer than my hand, and soft as she clings to my fingers when we start down the road toward the railroad tracks. She skips away again, and I feel only the stickiness of the candy from her hand in mine.

Goldfish . . .

MISS LIZ is sitting on the steps by the closet. I never know any-more if she is staying in one place because she wants to or if she just can't get up. All of her presents have been opened and the stack of white boxes is in her lap, the paper wrappings torn and scattered around her feet. I watched her as Aunt Cecie took the last present from under the tree, Miss Liz's eyes following Cecie as she walked across the room and gave it to Uncle June. Her fingers started going around the satin loops of one of the bows. Now she has her fingers tangled in the ribbon and looks at her hand in silence.

"Mama, have you got your fingers caught?" I ask.

She looks up at me and her eyes fill with tears, but I can't tell anymore if she's really crying or not. Her eyes are watery all the time and she rubs them with her fist until they get red. She just stares at me and her mouth drops open when I speak, but she doesn't answer me. She holds up her hand to me, the old fingers twisted and trapped in the green ribbon. I take the hand in mine and hold it for a moment. It is cold but I seem to feel some warmth still moving underneath. When I untangle the satin strands, I want to let go of the hand, so as not to feel its awful cold and rough skin, and not to see the cracked yellow nails. But

I would hold her hand and rub it for her if I thought it would make it so she could use it again.

Suddenly the ribbon is pulled from my hand and Miss Liz's hand jerks away from me.

"Mama, for goodness' sake," Aunt Cecie says. "There's no sense in treating you like a baby. Can't you get up from that dark corner for a while and go over there to your chair." Aunt Cecie is trying to talk soft so no one will hear her. "You won't get a chance to see everyone for a long time. They all came to see you and I think you ought to try to go over there and talk to them." Now Cecie bends her face down lower and whispers, "Do you want me to help you up? Do you need to go to the bathroom before you get settled?"

Miss Liz shakes her head slowly, and Aunt Cecie takes the boxes from her lap and puts them on the floor. I put Miss Liz's stick in her hand, and she waves Cecie back with the other hand. She starts to bounce up and down, each time her body rising a little higher from the steps, until finally she is on her feet. She grabs my shoulder with her hand and we start across the room toward the chair by the fireplace.

I hear Aunt Cecie talking about Miss Liz to the others as I sit down beside her on the floor. She says, "Well, I guess we all knew the time was coming when she couldn't do for herself. I came out last Sunday to check on her after Ramie had been out, and she had mud from head to toe, sitting there in front of that fireplace with the fire out and her feet cold as ice. I'm certain it must have been a slight stroke. The doctor said she was strong enough to last quite a few more years if she would just . . ."

Miss Liz starts to rock slowly in her chair. I can't tell if she hears Aunt Cecie and the others or not.

"Mama," I say. "You know those fish I gave you?"

She looks down at me and smiles, "Uh-huh, prettiest little yeller things."

"Well, I think I better tell you how to take care of them. Don't try to change the water — I mean I know you could change it, but I saw this girl at school let one of her goldfish slip out of her hand and go down the drain."

"Woo, where do he go then?" she asks suddenly.

"Oh Mama, I didn't mean that. Well, I don't know really. I guess he either got caught in the pipes or washed out in the sewer somewhere. But what I meant was, you have to be very careful when you're changing the water, so why don't you just add a little now and then, when the old water evaporates, to keep it fresh, and I'll change it for you each time I come out here."

"Do he go down under the house when he go down the drain? Do he go under the house and flip around in the dirt? A chicken'll peck him up!" Miss Liz starts to giggle and holds her hand to her mouth. I look at the fire and try to laugh too, but I can't really laugh.

"I wanted to tell you about feeding them," I say. "They don't need much food at all, just two of those little pellets in the can I gave you will feed them for all day."

Miss Liz doesn't say anything. I look up and she is looking over her shoulder at the other people. Uncle Buck is sitting on the end of the sofa and he watches Miss Liz. I jump as Miss Liz says loudly, "You making kindling a plenty, Buck?"

"What's that, Lizzie?" he says.

"I say you making me a lot of kindling these days?"

"Oh. Well, I don't know as how I would refer to it as making kindling, Lizzie. But I been making right smart much furniture and that makes kindling." Then he laughs. "Lord above, Lizzie, you could burn from now to doomsday and still not make a dent in that stack out back."

"When you bringing me another load?"

"When you need it, I guess," he says and starts to make a humming sound in his throat. He looks at the ceiling like he's thinking of something to talk to Miss Liz about. He drops his chin, thumping his fingers on his knees and says, "How you like that woman that's staying with you, Lizzie? I ain't met her myself."

"Pshaw. Pshaw," Miss Liz says, and turns back and stares at the fire. I watch Uncle Buck as he looks at her a moment then slides down the sofa and starts talking to the others.

"Sorry thing," Miss Liz mumbles.

"Who, Mama? The woman who's staying with you?" I ask.

"Think they're so smart sending her out here. Thinking I don't know what she's doing. Stealing everything she can get her hands on, stealing the stuff in the pantry. But she won't find my money, I hide it; I hide it good. She's near 'bout cleaned out the pantry and I heared them come in the night even, hauled off my wood in a truck. Seen the tracks in the yard and . . ."

"Did you tell Aunt Cecie that she was stealing? I don't think she believes that."

"I told her all right. I told her. Cecie thinks I don't know nothing, thinking I ain't got good sense, turning her nose up when I try to tell her. Thinking I can't manage. And letting that woman come in my house and in my kitchen like she owns the place . . . pshaw . . . pshaw."

Miss Liz starts to rock faster in her chair. "Mama, don't you think it's awful hot here in front of the fire? Would you like to walk down to the pond with me and feed the ducks? It's sort of boring to listen to all these people talking, don't you think?"

"Feed the ducks. I declare I plumb forgot about them, ought to be ashamed. Reckon they're dead. Reckon they are."

"Oh no, they aren't dead. All five of them are still there. I've already been down. They look fine, even whiter than ever with their winter feathers and since everything else is dead . . ."

"Reckon they done perished to death. Ain't a scrap to feed them. It's been hard times, have to feed what you can, but hard times. Have to let some things do for themselves and hope the good Lord will care for them in hard times. Bad winter, Papa should have knowed it was going to be a bad winter, he should have seen the fall won't right, nary a yellow leaf, just turning brown and dying. But the good Lord will have to care for them. A man got to care for what's his, he do."

"Mama, why do you say that? That's silly to say when I tell you I saw them and they were all right. Come on in the kitchen and I'll get your sweater."

She doesn't look at me and doesn't even act like she hears me. Why should she say they are dead when I just said they weren't? "You get some biscuits for the ducks, Mama. I want to show you they're all right. They're really pretty now with their feathers all fluffed up and white. Come on, get up."

Miss Liz puts her hand on my shoulder, pressing down as she stands up. She just got up because I said to; I still don't think she believes me.

"All swimmy-headed, all swimmy-headed," she mumbles.

She starts toward the kitchen and I follow her, but stop as Cecie says to me, "Ramie, where is she going?"

Everyone stops talking as Miss Liz disappears into the kitchen, and it is silent as I answer Aunt Cecie, "We are going down to feed the ducks. I thought it would be good for her to go outside for a while."

Uncle Buck shakes his head and says, "Now Ramie, I don't think that's a bit wise. There's not going to be a thing you can do if she takes a notion to fall. And she might get it in her head that she can take off by herself someday when no one's here to watch out for her."

"Well, I just think it's ridiculous," Aunt Cecie says. "Ramie, be a little sensible. Just get her back in here and let her sit down and talk to people. It's not going to do her one bit of good to go traipsing off down to the pond."

I look through the door and see Miss Liz at the table, filling her apron with biscuits.

"Aunt Cecie. Aunt Cecie," I say again until I have my steady voice. "Miss Liz and I are going down to the pond." Cecie puts her hands on her hips and looks embarrassed but doesn't say anything to me.

"Miss Liz and I are going to the pond. I don't think it's right for her to have to sit here and especially if you're going to talk about her." My eyes start to burn as I push through the kitchen door and shut it behind me. I can hear their voices rise and fall when I lean back against the door. Miss Liz is by the table in front of the window with her back to me. Her big square body is dark, as the light from the window burns around her.

"Ramie, that you? That you?" she says and squints her eyes at me. She is rubbing her eyes with her fist and when I walk to her, I see they are red and runny again. She smiles at me and says, "Fed my fish, Ramie. Found we had enough after all, ain't going to let them pretty little yeller things perish."

I look at the fish bowl and see what she has done. The top of the water is covered with white bread that is sinking around the fish. The bottom of the bowl is beginning to fill up and the water is clouding. "A biscuit. You fed them a biscuit?" My voice is thin and weak as I try to find the words, "Mama, they don't need that much, just a little fish food. They couldn't eat all of that in a million years."

The bread has disappeared from the top of the water, and only a scum of grease is left. It swirls and hangs on the water top like transparent paper, and when the light hits it, I see a rainbow of colors like oil on the street in the rain.

"Miss Liz, look. Can you see on top of the water? There's a rainbow."

"Can't make it out, can't. My eyes have gone bad, gone bad on me," and she walks toward the door. The fish rise to the top and

I hear them smacking at the water and see them looking up at me through the oil scum. I go to Miss Liz's bed and pick up her sweater. She is standing at the door panting and trying to turn the knob that keeps slipping from her hand. I put the sweater against her back, taking her arm in my hand and pushing it down the sleeve. I take her other arm in my hand as she changes hands on her apron full of biscuits. Her arms are heavy and limp, and she doesn't move as I try to smooth the sweater around her. I open the door and shiver as the cold air hits me, but Miss Liz walks out onto the porch like she doesn't feel the cold. I hurry to her side and she presses her hand against my shoulder when we start down the steps.

We are going across the yard, down the path under the clothesline. Miss Liz's black pot sits among the dead grass and she stops walking as we come to it, staring down at it. Then she starts walking slowly again. In the center of the path we come to the web again, the same web I ran into last fall. It is badly broken now, the birds have flown through it, leaving its thread broken and dangling down. Miss Liz and I stop as we get close to it and see that the orb, where the spider had woven it thick and carved its letters, was still strong. Clinging to the orb is the dried form of the spider.

"Oh, he done died. He done died," Miss Liz says.

"No, Mama. She's not dead. She is around here somewhere. Look closely, that's not a dead spider."

Miss Liz bends her face toward the web and lifts her finger to point. "Ramie, you look good. I declare I thought I was the one going blind. He's dead right there, sure as I'm standing here." She laughs and adds, "He's too wrinkled and shriveled up to be playing possum on me. None of that tomfoolery."

"I know it looks like it, Mama, but that's just the casing, the skin. She shed it and left it there. They do like snakes, but she is alive somewhere."

I pick the skin from the web and hold it in my hand. "Funny, Mama. How I'm not scared to touch it, now it's not in its skin. I thought I was scared of it because of the way it looked, but I was really scared of it because it was alive and because I couldn't understand it. I don't like to think I'm scared of things that are alive, but I guess I am."

Mama looks at the skin in my hand. I feel a movement and turn to look at the tree beside me. The spider is moving up the bark toward the long strand that holds her web to the tree. Chills run across my body as I sling the skin from my hand and rub my palms together. "Mama, there she is!"

Mama raises her head, but the spider has disappeared around the tree. I grab Mama's arm and feel its warmth under my hands. I don't want her to look at me and see that I am frightened again.

"Don't see a thing," she says.

"She's gone. She must have seen us." I look at the dark bark of the tree and wonder now if I really did see the yellow spider there or if it was just a leaf.

We start back down the path and I hold tightly to Miss Liz's arm. "You know something, Miss Liz. I read some of the strangest things about spiders. Did you know that the female kills her mate and that she's a lot bigger . . ."

"She do that?" Miss Liz asks.

"Uh-huh. The book said her appetite was a lot stronger than her love, and that she kills the male and eats him sometimes."

"Woo, that's awful sounding."

"There are some funny things they do too. When the male spider goes to see the girl spider, sometimes he takes her a fly all wrapped up in silk for a present. I think he is just hoping she'll eat the fly and decide she's not hungry anymore."

Miss Liz starts to giggle, so I go on.

"And some of the males are sort of dumb, and they suck all the juice out of the fly before they get there, which really makes the girl spider mad."

"Flies ain't got no juice."

"They do to a spider."

We are by the edge of the pond and Miss Liz is crumbling the biscuits in her apron. "They ain't here, Ramie. They're all dead. I told you they was dead."

"Mama, don't you hear them? They're over there, in the willows, listen. Here they come." The five white ducks splash out of the willows and glide over to us.

"Well, I declare. I declare, there's every last one of them."

Miss Liz lets go of her apron, but all the biscuits tumble at her feet when she tries to sling them out.

"Oh, Ramie. Look what I went and done. I meant to give them a good throw."

"Don't worry about it, Mama." I scoop the bread up and toss it on top of the water. The ducks rise up on their orange feet and walk quacking over to Miss Liz.

She watches them a moment and says, "Ain't no wonder you get et. I could eat you myself if I was a mind to." She starts to giggle again and looks over at me. When she stops laughing, I watch her face change; it's like a piece of crumpled paper that someones has tried to smooth out again.

"Ain't it a fine farm, Ramie? A fine farm. The ground just busting with stuff. I'm great-minded to pull us some fresh 'maters, give you some to take back. We got a plenty."

Her eyes are glazed over again, one minute they're wet and shiny, then it looks like the wetness just turns to frost. One of the ducks is tapping its beak on the bread in my hand. My hand feels cold and dead as I run it around the warm feathers of the duck. She darts away from me and splashes back into the water.

Miss Liz is smiling down at me and I say to her, "Your oats are sprouting, Mama. The ground is pink with them and even a little green is showing. I saw them when I was out walking yesterday."

"Are they? Are they now? Well, I can rest a mite easier. Once they broke ground, it's no need for more fretting, no need a'tall."

I stand up and we start climbing slowly back up the path to the house.

Miss Liz is back in the living room, in front of the fire and the talking and laughing is still going on, though some of the people have gone home. I have her two goldfish in the dishpan and am washing the biscuit out of the bowl. I fill the bowl with fresh water and drop the water grass back in, watching the little air bubbles that are on the grass float to the top and disappear. I wrote a note to the lady who stays with Miss Liz and put it under the fish food, telling her not to feed the fish but two pellets a day and to try to keep Miss Liz from dumping bread in the water. I set the bowl on the window sill and the sunlight pales the grass into light green. When I reach in the dishpan for the fish, I close my hands around his wiggling body and don't lift him from the water until I'm sure he can't slip out of my hand. I drop him in the bowl then catch the other one, who stops moving just like he is dead when he is in the air on the way to the bowl. As soon as he hits the fresh water, his long fins open up and he swarms around in the bowl. I hear the door to the kitchen swing open and turn around as Cecie walks in.

"I think maybe you were right in taking her outside for awhile. She is certainly more cheerful and agreeable now."

I don't say anything but I know Cecie is waiting for me to answer.

"The bowl looks nice," Cecie says. "I saw what she did to it."

"I left a note for the lady that's staying with her to try to keep her from doing it again."

"Oh, fine. Fine. That's a good idea."

"Aunt Cecie?"

"Yes, dear."

"Can I take off these hose and put on some old socks I left out here?"

"Whatever for?"

"Well, I skinned my knee playing basketball and the hose hurt it."

"I certainly noticed that your knee was skinned, Ramie. I thought you would put something over it, a bandage or something."

"Nope."

"Yes, you can take off the hose if you will put something on your legs so you don't catch cold. Where were you playing basketball? At school?"

"Sort of. Last week at this boy's house named Gary. He lives near school and his daddy is a teacher."

"Does the school approve of this?"

"Of what?"

"You playing basketball off the grounds. I mean in an unsupervised place. I'm not sure I approve and certainly not your playing with a bunch of roughneck boys. That's not why I am sending you to St. Anne's. Can't you get enough basketball in your own gym class?"

"They didn't make me fall down. I fell down all by myself." self."

Cecie turns to go back in the living room and stops at the door, her eyes on the table.

"Nice," she says and points. I look down and see a rainbow of colors from my fishbowl flickering on the table, as the door to the living room shuts and Cecie disappears. I take the bowl from the window sill and put it back on the table by Miss Liz's bed.

Millstone . . .

Who then is the greatest in the kingdom of heaven? And
he called to him a little child, and set him in the midst of
them, and said, Verily I say unto you, except ye turn and
become as little children, ye shall in no wise enter into the
kingdom of heaven . . . But whoso shall cause one of
these little ones that believe on me to stumble, it is profit-
able for him that a great millstone should be hanged
around his neck, and that he should be sunk in the depth
of the sea.

Matthew: 18

MISS LIZ is in her bed, and I hear her breathing like an animal
growling somewhere in a dark hollow. In my lap is the heavy
Bible. I turn to the front page marked in brown ink; all the people of the family are there: Miss Liz's grandmother, burned in
her house by the Yankees, her Uncle Tom tied to a tree after a
mad dog bite and dying there, all the children, when they were
born, Cecie, Mother, and me, and then Gregory and when he
died, and written again by his name, "Suffer little children," in
Miss Liz's handwriting.

Under Gregory's name I put Dummy's name, printed just like

Miss Liz would write it. Miss Liz will never know, not until she opens the Bible again when someone dies. Maybe she won't open it again, maybe it will be opened for Elizabeth Marshall, to put the last date by her name, the same date that will finish her stone at the church. And she is sinking in her heaviness and sickness in the bed, with a great invisible stone around her neck, for Gregory, for Papa, for my Daddy, for Dummy.

What things soever shall bind ye on earth, ye shall be bound by in heaven, and in heaven in a white dress is Dummy with the angels, but he has no voice to sing. If God were to give him a voice and were to let him speak . . . but he had no voice on earth. Will he be bound in heaven? What would he speak? If God were to say, "You can speak now, Dummy," what would he speak? He would sing loud and never say ugly of anyone . . . no . . . he would ask not to be able to speak and would be silent again. Then he could always be as a child.

And Miss Liz, here in her house until she will die too, but in her own house with no strangers like the ones who came to Papa. I don't want her to have the millstone and have the sea take her. It is strange there, and it would beat her and whip her. She did what she thought was right. She would whisper to me, "It's all right now. There are some things I can't whip. It's all right now, isn't it, Ramie?"

And she would like to be there in heaven, she likes to listen to the singing, and she would sit there in her red dress with her rhinestone pin on, all dressed for church with her chest powdered, and she would smile because the woman with the hateful voice wouldn't be there to mess up the singing.